RAINBOW high

RAINBOW high

alex sanchez

SIMON & SCHUSTER
New York   Toronto   Singapore
London   Sydney

SIMON & SCHUSTER
1230 Avenue of the Americas, New York, New York 10020

Book design by Paula Winicur
The text for this book is set in Mrs. Eaves.
Manufactured in the United States of America

2 4 6 8 10 9 7 5 3

Library of Congress Cataloging-in-Publication Data
Sanchez, Alex, 1957-
Rainbow High / Alex Sanchez.—1st ed.
p. cm.
Sequel to: Rainbow boys.
Summary: Follows three gay high school seniors as they struggle with issues of coming out,
safe sex, homophobia, being in love, and college choices.
ISBN 0-689-85477-3
[1. Homosexuality—Fiction. 2. Coming out (Sexual orientation)—Fiction.
3. High schools—Fiction. 4. Schools—Fiction. 5. Interpersonal relations—Fiction.] I. Title.
PZ7.S19475 Rak 2004
[Fic]—dc21   2003008252

To integrity—and our imperfect
strivings to attain it

With gratitude to my editor, Kevin Lewis, my agent,
Miriam Altshuler, and all those who contributed to
the creation of this book with their encouragement
and feedback, including Bruce Aufhammer,
Bill Brockschmidt, Jeremy Coleman, Jim Dalglish,
Jann Darsie, Alyssa Eisner, Toby Emert, Barbara Esstman,
the Fine Arts Work Center of Provincetown, David Gale,
Jim Howe, Jason Hungerford, Chuck Jones, J. R. Key,
Erica Lazaro, Elizabeth McCracken, Rob Phelps,
John Porter, J. Q. Quiñones, Bob Ripperger, Doug Rose,
Cosper Scafidi, Sean Sinclair, Jason Tifone, Mike Walker,
Jason Wells, and Mark Wersinger.
Thank you all.

prologue

"Words have power," Ms. MacTraugh told the students of Walt Whitman High's Gay-Straight Alliance. She made it sound more like a dare than a statement. "Today, how about if each of you writes a brief essay?"

"Not another paper," groaned a boy with lemon-tinted glasses.

A girl wearing a rainbow-bead necklace raised her hand. "Do we have to pass them in?"

"Only if you want to. The idea is to help you connect with your lives. Describe what's going on for you in school, your family. Write about your hopes and dreams—whatever is most important for you."

The rainbow-beaded girl chewed on her pen, thinking. A boy with a butterfly tattooed on his forearm gazed skyward out the window.

Three other boys began eagerly writing.

Nelson Glassman

Oy vey. *What a freaking senior year! Our petite opera de soap started in September, with Kyle and I going to the queer youth group downtown, like we do every boring Saturday. Except guess who walks into the meeting for the first time? Megajock Jason from school.*

Kyle's always had the hots for him. Ever since freshman year he's been all about Jason, Jason, Jason! Gag me.

I'd said a million times, "Old Jason's a closet case." But did Kyle believe me?

After that meeting he did. Overnight he and Jason became, like, best buds— and I became a vague memory. The story of my heartbreak life.

Well, maybe I exaggerate. Kyle didn't totally dump me. I guess I just assumed he and I would always be the heartbeat of each other's universe. But now he had Jason.

And me? The closest I'd ever gotten to romance was a warm computer screen. You know—chatting up guys on the Net, exchanging pics, all that crap.

Here I was, seventeen years old, bashed every day at school for being gay, and still a virgin. How pathetic is that?

So, one night I decided to real-life hook up with a dude. You should've seen his JPEG. Total boner magnet. The most amazing part was, it was his real photo!

We rode his freakin' motorcycle *to his place and did it—the full boink—my first time. It was so incredible! Except . . . I, um, sort of forgot to use a condom? Well, not exactly forgot. I knew I was supposed to, but . . . come on, do you seriously think I was going to stop in the middle of virginity-losing-hormone-raging-passion and bridle it with a condom? Hel-lo! Teenage boy here! Ever heard of testosterone? It's worse than drugs.*

After that night, things really got gnarly. Mom weaseled out of me what had happened and freaked. She yelled. She cried. She told me how she'd trusted me. Major drama. I felt so bad, I wanted to crawl beneath my sheets and never come out.

rainbow high

Anyway, she hauled my depressed butt to the doc, who said it would be a while before I could get an accurate HIV test result. I have to go back soon.

As for Motorcycle Dude? Never saw his hottie face again. After we'd done it he told me he had a lover. Ouch! Just toss me out with the garbage.

The one sunny spot in this supermess is Jeremy, a boy I've met at the queer youth group. Omigod, he's so cute—and kick-ass sweet!

I never thought he'd be interested in me, but we've gone out twice so far. He's a year and something older than me. I'm bouncing off walls, totally crushed on him. Mom hasn't met him yet. She wants to, but there's one teensy-weensy detail . . . he's HIV positive?

Yeah, yeah. I know what you're thinking. But there's no way I'm going to stop dating him. I don't give a crap what anyone says. I'm almost eighteen.

Besides, if I turn out to test poz too, then it's no big deal, right? Except . . . I'm not sure I'm ready to deal with that.

Oh God, please don't let me have it. Not now! Not when for once in my boring life things are starting to look up.

Kyle Meeks

I first realized I was different in seventh grade, when my friends started being interested in girls. And I wasn't.

About the same time, all the boys started joking about "queers" and "homos." At first I laughed along, not really understanding, until I realized they were talking about people like . . . me.

I broke out in such a sweat that day my teacher sent me to the nurse's office.

Almost every afternoon for the rest of middle school, I spent hours alone in my room, pacing, examining my every movement in the mirror, telling myself I wasn't going to be this way. I felt so lonely I wanted to die.

Then came high school, where I met Nelson. And my whole world changed.

He's like no one I've ever known—out and outrageous, totally okay with who he is. He became the best friend I'd always longed for—someone who knew and accepted me, no matter what. I'd do anything for him.

When he first told me about his unsafe sex episode I wanted to clobber him. Now I mostly worry what his HIV result will be . . . and about his dating Jeremy.

High school is also where I first laid eyes on Jason Carrillo. He was a star athlete, in a clique I could never join, and had a girlfriend. I never thought I had any real hope with him. But still, I could dream. Every time I saw him in the hall with his arm around Debra, I thought: What I wouldn't give to be her.

The afternoon when he walked into the Rainbow Youth meeting downtown, I nearly fell off my chair.

After that, one day I gave him a ride home from school. I think he was as nervous as I was. He kept biting his nails. He said that in order to stay on the basketball team he needed to get his algebra grade up, so I immediately offered to help. Math is my best subject—what I want to major in.

A few weeks later he invited me to his house. He told me he'd broken up with Debra. I felt bad about it, but I also wanted to whoop and holler.

Then, things really got moving fast. We went to the movies and held hands. My heart felt like it would burst from my chest. A few weeks later I somehow mustered the boldness to kiss him. And he kissed me back.

Then one evening when we were supposed to go out, his dad left home. We were alone in his house. I'd never seen Jason cry. Before I knew it, we were making love.

Ever since, I've walked around singing and bumping into things. I can't help it. My mom and dad look at me like I'm crazy.

This past fall I finally came out to them. It was the hardest thing I've ever done. My mom cried that she'd never have grandkids. My dad argued all this stuff about it being a choice—the wrong choice. I told him it's not like I asked to be gay. It's just the way I am.

We're getting through it—some days better than others. At least they like Jason. Sometimes it seems as if Dad likes him better than he likes me. After all, Jason is the star athlete Dad always hoped I'd be.

Jason even got a basketball scholarship to Tech. That's where I'd applied, too, even before all this happened. Every day I check the mail for my acceptance, wishing it would hurry.

rainbow high

My dad also insisted I apply to his **alma mater**, Princeton. My grades are good, but I doubt I'll get accepted there. It's one of the top math programs in the country—where Einstein lectured! Of course I'd love to go there, but . . .

My dream is for Jason and me to go to college together. Who knows? By the time we graduate, gay marriage might even be legal. Jason and I could have a house in the 'burbs. Maybe adopt kids. My mom could be a grandmom after all.

That's my dream. And every time I'm with Jason, I feel like it's coming true.

Jason Carrillo

So far senior year has been the five **best** months of my life—and the worst.

It really began spring of junior year, when I saw an ad in our high school paper for the Rainbow Youth Group. It took me all summer to build up my nerve to go. I was so confused—**beyond** confused.

On the one hand, I had a girlfriend who I loved. Debra and I had been dating for two years. We had sex and everything. I enjoyed it, except . . . at night I'd have dreams . . . about guys.

I tried to convince myself that I wasn't gay—that what I was going through was just a phase. My image of being gay was someone like Nelly—I mean, Nelson someone kind of girlish. I definitely wasn't like that. And I didn't want to be.

Part of it also had to do with my dad and what happened with my friend Tommy when I was little, and how my dad beat me up for it afterward.

My dad's a jerk—totally out of control. I don't know what his problem is. It goes beyond his temper, beyond his drinking. It's as if someone did something to him when he was a kid and he thinks that gives him the right to take it out on the world—especially me.

But with everything going on, I couldn't take his beating up on me anymore.

I finally stood up to him. And I came out. You should have seen the look on his face when he heard his son was a **maricón**.

He moved out, telling me I was disgusting. But I think it was also a **machismo** thing—because I'd been able to deck him. I hate to admit it, but I kind of feel sorry for him. Don't get me wrong, I'm glad he's gone and hope he never comes back. But sometimes I wonder if he could ever accept me. Not that I care if he does.

I'm going to live my life the way I want. I don't care if anybody thinks I'm disgusting or worthless. I know myself that I'm worth something.

I do feel bad about how everything turned out with Debra, though. I didn't mean to hurt her, but I know I did, and I couldn't blame her for hating me. I felt so happy later when she said that she still wanted to be friends. She means a lot to me.

Throughout all this, I've tried to keep focused on the one thing that's always helped me get through life—basketball. So far this season our team is 19 and 1. Coach Cameron says if we keep it up, we could be state champions again. It would be our second year in a row!

I want to come out to Coach, but I'm kind of scared. What would he say? And what if the team finds out? Coach and the team have been among the most important people in my life. If it weren't for them, I'm not sure I would've made it.

And another thing about coming out: What would happen with my scholarship to Tech? And if I lost that, what would happen to Kyle and me?

I'd known Kyle since freshman year as the shy kid with glasses. When we passed in the hall, I'd say "Wha's up?" but that was about it. I knew he hung out with Nelson, but I never suspected Kyle was gay. He looked too normal.

When I saw him at the Rainbow meeting, it totally blew me away. I thought, If someone like him is okay with being gay, then maybe I could be, too.

I decided to get to know him. While he helped me with math I told him things I'd never dared tell anyone—not even Debra or my best friend, Corey. And each time we got together, we became closer.

Man, so much has changed this year! I've changed so much.

If you'd told me a year ago that I'd hold hands, or kiss, or actually do it with another guy, I would've said you were loco. But that was before I got to know Kyle.

I like him a lot. He's good-hearted, smart, plus he has a great swimmer's bod. We've even told each other, "I love you," if you can believe that!

rainbow high

But sometimes I get nervous. I wonder, What does it mean to say that to a guy?

This is all so new to me. Every day I ask myself, What's going to happen next? And I just hope I don't screw it all up.

jason kyle

nelson

"Do you realize," Nelson said, hopping into a pair of freshly washed jeans, "it's my third date with Jeremy and we *still* haven't had sex?"

"I'll call the *Guinness Book of Records*," Kyle mumbled as he searched Nelson's jumbled sock drawer for a matching set. "You *are* going to wait till after your HIV test, right?"

Nelson groaned. Why did Kyle always have to bring up the serious crap? He'd invited him over to help him dye his hair, not lecture him.

"Yeah, yeah. Chillax." Nelson yanked up his zipper and gazed in the mirror at his flame-blue hair. "You think it's too bright?"

"Nah." Kyle grinned a crooked smile and tossed him the socks. "Not if he wears sunglasses."

"Thanks! Like I'm not nervous enough already." Nelson

pulled the socks on. "Hey, turn this song up!"

While Kyle cranked the stereo, Nelson danced in front of the mirror, tugging a shirt on and tearing it off again. A knock thudded at the door. "Yeah?" Nelson shouted.

His mom leaned into the room, and then reeled. "Oh, no! Honey, your hair!"

"You like it?" He took her hand and twirled her in his arms—first in one direction, then the other—until she patted her chest, out of breath.

"So when are you going to invite this boy over?" she asked, turning the stereo down, while Nelson buttoned his most recent shirt.

"Yeah, right. For what? To play Scrabble?"

"No! So I can meet him." She began returning the shirts on the bed to hangers as Kyle handed them to her.

"Are you afraid I won't like him?" she asked. "Or is there something you're not telling me?"

"Jeez, Mom! Don't you trust me?"

Granted, he hadn't told her about Jeremy's HIV yet. But what difference did it make since they weren't having sex? Yet.

Kyle stared expectantly at Nelson, silently mouthing the words "Tell her."

"Okay." Nelson let out a deep sigh. "Mom, I need to tell you something. You should know. He's . . . this is really hard for me to say . . ."

His mom and Kyle stopped their shirt hanging as Nelson choked up.

"He's . . . really a girl named Francine. I think I'm straight."

Kyle rolled his eyes. Nelson's mom shook her head with resignation.

"Gotta go!" Nelson grabbed his leather jacket, tossing his

rainbow high

mom an air kiss. "Kyle, can you give me a ride to the metro? Please? I'm *so* late."

As Kyle pulled into the station driveway he asked, "When are you going to tell her?"

"I'll tell her," Nelson said. "Just not yet." He reached over and squeezed Kyle's shoulder. "Let me enjoy it a while, okay?"

Kyle nodded. "But no more jokes, all right? Say hi to Jeremy for me."

When Nelson's subway reached his destination, he bounded off the train, wishing he'd brought Jeremy something to make up for being late. As he passed a convenience store he darted inside. On the counter stood a vase of cellophane-wrapped individual roses. *How cheesy,* Nelson thought, *but at least it's something.*

In front of the movie multiplex, Jeremy stood waiting, gazing from side to side. He'd grown a cute little brown goatee highlighting his eyes since Nelson last saw him. And his bomber jacket made his shoulders look even hunkier.

"I'm late, aren't I?" Nelson asked, rushing up. "I'm sorry." He quickly handed Jeremy the rose. "For you. Hey, I like your goatee."

Jeremy gave a little pout. "Thanks." He glanced at the top of Nelson's head. "I like your hair."

"Oh, thanks." Nelson grinned back, ogling.

"Why are you staring?" Jeremy asked.

"Um, just glad to see you."

Blushing, Jeremy glanced at his watch. "Well, the movie sold out."

"Oops. Sorry." Nelson tried to think fast how to unwreck

their date. "How about if we get tickets for the next show and have dinner first?"

"That won't work." Jeremy sighed. "I just took my meds. I have to wait before I can eat."

"Oh." Nelson remembered that Jeremy had to schedule his meals. Now he really felt like a turd. "Well . . . is there another movie here we can see?"

They checked the schedule board and found a different film. World crisis averted.

At their seats, Jeremy carefully laid aside the rose and dug into his pocket. "I have something for you, too. I remembered all the buttons on your backpack." He handed Nelson a button that read: 2Q2BSTR8.

"I love it!" Nelson laughed. He pinned the button onto his jacket, wondering if Jeremy really thought he was that cute.

The lights dimmed. It was the second time they'd been to a movie, and Nelson eagerly took hold of Jeremy's hand.

Jeremy slid his fingers between Nelson's and squeezed back. This was what Nelson had always wanted—a boyfriend to lean close to . . . if only the HIV issue didn't keep coming up.

After the movie, as they walked out into the cool night, Jeremy asked, "What are you in the mood for?"

Nelson responded with a suggestive grin.

Jeremy shook his head, smiling. "I mean to *eat*."

"Oh." Nelson gave a hugely disappointed sigh, then laughed.

Eventually they decided on a pizza parlor.

"What kind of pizza do you like?" Nelson asked, looking over the menu. "Sausage makes me sick. One time, yuck, it was so gross!" Nelson stopped. Why was he jabbering?

Fortunately a waitress interrupted and took their order.

"By the way," Nelson resumed after she left. "Kyle says hi. We're both waiting to hear from Tech. I'm sure he got accepted. He's such a brain. I hope I did, so we can dorm together. Can you imagine if they put me in a room with some straight dude? How do you spell disaster? Do you really like my hair? Some little rug rat on the metro asked if I was from *Sesame Street.*" Nelson grinned. "It's such a pain being a supermodel."

Jeremy laughed, but even so, Nelson reprimanded himself. *Queen it down.*

He fidgeted with his earrings, continuing: "School sucks, as usual. I've got to do some dumb-ass paper on bicameral legislatures. Who gives a crap? Our GSA posters keep getting torn down, but we put more up. My dog has dry skin. I have to put stinky cream on him twice a day. Thrills. That's my life. Me, me, me, me, me! Enough about me. I want to hear about you. What do you think of me? Just kidding. I'll shut up." He made a clamp with his fingers, pinning his lips together.

Jeremy smiled. "School's fine. I'm taking a psychology class. I really like it."

The waitress brought their pizza—black olive and mushroom.

"My brother?" Jeremy continued. "The one I live with? He's traveling a lot for work. My mom and dad went to Florida for the winter. My job at the video store sucks, but at least I get benefits. That's real important. I have this one friend who's taking a year off, traveling through Asia. I wish I could do that, but I'll never be able to. . . ."

There it was again: The Issue.

"I heard they're coming up with better meds," Nelson said, trying to cheer things up again.

"Yeah," Jeremy replied, "but I'd still need to work for insurance to pay for them."

"That sucks! It's like slavery."

"Yeah." Jeremy shrugged, lifting a slice of pizza.

"I'm supposed to take my test Monday," Nelson said. "The doctor says it's been long enough for antibodies to show up."

Jeremy quietly chewed his pizza slice and then put it down. "I've been thinking. . . ." His tone sounded uncertain. "What if you test negative?"

Nelson had tried not to think about his result. Naturally he hoped he'd test negative. But then what would happen with his dating Jeremy?

"Well, if I do test neg, it won't change anything. I'd still want to go out with you." He looked over at the rose he'd given Jeremy, laying on the checkered tablecloth, wilting. "Are you afraid I'd get it?"

Jeremy nodded. "That's part of it."

Nelson shrugged. "But you said you only have safe sex, right?"

"Yeah. But something could happen. A condom could break."

Nelson grabbed some water to swallow his bite of pizza. "Have you ever actually *known* anyone who had a condom break?"

"Yeah." Jeremy nodded. "A couple of people."

"Oh." Nelson paused and regrouped. "Well, I'm willing to take my chances. I'll probably get it eventually anyway. If I do, I'll go on meds. *You* do it."

"And it's a pain in the ass!" Jeremy's voice rose with alarm. "It's not like you get a cold and you can take pills for a week, then it goes away. It's every day, on schedule, no matter what, for the rest of your entire life!"

His voice continued growing louder. "Until you get it, you have no idea how it changes everything. Hardly a minute goes by when you don't think about it. And there's no escaping. You have to deal with it every damn day—forever."

Nelson wrapped a finger around his silver neck chain. He'd never seen Jeremy so upset.

"Look," Nelson said soothingly. "I know it's a big deal."

"*And,*" Jeremy said, still insistent, "if I'm dating someone, it affects him, too. The last negative guy I dated couldn't handle it."

"I know the risk I'm taking," Nelson said. "I can deal with it."

Even though he tried to sound like he meant it, the truth was he hadn't really thought about whether or not he'd be able to handle it. He'd just accepted HIV was part of being with Jeremy. And since he was probably going to test positive also, he could only benefit from Jeremy's experience.

Nelson plucked the rose off the table and stuck it in his water glass.

"I'm sorry," Jeremy said. "I didn't mean to vent on you. I guess I'm just anxious about how your test will turn out."

"Me too," Nelson said.

They sat silent till Nelson couldn't stand it any longer. "Can we talk about something else now? Please?"

Jeremy nodded. They discussed the movie, which Nelson thought had a downer ending—the girl left the guy. But Jeremy thought it was more realistic that way.

They talked about their favorite movies. Jeremy liked sci-fi and action pics. Nelson liked romantic comedies and fright flicks—anything conducive to hand-holding.

As for music, Nelson liked just about anything with a beat. "Except country. I hate, hate, hate country!"

Jeremy grinned across the booth at him. "That's my favorite."

"Don't tell me!" Nelson laughed. "Can you excuse me while I go vomit?"

HIV he could deal with, but *country*? That was a different matter altogether.

As they left the restaurant, Nelson hoped Jeremy would invite him back to his place. Though it would make Nelson late getting home and his mom would bawl him out, it would be worth it.

But after half a block of looking in store windows, still no hint of invitation had come forth. Precious minutes were passing and Nelson really, really wanted to suck face. He'd heard in safe-sex lectures that the chances of getting HIV through kissing were almost zip.

"Want to go to your place?" he finally blurted out.

Jeremy glanced up from the window display. "It's kind of late."

"It's barely eleven!"

"Yeah, but by the time we get to my place and then you get back home . . . I don't want to get in trouble with your mom."

"She's cool," Nelson said. "She's the freakin' vice president of the PFLAG chapter. She wants to meet you."

"Have you told her? About my being positive?"

Nelson shut his eyes. Not *that* again. "She hasn't even met you yet! Besides, I don't care what she says. It's none of her business. I'm not a kid. If she doesn't like it, tough."

"She's your mom, Nelson." Little worry lines furrowed Jeremy's brow. "I don't want to get caught between the two of you."

"I'll tell her," Nelson said, fidgeting once again with an earring. "Just not yet. Can she at least meet you first?"

Jeremy sighed. "Okay."

They continued walking to the metro, Nelson moping inside. As much as he adored Jeremy, sometimes he wanted to make him stop being such a stick-in-the-mud. Couldn't Jeremy just let himself be crazy in love for one minute?

At the station they paused on the landing amid a throng of people.

Jeremy inhaled the rose in his hand. Then his coffee-colored eyes looked up, softly intent.

Nelson jumped at the opportunity. "Are you sure I can't come over for just one teensy little minute? Please? I promise I'll be good."

Jeremy looked at Nelson's lips, hesitating.

"My train's coming." He gave Nelson one too-small kiss and pulled away.

"No way!" Nelson protested, clutching Jeremy's hand. "I'm not letting you go till you give me a *real* kiss."

Jeremy darted an anxious glance around the platform. "People are watching."

"I don't care," Nelson said. "I mean it."

Jeremy's lips curled into a smile. Then he leaned toward Nelson, who eagerly took the cue, aiming his mouth—first this way, then that—until, guided by the goatee's tickle, their lips met.

Nelson wrapped his arms around Jeremy's shoulders, taking in the juniper smell of him, and was lost to the world. Then all too quickly, the noisy gust of the incoming train delivered him back.

"Thanks," Jeremy whispered, his auburn hair blowing across his forehead.

For a moment Nelson thought—hoped—maybe Jeremy would forget being so freaking responsible and invite him home.

But the train's door chimes rang and Jeremy stepped on board just as the doors closed. He waved through the window, pressing his nose to his rose.

The train started and Nelson moved alongside, following faster and faster, just like in one of those old Bogart movies, till the last car disappeared into the dark tunnel.

When Nelson arrived home, *Saturday Night Live* sounded from the living room. No doubt his mom was waiting up for him.

"Did you have a nice time?" she called. "With Francine?"

"That was a joke, Mom." He sat down beside her on the sofa. "Don't call him that."

"I'm just kidding." She put her arm around his shoulder, pulling him to her. "Can't I joke too?" She turned the TV down with the remote control. "Is that a new button?"

Nelson glanced at the 2Q2BSTR8 on his jacket and rested his head on her shoulder. "Jeremy gave it to me. I think he's totally infatuated."

She stroked her son's hair. "And how do you feel about him?"

Nelson wanted to tell her how much he liked Jeremy in spite of the HIV and his being such a stodgy-wodge. He wanted to confide how confused he felt about what would happen if his own test came back negative. But how could he tell her all that?

"Mom, that's kind of personal." He grabbed the remote control, turning up the TV, and cradled into her shoulder.

jason kyle

nelson

Monday after school Kyle offered to go with Nelson to his HIV test, hoping it would help calm his own worries. But as they pulled into the parking lot, a new unease came over Kyle. "You think I should get tested too?"

He had, after all, made love with Jason. And Jason had made love with Debra.

"It depends," Nelson said. "What did you and Jason do together?"

Kyle shifted in his seat. Such detail made him uncomfortable, even if he and Nelson were best friends. "Well . . . we didn't exactly . . . you know . . . s or f."

Nelson's eyebrows arched. "'S or f'? Come on, Kyle, be a big boy. You're allowed to use grown-up words. "Why don't you ask the doctor what he thinks?"

In the reception room Kyle thought back to his night with

Jason. They hadn't done anything truly unsafe—like Nelson had—but he'd read so many conflicting things about what really was safe. The more he thought back on it, the more he squirmed in his chair. When Nelson's name finally got called, Kyle whispered, "I want to go in with you."

Nelson's pediatrician, Dr. Choudhury, was a wrinkly South Asian guy with glasses perched on the tip of his nose. "That's very interesting hair," he told Nelson in a high, cheery voice.

After studying Nelson's folder the doctor explained the test procedure. He placed a specially treated pad with a handle between Nelson's cheek and gum. "Now we leave it for two minutes."

While Nelson held the swab in his mouth, the doctor monitored the time on his watch.

Kyle wiped the sweat from his palms, debating whether to speak up. The procedure looked painless. It wouldn't hurt to at least ask about it. He cleared his throat. "Um, Doctor? I was wondering . . . if I should get tested too?"

The doctor tilted his head back, squinting through his bifocals. "You too? Don't you boys know to use precautions?"

Kyle squirmed in his seat, wishing he'd kept his mouth shut.

"Tell me," Dr. Choudhury asked impatiently, "did you engage in unprotected penetration?"

Kyle cringed, sinking into his chair. "Um, no."

"Any exchange of body fluids? Blood? Semen? Preejaculatory secretions? Breast milk?"

Kyle slid farther down his seat. "Um, no, not really."

The doctor threw his hands up in exasperation. "If you want, I can test you. But my suggestion to both of you—" he pulled the handle from Nelson's cheek and sealed the swab into a plastic tube "—is to wait till you're older before you

rainbow high

start fooling around with this sex business."

Kyle decided there wasn't much point in being tested now, though he should definitely ask Jason: Had he and Debra used condoms?

But how could he ask Jason that?

Kyle's parents' cars were already in the driveway when he arrived home. He hadn't told his mom or dad he was taking Nelson to get tested. No sir. No way. When Kyle came out to them, one of their biggest concerns had been his health. Now that they'd calmed down some, he didn't want them getting hyper again.

Kyle kicked his shoes off in the foyer and followed his parents' voices to the kitchen. "Did Jason call?"

His dad glanced up from the tomatoes he was slicing. A goofy smile lit up his face. "The future college student is home!" he sang out.

Kyle ignored his dad's goofiness, turning to his mom. "Did Jason call?"

"No, honey." She smiled, lifting a head of lettuce from the sink. "But you got a letter from Tech." She dried her hands on a washcloth and handed him an envelope.

At the sight of the letter Kyle's heart jumped. The return address was from the admissions office. This was it—his acceptance to Tech; the start of his college life with Jason—unless . . .

"Come on," his dad encouraged him. "Open it."

"Honey," his mom chimed in. "With your grades I'm sure you got accepted. Go ahead."

Kyle turned the envelope over, his hand trembling as he ran his finger beneath the flap. Slowly he unfolded the letter and quickly scanned the page. Halfway down, he looked up again.

His mom and dad were staring at him, their faces crinkled with worry and hope.

"I got accepted!" Kyle gasped.

"Honey, that's wonderful!" His mom wrapped her arms around him.

"That's great news, son." His dad patted him on the back. "You should be hearing from Princeton next."

Kyle bristled. "Can't I just enjoy the fact I was accepted to Tech?"

"Of course," his dad agreed. "Didn't I say it was great news?"

Yeah, but Kyle knew where his dad really wanted him to go— his *alma mater*.

Kyle gave a sigh, turning to his mom. "Can Jason come over?" Kyle wanted to share the news with him in person.

"All right," she said, "but—"

Before she could finish, Kyle was racing up the stairs. Grabbing the cordless phone, he speed-dialed Jason. "I've got a surprise," he said as soon as Jason answered. "Can you come over?"

"Um, I don't think so. My mom's going to a meeting, and I've got to watch Missy. What is it? Can you bring it here, or is it, like, an elephant or something? Is it a car? Did you get us a car?"

Kyle smiled to himself, stretching out across the bed. Had Jason really said "us"? "It's better than a car," Kyle told him.

"Hmn," Jason said. "Better than a car? Can you give me a hint?"

"No hints," Kyle said as the phone's call waiting beeped. "I gotta go. I'll be over soon as I eat, okay? Laters!" He pushed the flash key. "Hello?"

"Woo-hoo!" Nelson shouted, announcing news of his own acceptance to Tech.

"Awesome!" Kyle leaped off the bed. Not only would he be going to college with Jason, but also with Nelson.

"You got yours, too?" Nelson asked. "Of course *you* got accepted, but can you believe they accepted *moi*? This is going to be so cool!"

Nelson's dog started barking. "Uh-oh, Mom's home. She'll probably have a heart attack when I tell her I actually got—" his fingers snapped in the background "—ac-cep-ted. Woo-hoo!" He hung up.

Eager to get to Jason's, Kyle wolfed down dinner, but slowed down for dessert. His mom had bought an awesome chocolate-raspberry cake. "Can I take a piece to Jason?"

"All right," his mom said, cutting a slice. "But remember it's a school night. Don't stay too—"

"And one for his sister?" Kyle asked before his mom could put the knife down. She cut another wedge.

"And one for his mom?" Kyle added. "And another piece for me later?"

"Why don't you just take the whole cake?" His dad laughed.

"Okay," Kyle said, pretending his dad was serious.

Melissa, Jason's six-year-old sister, answered the Carrillos' door. Behind her the TV blared. Dolls and toys lay scattered before it. She grabbed Kyle's hand, pulling him in, her eyes opening wide at the box he carried. "What's that?"

"Mm . . ." Kyle rubbed a circle on his stomach. "Cake!"

Jason strode in wearing jeans and a flannel shirt that hung wide over his broad shoulders. A toothbrush handle protruded from his mouth as he vigorously brushed up and down, causing his left cheek to bulge and jiggle.

At the sight of him, Kyle fell in love all over again.

"Wha's up?" Jason said, popping the brush out. A perfect circle of foam ringed his mouth.

"I like your green lipstick," Kyle said, kidding.

Jason looked in the wall mirror. "Whoa!" He jogged back toward the bathroom.

With Melissa's help Kyle dished out cake and set the plates on the kitchen table.

"Oh, wow." Jason sauntered in. "You were right. This is better than a car."

"That's not the surprise," Kyle said, handing Jason the Tech letter. "This is."

Jason scanned the page, his lips moving to the words: ". . . pleased to inform you you've been accepted for admission—"

He glanced up at Kyle, high-fiving him. "Awesome! Congratulations, man."

"Can I take my cake to watch TV?" Melissa asked.

"Sure. Wait. You want some milk?" Jason poured them each a cold glass. "Careful you don't spill."

While Kyle sat down, Jason held the door for Melissa, then he returned to Kyle. "Of course, did you ever really think you wouldn't be accepted? You've got a four-point-o!"

"I don't have a four-point-o," Kyle said in mock protest. "It's a three-point-nine."

"Oh, right. Ex-cuuuze me." Pulling out a chair, Jason sat down, his knee grazing Kyle's.

The touch sent a spark through Kyle's body. Two excruciatingly long weeks had passed since they'd been alone together. It wouldn't take much for Kyle to jump Jason's bones right then and there.

"Nelson got his letter too," Kyle said in an effort to calm himself down. "So we'll all three go to Tech. It's going to be such a blast."

Jason studied Kyle, then glanced down at his cake.

"What's the matter?" Kyle asked.

"I've been thinking . . ." Jason paused, gulping a swig of milk as if fortifying himself. ". . . about coming out to Coach Cameron."

Kyle's throat clenched as he swallowed his cake. Had he heard right? He knew Jason's going to the Gay-Straight Alliance had been an enormous step toward coming out. Practically the whole school knew who went to the meeting, and even straight people who attended got crap for it. Jason telling his coach would be an even huger step for him.

And for Kyle it would also be a tremendous relief. He hated pretending they were just friends. While Jason garnered praise on the court or got interviewed by press, Kyle had to stand by anonymous. When Jason jaunted off to some postgame party, Kyle trudged home alone. Unlike Jason's ex-girlfriend, Kyle couldn't receive public recognition.

But if Jason came out . . . Kyle reveled in visions of the prom, whirling around the dance floor with Jason, arm in tuxedoed arm.

"Are you sure?" Kyle asked, not wanting to get his hopes up.

Jason gave a weary sigh. "I don't know. It's just . . ." His voice became agitated. "Sometimes I feel like I'm going to explode—or implode—if I keep hiding. It gets to where I just want to tell everyone and get it over with—not just Coach, the team, too. Does that sound crazy? What's happened with you and the swim team since the locker thing?"

The "locker thing" had happened after December break.

Someone scratched QUEER on Kyle's hall locker. Kyle repeatedly asked the school administration to repaint it, and they did nothing. Finally he got fed up. One morning he marched to school, and beneath the word QUEER he spray-painted AND PROUD!

The news raced around school. The following day his locker was repainted, but not before some teammates took notice.

"A few of the guys won't talk to me anymore, but they were never really friends to begin with. Besides, swimming is different from basketball. Except for relays, you're really on your own. In team sports, you're a lot more reliant on each other."

Jason nodded, slowly chewing a bite of cake. "So you don't think I should do it?"

Kyle immediately thought, *Of course you should do it!* He had always encouraged Jason to be honest and accepting of himself.

But before he could say anything, Jason confided, "I'm afraid I'll lose my scholarship."

Kyle set his fork down. "For coming out? They wouldn't dare. Look at how we fought for a GSA and won. If they tried to take your scholarship, we'd fight that, too. You're not going to lose your scholarship. You'll come out; we'll go to Tech together and graduate side by side."

He almost added how gay marriage would hopefully be legal by then, and about the kids they'd adopt and how they'd live happily ever after. But he decided he'd leave that discussion for later.

"Just suppose," said Jason, tapping his fork, "I did lose my scholarship—"

"Jason," Kyle interrupted. "I told you, you're not—"

"But just suppose," Jason insisted. "Would you still go to Tech?"

"Well," Kyle said, "could you still go without a scholarship?"

Jason shrugged. "I don't know how I'd pay for it. My mom can't afford it, especially with my dad gone. I could get loans, but not enough to go away. I'd probably stay home and go to community college, then transfer later."

Kyle felt his heart sink. More than anything, he wanted to be with Jason. But did he want it enough to put aside his dream of going away to a university?

"I hate this!" Kyle blurted out. "Our society is crazy. Why should we even have to deal with this? Our whole future together shouldn't hinge on whether you're honest and come out. It's homophobic *BS*."

Jason leaned back, looking a little blown away by Kyle's outburst.

"I'm sorry." Kyle took a deep breath. "I didn't mean to go off like that."

"It's okay. I'm sorry I brought all this up. It isn't your problem."

"It *is* my problem," Kyle told him. "If you don't go to Tech, where would that leave me? What you decide affects both of us."

Jason looked back at him, a solemn expression on his face. "Maybe I should forget all this," he said softly.

"How?" Kyle said. "It's not going to go away. Do you want to go through college like this? What happens if they find out after you're already there and take away your scholarship *then*?"

Jason bit into a fingernail. "I hadn't thought of that."

"At least," Kyle said soothingly, "if you come out now, you'd be, I don't know, like, a role model—someone people would look up to."

"Yeah, right," Jason said. "No one's going to look up to me."

"I do," Kyle said, staring deeply into Jason's brown eyes.

Jason pursed his lips into a little pout. "Yeah, well, you're biased. *You're* the role model, not me."

"Oh, yeah?" Kyle asked. "And you're not biased?"

Jason's mouth opened in a wide show of teeth. "Maybe."

Kyle thought how much he loved those teeth, that mouth, this boy. He considered what he was about to say and, fighting all common sense, he said it: "If you feel you need to come out to your coach, then I think you should do it."

Jason gazed back at him, sighing, and slumped down in his chair. In the process, his knee bumped against Kyle's.

Kyle let it rest there and reached across the table for Jason's hand.

Jason flashed a glance toward the door. An instant later they were on their feet, pressed against each other. Jason's lips devoured Kyle's, tasting of chocolate-raspberry cake, sweeter than the original.

As Kyle's tongue rolled across Jason's, he no longer cared about college next year. He only wanted to live this moment, forever. Except . . .

From the doorway came a giggle. Startled, the boys jumped apart.

Melissa stared at them, carrying her empty plate and milk glass. "Were you two kissing?"

Jason, bright red, darted a questioning glance at Kyle, but Kyle looked away, embarrassed. It was up to Jason what he told his sister, though Kyle hoped he'd be truthful.

Jason cleared his throat. "Um, yeah." He hurriedly took her plate and glass. "Don't tell Ma, okay?"

Melissa glanced at Kyle. "I won't." Giggling, she skipped out of the room.

rainbow high

"Oh, man!" Jason brought his fingers to his forehead. "I can't believe she saw us."

"At least you were honest with her," Kyle said, patting him on the shoulder. "That's great."

Jason rubbed his temples. "I'm glad you think so."

The front door sounded as Mrs. Carrillo came home. Melissa kept her word, not saying anything about the boys' kiss while Jason's mom chatted with them, thanking Kyle for the cake.

Before Kyle left, Jason handed him a pair of tickets for the game against Chesapeake High Friday. "For you and your dad. Can you come?"

"Of course!" Kyle beamed.

As he walked home through the cold, dark night, past brick houses with blue-hazed windows and dogs barking in yards, he thought how clear his life had seemed only two hours earlier. Now everything seemed so uncertain. What if Jason did lose his scholarship? Would Kyle stick by him no matter what? Wasn't that part of loving someone?

Kyle felt the game tickets in his pocket, desperately hoping he wouldn't regret encouraging Jason to come out to his coach.

chapter 3

jason   kyle

nelson

Friday evening, prior to the game against Chesapeake High, Jason suited up in the locker room, pulling on his blue and silver uniform. He replayed his conversation with Kyle in his mind, still wavering whether to come out to Coach and the team.

Wasn't it enough that he'd stood up to his dad and confided in most of the important people in his life—his best friend, Corey, Debra (his ex), his mom and little sister? He was free of his dad; he was discovering his feelings with a boy whom he'd told he loved; and he had a university scholarship in hand. For the first time in his life, everything was going his way. Did he really want to screw it all up?

Three lockers down, Dwayne Smith was spouting off about how tonight he was going to kick Chesapeakes' asses.

"And you faggoty fairies better not foul all over the place, like last game."

The jerk hassled everyone, then claimed he was only joking. He'd already tried to get into it with Jason twice during the past week at practice. On both occasions Jason had turned away, refusing to be goaded.

Now, as Jason finished tying his shoelaces, he felt Dwayne's sharklike gaze lock onto him. "Hey, Carrillo," Dwayne shouted, loud enough for the entire locker room to hear. "What did you go to that fag group for?"

Jason's heart thundered like a basketball on the court. A couple of teammates turned to Jason, awaiting his response. For a moment Jason regretted having gone to the GSA meeting. But didn't he want to come out to the team? Dwayne had yanked the door wide open for him. All Jason had to do was step out.

He hesitated. The words dangled from his tongue. But he refused to come out in reaction to Dwayne's provocation.

"I went to the group," Jason said, swallowing the knot in his throat, "'cause I wanted to."

The answer was true enough. Its force effectively terminated the discussion.

As Jason scanned his teammates' faces, he knew the issue wasn't over. With the exception of Dwayne, those in the locker room had been among the most cherished people in Jason's life. They were like brothers to him—even more than brothers.

First among them was Corey, Jason's best friend since freshman basketball tryouts. He was like a big brother to Jason, knowing him better than anyone. On many a night, when Jason's dad came after him in a drunken rage, Jason had fled to Corey's. And in turn, when Corey's own parents fought a bitter divorce, Jason was there, helping Corey get through it.

Then there was Odell, Jason's roommate at sports camp sophomore year. During their second week, Odell had gotten news his grandma died. He cried uncontrollably to Jason the entire night, apologizing between sobs. But Jason dismissed his apologies, staying up to console him.

There was Skip, who only three weeks ago had confided to Jason he'd accidentally gotten his girlfriend pregnant. "I don't know what to do!" he told Jason. "What the hell should I do?"

Jason didn't know either, so he just listened, hoping Skip would figure it out.

Andre was the heartbreaker of the group. His cologne filled the locker room at the end of each game. And his much-admired ability to win girls filled the rest of the team with awe. Jason remembered when he'd first courted Debra and asked Andre's advice. How could he come out to him *now*?

There was "Comeback Kid" Wang, who after a knee injury, feared he'd never play again. But everyone, including Jason, took turns massaging and exercising with him, pleading with Coach to let him return to the team, till at last Coach accepted him back.

And there were others, each holding a special place in Jason's life. He'd bonded with them, on the court and off—through back-slapping triumphs and somber defeats, memorable awards dinners and forgettable fast-food feasts; through birthdays getting tossed fully clothed into the shower and pay-back times when someone else's birthday came round; through the bus songs and diesel smells and awkward moments awaking on one another's shoulders; through winners' hugs and worries about grades; through being praised by Coach, then chewed out, then praised some more.

These were Jason's "boys," like family to one another.

And yet, in the very midst of their closest friendship, erupted the pervasive fag jokes and constant innuendo. Even now, as Jason closed his locker, Odell reached into Andre's shorts, snapping his jockstrap.

"Hey, honey. Gonna score another heart tonight?"

"Fag." Andre burped, grabbing for Odell's crotch in return.

"Homo." Odell laughed, pulling away.

It was like this all the time—as if they were all afraid of getting too close, so they had to make fun of it.

"That's enough," Coach Cameron bellowed, calling the team together for the pregame meeting.

Jason let out a breath of relief, eager for the pending game—where the rules were clear and made sense.

With the basketball season ending, Whitman ranked in the state's top ten. As the team jogged out to the court, the packed gym cheered.

But the game got off to a bad start. Whitman turned over the ball twenty-four times in the first twenty minutes. By halftime the team trailed 29-48.

In the locker room Coach Cameron did his best to rally them. "Come on, boys. Their team is crap. Show 'em who you are."

As the third quarter got under way, it seemed as if the game had turned round. Jason freed Corey up to get three shots, but then Jason missed a layup.

"Get with it," Dwayne hissed. "Stop playing like you're gay."

Jason disregarded the taunt, more angry at himself for messing up than at Dwayne. Nevertheless, the comment rattled him. And during the next play, he lost the ball.

Dwayne shouted, "Man!" and elbowed him in the side. That was too much. Jason spun around, shoving Dwayne. The referee blew his whistle.

Corey intervened, thrusting his arms between the boys.

The coach yelled, "What the hell's the matter with you two?" He shot Jason a disappointed look, as if Jason had let him down, and ordered both boys to the bench. In the stands the crowd booed.

Jason hung his head and stared at the floor. It was the first time in his career he'd been benched for an altercation. To make matters worse, Whitman lost the game.

In the locker room afterward, amid the shouts and lockers slamming, Coach called Jason and Dwayne aside. "All right, you two, what the hell happened?"

"I didn't mean to bump into him," Dwayne whined. "I don't know why he got so upset. He's so . . . *sensitive*!"

Jason strained every muscle not to strike the jerk.

"That's crap!" the coach told Dwayne. "I don't know what's with you two, but I won't tolerate it, understand? I want to see each of you Monday."

Jason nodded, too angry to think beyond the present moment. Quickly he undressed, hurrying to cool off in the showers.

Not even Kyle and Mr. Meeks, who were waiting eagerly for him, buoyed his spirits.

All weekend Jason racked his brain, debating what to tell Coach. He knew he'd let Coach and the team down by getting into it with Dwayne. But he was sick of the name-calling, sick of rumors, sick of hiding. The fight wouldn't have happened in the first place if Dwayne weren't such a homophobe.

He should simply be up-front with the coach. Even though Coach yelled all the time, he'd always been fair with Jason. And it was thanks to him that Jason had the scholarship to Tech. Except . . .

This was different from missing practice or screwing up a reverse. He'd heard Coach himself use the word "fag" enough times. How could Jason admit to being one?

rainbow high

Monday morning at school Jason headed toward Coach's office—one moment stepping quickly, determined to come out, but with the next step slowing, as his resolve flagged.

Turning the hallway corner, he saw Coach. In one hand he carried a steaming coffee mug, captioned WORLD'S GREATEST DAD. With the other hand he hauled a nylon bag of kickballs.

"Hi, Coach," Jason said, his voice quavering.

"Carrillo, give me a hand with these."

Jason grabbed the mesh bag and followed the coach to his office. On the wall hung photos of Coach standing proudly by past years' teams, alongside a picture with his wife and kids—known to Jason from the times Coach and his wife had the team to their home for dinner.

Coach took the bag of kickballs and placed it by his gray metal desk. "Close the door, Carrillo. Take a seat."

Jason thought back to the last time he'd sat in the low vinyl chair, only a few weeks earlier, when Coach handed him the scholarship offer from Tech.

"Smith was here earlier," Coach said, bringing Jason back to the present.

What had Dwayne told Coach? Jason wondered. Had he mentioned the GSA meeting?

"Carrillo . . ." Coach cleared his throat. "What the hell happened the other night?"

Jason shifted his feet, glancing down at his sneakers. "Well, first Dwayne said something, then he jabbed me—"

"Carrillo!" Coach brought his hands together, cracking his knuckles. "I don't want to get into this who-started-what, as if you were a couple of playground sissies."

Jason kept his gaze fixed on the tile floor as the word "sissies" echoed in his ears.

"If there was a problem," Coach railed on, "you should've come to me. All this year you've been holding something back— in your game, with the team, with me. Now, I want to know: What the hell is going on?"

Jason slid his feet, trying to think what to say. "Um, I've been dealing with a lot. My dad . . . I told you he left home. I guess it's bothered me."

He glanced up, checking to see if that explanation might suffice.

The coach leveled his eyes and took a sip of coffee. He set his cup down and rubbed his forehead above his glasses, all the while studying Jason. "Look, Jason, I know you've got a tough home situation. But you can't let that interfere with your game."

"I know," Jason mumbled, but the coach spoke right through it.

"You've got your scholarship to think about. I imagine to you that means getting away to college, the thrill of playing NCAA. But to the university, it's strictly business. You've got to understand that. They're not going to pay for someone who flies off the handle like you did. The way these signing letters are written, they can take it away from you just like that!" He snapped his fingers. "For any damn reason. That's the reality. I don't want to see you screw this up for yourself."

Jason sank into the cracked-vinyl chair, relieved by the coach's softening tone, but more confused than ever.

"Not to mention," Coach added, "I don't know if you realize it, but many of the younger boys look to you as a role model."

Jason recalled Kyle using the same two words. Was this some sort of conspiracy?

He flashed back to times he'd helped the freshman and JV squads. But what kind of role model lived a secret life? And if people already saw him as a role model, why should it matter if the special someone he liked was a girl or a guy?

Jason's thoughts returned to Kyle—his soft hazel eyes looking up at him as he encouraged Jason to tell Coach the truth. If the whole world expected him to be a role model, he had to be honest—with both himself and them.

Jason clasped the wooden arms of the chair and took a deep breath. "Um, Coach, can I ask you something?"

The coach swigged the last of his coffee. "Sure, but hurry up. I need to get ready for class."

Jason glanced down at his hands gripping the chair arms. His knuckles were bone white. A voice screamed inside his head, *Don't say it!* He gave an anxious cough. "Um, what if someone on the team told you they were, um, gay?"

In the gaping silence that followed, Jason swore he could hear the sweat trickling down his back.

Coach Cameron stared at him, adjusting his glasses, as if to make sure he wasn't seeing things. Then he broke into a wide grin, as if he'd been told a joke. "Carrillo, are you pulling some kind of crap on me?" His smile abruptly vanished and his face turned red with anger. "'Cause if you are—"

Jason squirmed in the chair. The back of his sweat-soaked shirt slid across the vinyl. "No, Coach. I wouldn't joke."

Coach Cameron turned silent. Then he gave the deepest sigh Jason thought he'd ever heard. When he spoke again, his tone was gentler. "Look, son, when you're young, it's not uncommon to go through phases when you feel, um . . . close to another boy. That doesn't mean . . . you know . . . I mean, what about Debra? You've been together for how long now? Two years?"

Jason shook his head, and though he hated to disappoint

Coach, told him, "We broke up a couple of months ago. We're just friends now."

"Oh," Coach said. He rubbed his chin, his gaze softening.

Jason felt his grip on the chair relax. "I've wanted to talk with you about all this, but I was afraid what you'd say. I guess it's what I've been holding back."

The coach leaned back in his swivel chair, folding his arms, and peered at Jason, as if unconvinced. His mouth opened to say something but closed again. He scratched his head. At last he leaned forward.

"Have you told anyone on the team?"

"Only Corey. I wasn't sure what everyone would say. I *want* to tell them."

Coach raised an eyebrow. "How did Corey react?"

"Well, at first he didn't believe me. Then he said it didn't matter to him. Except he's scared . . ."

Jason heard his voice breaking. His throat was choking up. He took a breath and swallowed, composing himself. "Coach, what'll happen to my scholarship?"

"I don't know," Coach muttered. "I recall the NCAA added sexual orientation to the charter's nondiscrimination clause. With no opposition, in fact. But whether a school would actually abide by that . . . Are you participating in that new group?"

Jason knew Coach meant the GSA. Dwayne must have ratted on him. "Um, yeah. I went to the first meeting."

"Was it helpful?"

Jason hesitated. "Um, yeah. I mean, I guess so."

The coach picked up a pencil and tapped it on his desk, as if thinking. "Who's in charge of that group, MacTraugh? Have you spoken to her about all this?"

"Not yet."

rainbow high

"Maybe you should. Maybe *I* should. Would you mind?"

Jason shrugged, not sure why Coach wanted to talk with her.

As if reading Jason's thoughts, the coach continued: "She might have some ideas about the team and how . . ." He tossed his pencil aside. "Have you thought about how you'd tell the team?"

Jason shook his head. "I hadn't thought that far ahead. I guess I'll just start telling people."

"Hmm," Coach grumbled. "I should probably mention it to Mueller, too."

Jason sat up in his chair. Principal Mueller? "Why?"

"He's the principal," Coach said grimly. "If you're going to do this, I think he should know. It could have an impact on the whole school."

Jason bit into a fingernail. He hadn't expected all this. It felt like his life had suddenly accelerated to fast forward.

"In the meantime—" Coach's voice became stern "—the same thing I told Smith goes for you. At practice this afternoon I expect you both to shake hands and play like a team. Is that understood?"

"Yes, sir." Jason stood up, taking the hall pass Coach handed him. "Thanks, Coach. I mean it."

Coach leveled his gaze at him. "Don't thank me yet, Carrillo. This is one hell of a move."

Outside Coach's office, Jason slumped against the concrete wall and closed his eyes. Not only had Coach failed to reassure him about his scholarship, he'd dragged MacTraugh and Mueller into it. What was *that* all about?

"You okay?" a voice asked, startling him.

Jason's eyes opened to a shocking blue head of hair.

"Wha's up?" Jason said. He'd grown to kind of admire Nelson, partly for his nerve to do over-the-top crap like dye his hair blue.

"You feeling okay?" Nelson repeated.

"Yeah," Jason said, standing away from the wall. He debated a moment before telling Nelson about having come out to Coach.

Nelson snapped his fingers in approval. "That's awesome! Can I tell Kyle?"

"I guess so. Just don't tell anyone else, okay?"

"Don't worry." Nelson patted him on the back. "You're doing great."

"Hey!" A voice boomed from the end of the hall. Jason turned to see Mueller marching up, his eyes darting between Jason and Nelson, as if puzzled. His scowl settled on Nelson's blue hair. "Glassman, you have a hall permit?"

He grabbed Nelson's pass and scrutinized it. "Get back to class." He snorted and shoved the pass back. "Hurry it up."

Nelson made a defiantly bored face and said "later" to Jason before strolling away, not at all hurrying.

Jason held out his own hall pass, but Mueller showed no interest. Instead he rested a hand on Jason's shoulder and began walking alongside him, giving him a lecture for having lost the game.

Jason had known it was coming. Whenever the team won, Mueller always gave Jason a pat on the back, telling him, "We did it! Let's keep up the good work."

But if they lost, he'd frown and grouse.

Either way, Mueller took the team's performance personally—as if he were part of the squad.

How would he react when Coach told him Jason was gay? Would he take that personally too?

chapter 4

jason

kyle

nelson

"I saw your future husband today," Nelson told Kyle as they
drove to the doctor's. "He said he came out to Coach
Cameron."

"He did?" Kyle's voice rose, excited. "Did he say anything
about his scholarship?"

"No. Mueller nabbed us—me, anyway. He treats Jason like
some jock goddess."

Nelson flicked his cigarette out the window and lit up a new
one. Ever since his HIV test, he'd practically been chain-
smoking.

"This has been worse than waiting for my SAT scores. What
if I test positive? Tell me honestly, Kyle. Do you think I got it?"

"Nelson . . ." Kyle let out a sigh. "Whatever happens, we'll
deal with it." His calm reassured Nelson, but annoyed him too.

"You *do* think I got it, don't you?"

"Nelson! I don't know." Kyle pulled into the doctor's parking lot.

"I'm so stressed," Nelson said, exhaling a stream of smoke. Inside his head he promised God that if he tested negative, he'd always use condoms from now on. But what if he slipped again? What guaranteed he wouldn't mess up a second time?

"Maybe I'll become a monk," Nelson said, pointing to a parking spot.

"Nelson, you're Jewish."

"Barely," Nelson grumbled. Didn't Kyle realize he was trying his hardest to avoid being serious, in order to keep from totally freaking out?

"Well . . ." Kyle grinned. "If you're going to convert, I see you more as a nun."

Nelson swatted him. "Seriously, I'm scared."

"You'll be okay," Kyle told him. And Nelson wished he could believe him.

Inside the reception room Nelson signed in and huddled into a chair beside Kyle, while Kyle picked up a *Reader's Digest,* turning to an article titled "Sex Secrets for a Happy Marriage."

Oh, puke, Nelson thought.

Why couldn't Jason just go away to some remote sports camp for indecisive bisexual jocks and never return?

Granted, Nelson had grown to like him—especially after Jason rescued him from getting beat up. And it was heartwarming to see Kyle and Jason finally together, after hearing Kyle pant over him *ad nauseam* since freshman year.

But why couldn't Kyle have become *his* boyfriend instead of Jason's? Then none of this HIV crap would've happened in the first place. It still irked him that Kyle couldn't see how perfect they were for each other. They liked the same music, same TV shows, same foods. They liked *each other*.

The door by the reception counter swung open, snapping Nelson back to the present. Some amazon-looking nurse appeared, folder in hand. *Omigod,* Nelson thought, *this is it.*

But she called someone else's name. A mom with a screaming toddler strained to lift him up, and in the process dropped his toy gorilla. Nelson picked it up and handed it to her.

"Thanks," said the mom and carried the shrieking kid over to the nurse.

Nelson sat down again, desperate to get this over with and dreading it too. A stream of questions hounded him. How would his life change if he tested positive? What if people at school found out? What would his so-called dad say about it?

His cell phone rang, displaying his mom's office number. She'd bought the phone for him as a result of the whole night-he-had-sex-and-didn't-call-her mess, though she admonished him not to think of it as a reward. Yeah, right, whatever.

"Have you seen the doctor yet?" she now asked.

"No. I told you I'll call you soon as I find out."

After Nelson hung up, he told Kyle, "I need to go for another smoke."

Kyle glanced up from his magazine. "Stay. They'll probably call you soon."

Nelson hoped so, or he was going to scream. Verging on despair, he reached beneath the *Reader's Digest,* grasping hold of Kyle's hand. Without missing a beat, Kyle gently squeezed back. And for the first time that day, Nelson felt a semblance of peace.

Even though Kyle had betrayed him for frickin' Jason, Nelson knew he couldn't really blame Kyle for this mess.

Nelson accepted full responsibility for it. He only hoped he wouldn't have to suffer massive consequences.

The door by the reception desk opened again and the behemoth nurse shouted, "Nelson Glassman!"

"That's us!" Nelson said.

Kyle got up to go with him.

"I'm sorry," the nurse told Kyle. "Results can only be given to the person tested."

"But he's my best friend," Nelson protested.

"Sorry," the nurse repeated, holding the door open.

That must mean I got it, Nelson thought, horrified.

"Don't worry," Kyle whispered. "I'll be here waiting."

Reluctantly Nelson followed the nurse to the examining room. After checking his blood pressure and taking his temperature, she left him. Alone.

Please, please, God, he silently repeated over and over as he waited on the examining table. *Don't let me test positive.* It was the first time he'd prayed in ages.

On the wall an illustration of a woman's reproductive system stared back at him, as if taunting. Nelson turned away, wondering what on earth was taking pruney old Dr. Choudhury so long?

The sound of someone whistling approached from the hall outside, followed by a knock. The door opened and a beefy black guy strode in with a folder.

"Wow," he said to Nelson. "That's some hair!"

He was built more like a cop than a doctor, his white medical jacket hanging tightly over his chest. "I'm Doctor Houston," he said, firmly grasping Nelson's hand. "Doctor Choudhury had to run to the hospital. You must be Nelson."

Nelson nodded speechlessly, a little taken aback. He'd never

rainbow high

expected anyone other than his regular doc—especially not someone young and gorgeous. Suddenly the tiny examining room seemed downright intimate.

"Let's see," Dr. Houston said, sitting on the stool. He opened Nelson's file. "You're here for your HIV antibody test result?"

Nelson snapped back to reality. *Omigod!* He grabbed hold of the examining table, his heart pumping at warp speed.

Dr. Houston lifted his brown-eyed gaze from the folder. "I'm happy to say your test came back . . . negative."

The word seemed to hang in midair as Nelson sat silent, taking it in.

"Negative?" he echoed back, just to be sure.

"Yep." Dr. Houston nodded. "I bet that's a relief."

"Yeah!" Nelson said, letting out his breath. He hadn't realized he'd been holding it. "Can I go tell my friend?" He leaped down from the examining table.

"Whoa!" The doc raised his arm, blocking him. "Not so fast." His smile had faded, replaced by a stern gaze. "First you and I need to have a little man-to-man chat."

Man-to-man? Nelson thought. *Oh, please, spare me.*

"But he's my best friend! He's waiting."

"If he's your best friend, he won't mind waiting. This is important."

Reluctantly Nelson sat down again, crossing his arms. "Look, if this is a safe-sex lecture, I already know all about that."

"Oh, you do?" The doctor raised his thick black eyebrows. "Well then, what caused you to come in for testing?"

Nelson stared at the doc's massive shoulders, feeling like he'd been pinned against the wall. "Look, I knew I was supposed to use a condom, but I didn't. I was stupid, okay?"

Dr. Houston pressed him with his stare. "You seem pretty intelligent to me." He studied Nelson's file for a moment before looking up at him. "You're straight? Bi? Gay?"

"Queer," Nelson said defiantly.

Doc nodded, unfazed. "Did you and this dude discuss safe sex?"

"No." Nelson shook his head. "I know we should've. Look, I made a mistake and I'm sorry. I won't do it again. Promise. That what you want? Can I go now?"

Dr. Houston refused to be deterred. "How come you didn't talk about it with him?"

"I don't know!"

The doctor cocked his head. "Afraid Dude wouldn't like you if you said no?"

Nelson fidgeted with an earring. "Maybe."

"Nelson?" The doc's voice was still forceful, but had become tender. "Never let yourself be pressured into doing something unsafe. It's okay to say no. If Dude can't understand that, he's not worth it."

Nelson stared at the doc's lush eyelashes, thinking, *I can't believe I'm getting turned on in old Choudhury's office.* He forced himself to shift his gaze and concentrate on the illustration of the woman's uterus.

"Now listen up!" Dr. Houston said, tossing Nelson's folder onto the counter. "First of all, abstinence is always a choice."

Sure it is, Nelson thought, *if you want to go crazy.*

"But . . ." The doctor sighed. "Since you're already sexually active, you need to remember: Before anything gets started, tell the dude you only have sex using condoms. Okay? Will you do that? Nelson?"

"Huh?" Nelson said, gazing at the doctor's lips. "Um, yeah."

The doc gave Nelson a hard look, as if unconvinced. "All right. Before you leave, I want you to start Hepatitis A and B vaccines."

"What for?" Nelson asked.

"So you don't get hepatitis. Sex with guys puts you at risk. Any other questions?"

Yeah, Nelson thought, *are you single?*

Still sore from the shots, Nelson pulled open the reception room door.

Kyle immediately glanced up, tossing his magazine aside, eyebrows raised in expectation.

Nelson gave him the thumbs up.

"You're okay?" Kyle said, rushing over. "What took so long?" He squeezed Nelson in a bear hug.

"Ow!" Nelson protested. "My arm!"

"What's the matter?" Kyle said, pulling away.

"Hep vaccines. Since I'm so-called sexually active." He rolled his eyes. "I wish!"

"Probably a good idea," Kyle said, like he was some Nobel laureate in medicine.

"I better call the old lady," Nelson said, dialing his cell phone as they walked outside.

"Thank God!" his mom gasped upon hearing his result. "You know how worried I was? Promise me you won't ever make me go through anything like this again. Do you hear me, Nelson? I mean it." She was talking so loud he had to hold the phone away from his ear.

"Love you too, Mom," he muttered, and hung up. "Can you drive again?" he asked Kyle, tossing him the car keys.

"Aren't you ecstatic?" Kyle said, starting the car. "You just tested negative. That means you don't have it!"

Nelson shrugged. He knew Kyle was right—he should be jumping up and down, except for one thing: Now that he'd officially tested negative, what was he going to do about Jeremy?

He wanted to ask Kyle. But what if Kyle told him to dump Jeremy? Easy enough for Kyle to say. He was in the midst of a senior year kissyfest with Jason.

"I promised to call Jeremy tonight," Nelson told Kyle as they drove past the retail strip on Lee Highway, "to let him know the news—even though he'll probably dump me now."

Kyle glanced across the dashboard. "Well, you can still be friends, can't you?"

Nelson laid his hand on the armrest, preparing for the argument he was certain would follow. "I want to be more than just friends with him."

Kyle looked over at Nelson again, staring this time. "You're not serious."

"I want a boyfriend." Nelson nodded. "Like you and Jason—except not as closeted, of course—someone to date and hold hands with. I want to take him to the prom. This is our freaking senior year, Kyle. I want the whole rite of passage thing. Someone I can introduce to my mom—and watch him fidget."

Kyle turned the car into the strip mall parking lot. "Can I remind you of one not-so-minor detail?" He stopped the car. "What's your mom going to say when you tell her he's positive?"

"I don't care," Nelson said. He was lying, of course. "Why are you stopping?"

"So we can talk about this." Kyle shut off the engine. He turned in the seat to face Nelson. "Think for a minute about what you just went through. You'd actually risk putting yourself through this again?"

rainbow high

"No," Nelson said. "What I just went through happened because I didn't have safe sex. I'd be careful. We both would. Jeremy told me he only has safe sex."

Kyle shook his head. "Something could still happen. Condoms break, you know. You'd be putting your health at risk—maybe even your life."

"Oh, stop exaggerating!" Nelson stared out the window at the playground beyond the asphalt. "No one dies of AIDS anymore."

"Yes, they do!" Kyle protested. "People die of AIDS all the time."

"In Africa maybe. Ever heard of meds?"

"Meds don't cure the disease. Besides, you want to be on meds all your life? I don't believe this. An hour ago you were hysterical, terrified that you might have gotten it!"

"I wasn't hysterical."

"Yes, you were! You wanted to become a monk."

"I was joking, Kyle."

"Well, this isn't a joke. You know, you're not the only one who suffered with this whole HIV scare of yours. It scared me, too."

Kyle folded his arms across his chest, sulking. Nelson sat silent, letting him cool off, and thought carefully about what he wanted to say.

"I'm sorry, Kyle. I know it scared you too. I admit what I did was stupid, but I'm allowed to learn from my mistakes. I'm not going to go though life living in fear."

Kyle unfolded his arms and sighed. "Can't you just be friends with him?"

Nelson gave a shrug. "I like him, Kyle—a lot. I think I might even be in love with him. I need to find out."

Kyle glanced away, shaking his head.

"Kyle, look at me." Nelson waited until Kyle faced him. "You remember when you were ready to dump Jason that time after the cafeteria episode? I could've told you, 'Do it.' But I didn't. I told you, 'Don't you dare!' Remember? Now I'm asking you a favor in return. Please don't bail on me with this."

Kyle stared at him, then turned away again.

"Kyle?" Nelson insisted, his voice unyielding.

Kyle turned back toward him, took a deep breath, and sighed. "Okay, *but* . . . I'll say this once, then I promise never to say it again. I think you're making a huge mistake. I like Jeremy as a friend, but . . ." Kyle's eyes had become watery. "I'm really scared for you."

Looking at him made Nelson's own eyes film over. "Stop worrying." He reached across and gave Kyle's shoulder a squeeze. "Nothing's going to happen to me."

Kyle started the car again, and Nelson shook a cigarette from his pack, hoping it would calm his nerves.

jason   kyle

nelson

True to his word, Kyle didn't say another word to Nelson about
dating Jeremy for the rest of the drive. But inside his head, the
debate raged on.

How could Nelson even consider putting his health at risk
by dating someone whom he *knew* was HIV positive? If he
wanted a boyfriend so badly, why couldn't he find someone
negative?

After all, he was good-looking—thin, brilliant blue eyes,
colorful hair, even his million earrings looked cool. He was
funny, smart, good-hearted. You couldn't find anyone more
loyal. Whenever Kyle needed anything, Nelson was there. Even
when Kyle *didn't* need anything, Nelson was there.

Kyle wanted to shake Nelson and make him come to his
senses. But little good that would do. Once Nelson put his
mind to something, there was no stopping him.

Upon arriving at Kyle's, Nelson got out to switch over to the driver's seat.

"You're not still mad at me?" Nelson asked, pausing on the grass strip between car and sidewalk. "Are you?"

He looked so fragile, fidgeting with his earrings, his Dr. Seuss blue hair hanging into his face, that Kyle felt guilty for being angry.

"No," he lied. "I'm not mad."

Nelson's sheepish mouth turned up into a faint grin. "Thanks for going with me today."

"Sure. I just hope we never have to go through it again."

Nelson nodded somberly, then broke into a shameless smile. "I wish you'd seen the doc. He was *so* cute!" Patting Kyle on the cheek, Nelson laughed his invincible laugh. "See you later, stud."

He hopped into the car and drove off, disappearing past the green suburban lawns.

He's absolutely hopeless, Kyle thought, and wandered up the driveway.

His mom and dad weren't home from work yet. Kyle picked up the mail that had been pushed through the front door slot and quickly scanned through it—nothing interesting, just junk. Tossing the pile aside, he checked for phone messages.

"Hey, Kyle. This is Jason."

At the sound of the low, husky voice, Kyle swooned into the foyer armchair.

"Call me when you get home, okay?"

Three times Kyle listened to the message, relishing every word. Over the past months he'd saved all of Jason's messages, till the voice mailbox became so full his dad made him erase them.

Reluctantly he now deleted the new one and immediately dialed Jason.

Mrs. Carrillo answered. She was always sweet to Kyle, asking how he was and thanking him for helping Jason with school. Now she sounded out of breath.

"Hold on," she told Kyle. "Jason! It's Kyle!"

Kyle ran a hand through his hair, eagerly listening for Jason's approach.

"Wha's up?" Jason said. "Have you seen Nelson? Did he tell you about what happened with Coach today?"

"Yeah. Congrats. How'd Coach take it?"

"Okay, I guess. He didn't kick me off the team or anything. But he said he wants to talk to Mueller."

"No way!" Kyle sat up in his seat. "What for?"

"I don't know. Hey, can I call you back? I'm helping my mom move furniture."

"Well, you want to come over later?" Kyle asked, anxious to hear the rest of Jason's story. Happily, Jason agreed.

After hanging up, Kyle went upstairs and crashed onto the bed, wiped out from the doctor's visit with Nelson. He cupped his hands behind his head and stared at the movie poster Jason had given him tacked on the wall.

During the past few days Kyle had spent hours thinking back and forth about college and his future with Jason. Now once again his thoughts began turning. But before he knew it, he'd fallen asleep.

His mom woke him, brushing her hand gently across his forehead. "Honey, it's time for dinner."

She'd made lemon chicken, with cinnamon sweet potatoes and almond string beans. Kyle loved her cooking.

"Still no word from Princeton?" his dad asked. "Maybe I should call and ask when they're sending their letters out."

"Dad!" Kyle said, tossing down his fork. "Can't you just leave it alone? I'm the one going to school, not you!"

His dad drew back a tiny bit. "I'm just suggesting—"

Kyle's mom intervened, as usual. "Honey, Kyle's right. It's not going to do any good to call them."

As if scolded, his dad backed off. "At least they could tell us when we'd hear."

His mom tried to switch the conversation, asking Kyle what he knew about the Tech and Princeton swim teams, just as the doorbell rang.

"Jason!" Kyle gasped, suddenly realizing he'd forgotten to tell his mom. "Um, I invited him over." Kyle tried to keep himself from tearing to the door. "Is it all right?"

"Of course, honey. But it would be nice if you'd tell me ahead of time."

"Sorry!" Kyle yelled over his shoulder as he bolted to the foyer, his socks sliding across the tile.

Jason stood on the doorstep, warming his hands with his breath, dark eyes glowing brightly above his cheeks. "Wha's up?" he said, stepping inside.

Kyle pressed his hand against Jason's. "You're ice cold. You need gloves."

"I'm all right." Jason smiled, peeling off his coat.

Kyle hung it for him on the hook atop his own jacket. Then glancing over his shoulder and seeing his parents weren't looking, he quickly pecked Jason a kiss.

"Hey, cut it out," Jason whispered. But he was smiling and an instant later, he tapped Kyle a kiss in return.

"Have you eaten?" Kyle asked, grinning.

rainbow high

Jason gave a vague shrug that Kyle took to mean he wouldn't mind eating again.

"Hello, Jason!" Kyle's dad said, instantly on his feet as Jason came into the dining room. He shook Jason's hand, clapped him on the shoulder, and as Kyle set an extra place, his dad and Jason began talking excitedly about assists, steals, rebounds, and turnovers.

Although Kyle never doubted his dad loved him, he could tell Jason was the type of son he'd always wanted Kyle to be—self-confident, popular, winning.

Kyle tried not to feel jealous, listening politely till everyone finished eating and his mom interceded.

"Honey," she told his dad, "the boys probably want to go study."

"Huh?" His dad blinked. "Oh, yeah."

"There's apple pie when you boys get hungry again," his mom said after Jason helped Kyle clear the table.

"I hope my dad didn't talk your ear off," Kyle whispered to Jason as he led him upstairs.

"I don't mind." Jason shrugged. "At least he takes an interest. That's more than I could ever say for mine." He sat down in the desk chair.

"So, tell me everything!" Kyle said, sitting down on his bed. "What did Coach say? Why's he want to talk to Mueller about you?"

Jason recounted the story, as if recapping a game, and even though he seemed to be cool with the whole thing, the way he bit into a fingernail every once in a while hinted he was really kind of nervous.

"It sounds like you did great," Kyle said, trying to reassure him.

Jason shrugged and gave a slight grin. "It was so weird when

Coach brought up the role model thing. Almost like you'd told him to say that."

"I did," Kyle teased. "I phoned him over the weekend."

"Want to give Mueller a call too?" Jason kidded in return.

Kyle laughed, then turned earnest. "I think Coach's idea of talking to MacTraugh is great. She's awesome."

"I hope so," Jason said.

Kyle nodded, carefully considering what he wanted to say next. "I've been thinking. . . ." He sat forward on the bed, bracing his arms on the mattress. "About what you said—you know—about staying home and going to community college?"

"Yeah?" Jason's thick eyebrows rose with curiosity.

"Like you said," Kyle continued, "going to a community college wouldn't be the worst thing. I mean, I guess what I'm saying is . . . if that's what you had to do, well, I could do it too."

Kyle knew he was crazy to even entertain the idea, but wasn't the alternative—being apart from Jason—even crazier?

"I mean," Kyle pressed on, "we'd still transfer to Tech junior year, right?"

Jason ran a hand through his hair. "I don't know about this, Kyle. You shouldn't decide on your college based on me. You need to think maturely about this."

"I'm not," Kyle said. "I mean, I *am* thinking maturely. I wouldn't only do this because of you. I'd be doing it for me."

Jason raised an eyebrow. "What do you mean?"

Kyle wondered: How could he convince Jason how much he meant to him without sounding immature?

"I want to be with you," he said softly. "I don't want to be apart. We're boyfriends."

Jason gazed into his eyes. "Well . . ." His beautifully

rounded lips quivered anxiously. "Like you said before, this is all hypothetical."

Abruptly he glanced away, grabbing his backpack, and pulled out a book. "Can you help me with some math?"

His notebook accidentally dropped to the floor. Obviously he felt too nervous to talk any more about the future.

Kyle longed for some reassurance about his plan. But he knew from experience how skittish Jason could get, so he contented himself with Jason scooting his chair close.

For the next hour Kyle helped him with algebra, every once in a while finding himself leaning against Jason's shoulder. He'd force himself to pull back, to concentrate on the math. But the next moment Jason would rest his knee against Kyle's.

When they finished the last equation and Jason turned to him, Kyle had to close his eyes to keep from melting. An instant later, as in a dream, Jason's lips touched his, their tenderness putting to rest all of Kyle's worries about the future.

Losing all restraint, he pulled Jason by the hand onto the bed.

"What about your parents?" Jason said in a soft voice.

"Who?" Kyle said, half joking and half in dazed earnestness. "Oh, yeah." Reluctantly, he tiptoed to the door and quietly closed it. A thrill coursed through his heart. He couldn't believe he was actually doing this.

"What if they come up?" Jason whispered as Kyle lay back down beside him.

Kyle pressed a finger onto Jason's lips and kissed him. For a brief moment Jason resisted, but then relaxed into a kiss, telling Kyle, in a gravelly voice, "You feel so good."

Then they kissed passionately—their tongues touching, blood pounding, hands clutching as they pressed against each other.

"This is getting too intense," Kyle panted, about to burst.

"Yeah." Jason's chest surged and fell, mirroring Kyle's passion.

But neither of them could stop—till a knock rattled the door.

Jason scrambled from the bed. "Crap!" he cursed, springing to his feet.

Kyle leaped up beside him. "It's okay," he told Jason, knowing full well it wasn't. "Just a minute!" he called out, smoothing the bedspread.

Jason tucked in his shirt. "Your hair!" he told Kyle in a stage whisper.

Kyle glanced in the mirror and patted his hair down. Trying to slow his breath, he opened the door. "Oh hi, Mom." His voice squeaked out thin and false.

"I thought you might be ready for dessert." She held a tray of pie and milk.

Though she wore a tight-lipped smile, her eyes, dark and troubled, darted between the two boys. "Kyle, can I talk to you a minute?"

Kyle's stomach clenched. He shot Jason a nervous glance, handing him the tray, then he followed his mom into the hall.

"Honey," she said in a strained tone, "could you please leave the door open?"

"Huh?" Kyle tried to sound innocent, though he knew his face was betraying him. "Um, sure."

"Good." She gave his arm a firm pat. "Enjoy the pie."

"Thanks," he replied. Did she really expect him to eat after that?

"What did she say?" Jason asked in a hushed voice.

rainbow high

Kyle handed him a plate of pie, trying to appear calm. "She wants us to keep the door open."

"Crap!" Jason punched himself on the leg. "You think she knew what we were doing?"

"All we were doing was kissing." Kyle grabbed a plate and tried to eat, but his throat felt too dry to swallow.

Jason started pacing. "I can't believe this. You think she told your dad? How am I going to walk past them now?"

"Well, as far as my dad is concerned, you can do no wrong. I think he likes you better than he likes me."

Jason gave him a sarcastic smirk. "I better go. We shouldn't have done anything with your parents around."

Kyle didn't want Jason to go, but he knew he couldn't stop him. He followed Jason downstairs, wishing his mom hadn't come up and scared him away. Why had she made such a big deal of the closed door? Didn't she trust them?

She and his dad sat in the living room reading—his dad in the recliner, his mom in the wingchair. "Leaving so soon?" she asked Jason.

"Yes, ma'am," he replied, keeping his gaze lowered. "Thanks for dinner. Good night, Mr. Meeks."

"See you at the next game," Kyle's dad said, and gave Kyle a reproachful glance.

Kyle handed Jason his jacket. "Are you coming to the GSA at lunch tomorrow? It's Ms. MacTraugh's birthday."

"Okay," Jason said, pushing his arms through the sleeves.

Kyle recalled his cold hands when he'd arrived. "Take my gloves."

Jason brushed them aside. "I don't want to take your gloves."

"Take them," Kyle insisted. "I have another pair."

Jason took them. "Later." He stepped out the door and down the driveway, leaning into the wind. Kyle watched, hoping he'd turn around.

"Kyle!" his dad yelled. "You're letting in the cold."

Kyle pulled the door closed just enough so he could still watch until Jason disappeared down the dark, tree-lined street.

Sidling into the living room, he stood before his parents. "Why do I have to keep my bedroom door open?"

His mom glanced at him over the rim of her glasses. "Because," she said, calmly closing her book, "we'd feel more comfortable."

"About *what*? Whenever Nelson comes over we always close the door."

His dad peered over the newspaper. "That's different."

"Why's it different?" Kyle insisted.

"Because Nelson isn't your boyfriend," his mom said.

Kyle shoved his hands into his pockets. "So Jason and I can't have any privacy because you're afraid we'll do something? That's pretty homophobic."

His mom pushed a strand of graying blond hair behind her ear. "Kyle, that's not fair. Your dad and I are trying very hard to be understanding. If you had a girlfriend, we'd have the same rule. You can have Jason in your room, but keep the door open."

"Why? You afraid one of us will get pregnant?"

With that, he stomped up to his room and tossed himself onto the bed, where only minutes earlier he'd lain with Jason.

There was no way he could stay home and go to community college. What was the point, if Jason and he couldn't be alone together?

How would they ever make out again—much less make love?

They absolutely *had* to go to Tech. Once away from home, there was no way his parents—or anyone—could keep Jason and him apart.

Except . . . what if Jason lost his scholarship?

Kyle shut his eyes, not wanting to think about that.

chapter 6

jason   kyle

nelson

Jason trudged home, rehashing in his mind some of the things Kyle had said that evening and wondering since when had they become "boyfriends." They'd never discussed it.

True, they'd had sex. But that just sort of happened. Jason had wanted it to happen and wished it could happen more often—a whole lot more often. But did that make them *boyfriends*? What did it mean for two guys to be boyfriends?

He definitely liked Kyle a lot. He was funny, sweet, smart, and always there to help. There was never a better listener, and Jason enjoyed spending time with him more than with anyone else he'd ever known.

He also liked being physical with Kyle—not just in sex, but also kissing and holding him. He ached to be with him.

But it worried Jason the way Kyle was so ready to sacrifice Tech and jump on the forever bus. Sure, it was a total rush. But

rainbow high

was Jason ready for so much in-love-ness? Was *either* of them? What if Kyle got hurt—the same as Debra had?

As Jason walked down the street, thinking and fretting, a cold gust of wind blew into his face. At least his hands were warm inside Kyle's gloves.

The following day on the way to the lunchroom, Corey's voice called out, "Yo, Jason!" He jostled toward Jason across the crowded hall. "What's with you, man? Didn't you hear me?" He raised his arm to clasp hands.

"Sorry," Jason said, grabbing hold of Corey's hand. "I guess I was zoned out."

As they herded into the ketchupy-smelling cafeteria, Jason peered through the glass panes of the food line, and took a plate of something red—maybe pizza, lasagna, or cherry cobbler—he wasn't sure which. When they got to the cash register, he couldn't find his lunch ticket.

Corey lent him some money, whispering, "You sure you're all right?"

Jason shrugged. He hadn't told Corey yet about coming out to Coach or about everything going on with Kyle.

As they carried their trays through the rowdy lunchroom, Jason confided in a low voice, "Yesterday I told the coach about . . . you know . . ."

"Whoa!" Corey stopped in his tracks. "You did what?" He glanced toward the basketball team table. "Let's sit somewhere else."

They found an empty table by the wall. "How did Coach take it?" Corey said.

But before Jason could answer, Corey's girlfriend walked up. "Hi, guys!" Cindy plopped her tray next to Corey's.

Beside her stood Debra, wearing a formfitting pink cashmere turtleneck. "Mind if I sit?" she asked Jason.

Her familiar scent of rose perfume carried over. This would mark their first time lunching together since their breakup.

"Sure." He pulled the chair out for her.

"How come you're sitting way over here?" Cindy asked. She was always to the point like that.

Corey glanced at Jason, deferring to his response.

Jason bit into his lip. Should he tell *all* of them about coming out to Coach? He hated having to make daily decisions about when to tell who how much about what. It was ridiculous.

But since he'd already come out to Corey, Debra, and Cindy, he decided he may as well update them.

He took a deep breath. "I was telling Corey that I told Coach. You know . . . I came out to him."

He tried to gauge Debra's reaction. He hadn't discussed with her any more about his liking guys since he'd first come out to her and she'd responded by striking out at him, yelling that she hated him. Even though she'd since apologized and said she wanted to be friends, the episode had left its mark.

Now Cindy responded first. "So does that mean you're out to the whole school?"

"No," Jason said, glancing over his shoulder. "Not yet."

Debra took a sip from her Coke. "What did Coach say?"

Jason relaxed in his chair, relieved she wasn't freaking out. "He wants to discuss it with some people. I'm not sure what's going to happen. I just hope Tech won't take away my scholarship."

"They couldn't do that," Cindy said. "Could they?"

Corey nodded. "Oh, yeah!"

"That sucks," Cindy said. "It seems like everyone's coming out all of a sudden. First Kyle spray-painted his locker. Of

rainbow high

course, I always suspected him. I saw you two talking after the game. Are you friends?"

Jason felt a trickle of sweat start down his back. He hadn't mentioned to Debra about his relationship with Kyle yet, in part because he didn't want to hurt her feelings—everything with Kyle had happened so soon after she and Jason had broken up— and partly because it was still hard to talk about being involved with a guy, especially to an ex-girlfriend.

"Um . . ." Jason cleared his throat. "I guess you could say Kyle and I are friends. He started helping me with math and we, um . . . hang out sometimes."

"I've always liked him," Debra said. "I remember the day he helped me carry this *huge* load of field hockey equipment out to my car. And when my mom was in the hospital that time? He always asked how I was doing. He's a sweet guy. I didn't realize you'd become friends."

Jason nodded, hoping that would end the discussion, but Cindy gave him a mischievous grin. "So," she whispered, "are you two dating?"

Jason nearly slid off his chair. Did she really just ask that? He'd never thought of Kyle and him as "dating," but wasn't that what they were doing?

"Um . . ." He sipped his Coke, trying to quench the sudden drought in his mouth. "Yeah, I mean, I guess so."

Cindy's smile evaporated. "Oh," she said. "I was just joking."

Debra spun around to stare at Jason, her cheerful calm shattered. "You're *dating* Kyle? Since *when*?"

"Just recently," Jason said, trying to sound like it was no big deal. "Not till you and I broke up." His feet pressed into the floor, ready to propel his chair back if she swung out at him.

But Debra folded her arms. "Why didn't you tell me about it?"

Jason swallowed the knot in his throat. "I was afraid you'd feel hurt."

"Jason!" Debra said, her voice sounding exasperated. "I told you I want to be your friend!"

Great, now he felt even guiltier. "Well, I—I just didn't want to hurt you."

Debra pursed her lips as if disbelieving him. "What hurts is when you don't tell me things—it's like you don't trust me."

"Trust you?" Jason protested. "I was afraid you'd flip out again."

"Well, you've got to admit," Debra shot back, "after making love for two years, you could've given me some warning."

"I tried!" Jason muttered, letting his hand slam down on the tabletop. "But like now, every time I try, you make me feel like I've done something wrong."

"Guys?" Corey crossed his hands into a *T*, signaling time-out.

But Debra kept focused on Jason. "How do you think *I* feel? Like I wasn't able to please you, like you never really cared about me, like you used me."

"I didn't use you."

The bell rang and Cindy leaped up, obviously embarrassed by what she'd started.

"Jason?" Debra said over the clatter of chairs and trays. "I've got to get to class now, but we need to talk."

She hurried to the tray window, wiping her cheek.

Corey clasped a hand on Jason's shoulder and said something consoling, but the rumble of the cafeteria drowned it out.

Jason remained in his chair a moment, too dazed to stand.

Had he actually admitted to his ex-girlfriend, best friend, and best friend's girlfriend that he was dating a guy? It was all too confusing.

He wandered in a haze through the rest of the day. By the end of last period, he'd decided to talk to Ms. MacTraugh, as Coach had suggested. He pressed his way against the oncoming crowd of students, heading toward her classroom.

From amid the tide, a teammate high-fived him. "Aren't you coming to practice?" Odell asked.

"Can you let Coach know I'll be late?" Jason mumbled. "Tell him I, um, had to do something."

"Uh-oh!" Odell gave a suggestive grin. "Got some secret rendezvous?"

Yeah, right, Jason thought, envisioning tall, broad-shouldered Ms. MacTraugh—or "Big Mac," as students called her.

The afternoon sun shone brightly through the windows of her art classroom, illuminating the multicolored stained glass projects. Every inch of wall was covered with vivid paintings. And each side counter was lined with clay sculpture.

Ms. MacTraugh was bent over a table slicing the vestiges of what looked to have been a sheet cake. Jason suddenly remembered he'd forgotten the GSA meeting—and Ms. MacTraugh's birthday.

"Hi, Jason." She smiled, waving him closer. "We missed you at the GSA. Come have some cake."

"Um, no thanks." His stomach was too tied in knots. "But happy birthday."

"Oh, you've got to help me," she insisted, slicing a piece for him. "It's too much for me, and my cats won't eat it. Neither will Barb."

Jason accepted the plate and wondered, *Who is Barb?*

"Have a seat," Ms. MacTraugh said, sitting across from Jason. "Coach Cameron spoke to me yesterday. I didn't know you'd received a scholarship for next year. Congratulations!" She extended a hand.

Jason wiped the icing from his fingers and shook hands. "Thanks."

"I played college ball myself," MacTraugh said. "Of course, I was a wee bit thinner then." She grinned, dabbing her chin with a paper napkin. "In any case, Coach is concerned about you. I imagine your conversation with him must've been quite a big step for you." She patted his knee. "That was very brave."

Jason shrugged, proud but also a little embarrassed.

Ms. MacTraugh adjusted her wire-framed glasses. "Coach said you're thinking of telling your team?"

"Well, um, yeah, except . . ." Jason set his plate aside. "I'm not sure how they'd react. What do you think I should do?"

"Well . . ." Ms. MacTraugh wiped her hands. "I emphasized to Coach Cameron that coming out is a very personal decision. Only you can determine what's right for you, but . . . I think coming out publicly would make you an excellent role model."

Jason groaned softly. *Not again.*

"Can I ask you a question?" He sat up. "If it's not too personal . . . are you . . ." He scrunched up the napkin in his hand. "Are you gay?"

Ms. MacTraugh nodded, smiling. "I try not to make a big deal of it, but with so many of you students coming out now . . ."

Jason shifted his feet. "When did you come out?"

"Hmm," Ms. MacTraugh said, as if remembering. "It depends on what you mean. In college I first realized my feelings for other girls were more than friendship. Up till then I'd gone out with boys. I was playing ball sophomore year, when I met a girl and fell in love. This May will mark twenty-four years together."

Jason wondered, *Is that "Barb"?*

"Coming out is a lifelong process," Ms. MacTraugh continued. "Each time we meet someone new or move to a different setting, we're challenged to reveal who we are. It's not always easy. But no matter how difficult, it's something I've never regretted. So few things in life truly matter. Chief among them are being true to yourself, and being honest with others."

"But," Jason said, "what if that means losing my scholarship?"

"We could certainly fight it." Ms. MacTraugh's voice brimmed with optimism. "You're not alone in this. Coach Cameron thinks very highly of you, and you can count on my support."

"Thanks," Jason said, a little encouraged.

"Now, what about your family?" Ms. MacTraugh asked. "Have you come out to them?"

Jason shifted in his seat, uneasy. "After I told my dad, he left home. I thought my mom was okay with it, but now I think she was in shock. Or denial. She hasn't talked about it since that night. I don't think she really understands."

"Well . . ." Ms. MacTraugh gave an understanding nod. "Parents have to go through their own coming to terms process. Whatever you decide to do is okay. We each come out in different ways at different times in our lives. As I said, only you can determine what's the right decision."

Jason bit into a nail, wondering what *was* the right decision.

He glanced at the wall clock and realized he'd be way late for practice.

Coach wasn't thrilled by his tardiness. But when Jason said he'd been talking with Ms. MacTraugh, Coach let him off with fifty push-ups.

After dinner that evening Jason tried doing some homework. But Ms. MacTraugh's words about being true to yourself and honest with others kept interfering.

Finally he tossed his pen aside and headed to the kitchen. His mom sat at the breakfast table, wearing her red plastic drugstore reading glasses, writing checks to pay bills.

"Do we have enough money?" Jason asked.

"Honey, let me worry about that. You focus on school, okay?" She peered over her half frames. "Finish your homework?"

"Taking a break." He poured a glass of water and drank some, leaning against the sink. "How are we going to manage without dad?"

"Oh, we'll make do." She tore out a check. "I reminded him about the mortgage payment when we talked this morning."

Jason nearly choked. "You *talked* with him?" He'd assumed they weren't speaking. "What for?"

"Because he has two children to help support."

"Hah. He doesn't care." Jason sat down at the table, moving aside Melissa's coloring book. "At least not about me."

"Well . . ." His mom ran her tongue along an envelope. "He can't just walk away."

"Yeah? He already did."

Unwilling to argue, his mom glanced toward the counter. "Can you grab the stamps? How was school today?"

"Okay." Jason handed her the stamps. "There's something I want to talk to you about." He took a sip from his water, preparing himself. This would be the first time he'd discussed his coming out with her since he got into the fistfight with his dad.

"I, um, came out to Coach. I told him I want to let the team know."

His mom stared at him a moment, then she began busily shifting and sorting bills. "Honey, are you sure you don't want to talk to someone about all this?"

He knew she meant a psychologist.

"Ma, I'm not crazy. I just told you I talked to Coach. And I talked to the teacher who's adviser for the GSA. That's the group for people dealing with this stuff."

He knew his mom was big on groups. She'd been going to Al-Anon meetings because of his dad's alcoholism.

"And what did Coach and this teacher say?"

Jason nervously ran his fingers along the side of his water glass. "Different things."

"Like what?"

"Like that I could lose my scholarship."

"Oh, honey!" his mom burst out. "You've worked so hard for that. It's been your dream."

He shrank at his mom's protest, though he couldn't blame her for being upset. Through the years she'd always encouraged him. She'd bought him his first basketball. She always found money for new sneakers. She cheered him on at games. She pasted news clippings into a scrapbook. Now he felt he was letting her down.

"Well," he said, "I could stay home to help you."

"Honey, don't worry about me. You need to think about *you*. If this means losing your scholarship, then you shouldn't do it. You can't give up college!"

She'd always wanted him to have the opportunity she'd never had.

Jason sipped his glass of water, considering what his mom had said and comparing it to what Ms. MacTraugh had said, and what Coach had said, and Corey, and Kyle, and Nelson. . . . Trying to sort it all out was making his head ache.

"I'm going to finish my homework," he said, and wandered back to his room.

On the way he stopped by the bathroom for aspirin. Glancing out the window at the driveway, he recalled being a little kid, happily bouncing his first ball there, never imagining all his future would bring.

jason   kyle

nelson

Nelson sat on the carpet in his bedroom, glancing out the window at the quiet suburban night, and thinking.

Twenty-eight hours had passed since he'd gotten his negative test result, and he still hadn't called Jeremy, even though he'd promised to—and even though Jeremy had phoned twice, leaving messages both times.

But when Nelson had started to call, he remembered his night with the Motorcycle Dude and how easily he'd let slip all caution about using a condom, and how depressed he'd been for an entire week afterward, barely able to get out of bed, certain he'd been infected. It had been a close call—severely close.

Did he really want to take another risk of getting infected? Maybe Kyle was right.

He should forget Jeremy and date some nice HIV-negative

boy instead. But he hadn't met any boy nicer than Jeremy. And Jeremy was the only guy who hadn't tried to jump Nelson's bones their first time together. He liked Jeremy more than he'd ever liked anyone except Kyle.

But what would Jeremy's reaction be to the negative news? Nelson picked at a scab on his finger and glanced at the phone. What if Jeremy didn't want to go out anymore?

"Dumped again," Nelson said aloud.

His dog Atticus, lying beside him, looked up, and Nelson patted him. "Just you and me, boy. You'll never leave me, will you?"

Atticus leaned up, slurping his tongue. As Nelson hugged him in return, a new idea dawned on him: *Why not just lie to Jeremy and tell him I tested positive? That way he won't have any reason to dump me. Totally brilliant!*

Nelson grabbed the phone and started to dial, but stopped. *Wait a minute, that's totally crazy.*

He hung up. What was the matter with him? He should just tell Jeremy the truth.

Once again he lifted the receiver. Slowly he dialed and listened. The phone rang. Once. Twice. He still had a chance to hang up.

Just then, Jeremy answered. "Hello?"

Nelson took a deep breath. "Hi. It's me."

"Nelson! Hold on a sec. Let me get off the other line."

Nelson waited, picking at his scab some more, till Jeremy came back on.

"Dude, I left you two messages!"

Nelson brought the scab to his mouth. "I'm sorry."

"I was worried," Jeremy said. "How'd your test go?"

Nelson sucked on his finger, tasting blood, and trying to

rainbow high

decide how to tell Jeremy his news. "Can I come over? And—you know—talk in person?"

"Sure!" Jeremy said eagerly. "Come on over."

Jeremy lived with his straight older brother in a redbrick low-rise near the community college across town. Since Nelson's mom had gone to the supermarket, he left her a note and walked to the metro.

"Hi. Come on in," Jeremy said, answering the door. "You can meet my brother."

Nelson pulled off his jacket. "Kiss?" he asked, pursing his lips.

Jeremy took the coat and grinned, pecking Nelson on the lips. He turned toward the kitchen. "Hey, Bob! This is Nelson."

Jeremy's brother looked like a slightly older, taller version of Jeremy—same brown hair and eyes—though in Nelson's opinion, he wasn't nearly as cute, with a scruffy face and the start of a potbelly. "Howdy!" Bob waved from the kitchen pass-through. "Nice to meet you."

After pouring Nelson a Coke, Jeremy led him to the bedroom. Though it was Nelson's first time in the brothers' room, he could guess which half was whose. On one side hung an outdated babe calendar of a bare-breasted blonde. A disheveled pile of CDs lay scattered by the stereo. Tangled covers lay strewn on an unmade twin bed.

On the opposite side hung a framed arty photo of a guy in his underwear. College textbooks neatly lined the desk. On top of a perfectly made bed lay a pile of freshly laundered clothes.

From amid the jumble of shirts, socks, and gym shorts, a pair of bleached white undies shone out, bright as a beacon.

"Sorry about the laundry." Jeremy placed a coaster on the desk for Nelson's glass and pulled the desk chair out for him. "Have a seat."

Nelson noticed a photo of a grinning girl in sandals on the desk. "Who's that?"

"Celia," Jeremy said, sitting on the bed opposite Nelson. "One of those 'Save the Children' kids. We write letters. It helps keep me from getting too self-absorbed. So, how did your test go?"

Nelson eased into the chair and fidgeted with an earring.

"I, um . . . tested negative?" It sounded like a question, though he hadn't meant it to.

Jeremy's face scrunched up—either in confusion or disappointment, Nelson wasn't sure which. "Negative?" Jeremy echoed.

"Yeah?" Nelson said, his voice quivering.

"What a relief!" Jeremy sighed. "That's great, man. When you didn't call me, I figured you'd tested positive and were too depressed. I remember how down I got about my result. I didn't want to talk to anyone."

Hearing Jeremy's story, Nelson felt totally silly. He was probably the only freak in history to feel upset because he'd tested negative.

"So," Jeremy said. "Why didn't you call and tell me?"

"Well . . ." Nelson fussed some more with an earring. "I guess I was afraid, after all you said . . . you know . . . about dating someone negative. . . ."

As Nelson spoke Jeremy gazed intently back at him, his calm brown eyes only making Nelson's words that much harder to utter.

"I mean . . . if you don't want to go out with me anymore . . .

just tell me." His hand trembled as he reached for some soda and waited for Jeremy's response.

Jeremy studied Nelson. His tongue ran across his lips before he finally spoke. "Well, I guess I'm just a little scared. . . . Are you sure *you* want to go out?"

Nelson felt his shoulders relax. "Of course! Do you?"

"Yeah." Jeremy nodded slowly. "I do."

Nelson's heart leaped up in his chest. This whole thing felt so frigging goofy—like they were exchanging wedding vows or something.

"How about Saturday?" Jeremy asked, shifting on the mattress.

"Saturday's good," Nelson replied, imagining them together on the bed.

In fact, why wait till Saturday? Summoning his nerve, he moved onto the mattress. He brought his lips to Jeremy's. And they fell onto the pile of laundry, their arms entwined around each other.

Nelson breathed deep the fresh detergent scent. His tongue glided across Jeremy's, darting from side to side. His hands caressed the muscles of Jeremy's broad shoulders, holding him tight.

"Uh-oh," Jeremy whispered.

"What?" Nelson whispered back.

"Your face—" Jeremy laughed, blushing "– is on my underwear."

Nelson lifted his head to look. Beneath him lay Jeremy's tighty-whities.

Jeremy quickly yanked them away and tossed them atop the pile. "Sorry about that."

"I don't mind," Nelson said, grinning fiendishly.

Jeremy smiled. "Want to help me fold?" He sat up.

But Nelson pulled him back onto the bed beside him. "Stay," he begged.

"We'd better not," Jeremy protested. "My brother and I have a rule about . . . you know . . . when we're both here."

"We're not doing anything," Nelson grumbled, "except kissing."

But Jeremy stood firm—the spoilsport. Instead of engaging in wild raunchy passion, they folded clean laundry. Apropos, Nelson brought Jeremy up to speed on his boring life: his acceptance to Tech, his dog's dry skin, Kyle's obsession with Jason, and Jason's coming out drama with the coach.

In turn, Jeremy told Nelson about his job at the video store, his classes at the community college, and his brother's latest girlfriend.

"This feels so intimate," Nelson said, plucking Jeremy's underwear from the pile. He'd never folded another guy's clothes—other than Kyle's.

While Jeremy turned to put his T-shirts in the dresser, a nutty idea popped into Nelson's brain: Why not take the undies? Jeremy wouldn't miss them. But would it feel right stealing his date's underwear? He should at least ask. But then Jeremy would *really* think he was kooky.

"Can I have them?" Nelson asked in barely a whisper.

Jeremy turned and glanced at the underwear in Nelson's hands. "Are you serious?"

"Yeah." Nelson tried to sound coy, even though he felt his face turning red.

"Hmm," Jeremy said, eyeing Nelson from head to foot. "You're very interesting, you know that?" He gave a shrug. "I guess you can keep them."

"Thanks!" Nelson beamed, stuffing the underwear into his pants pocket.

Jeremy turned again to put another stack of clothes into a drawer. The contour of his jeans curved across his butt. Nelson reached his arms out, circling Jeremy's waist. Jeremy turned, his mouth beckoning. In an instant they were kissing and Nelson tried to pull him onto the bed again.

"Hey, stop." Jeremy pried away, laughing. "We both have school tomorrow. I'll borrow the car and take you home, okay?"

Nelson moaned. But at least he had the underwear to take with him.

When Jeremy started the car, the radio came on, blasting country music from the speakers.

Nelson covered his ears. "Can we please listen to something else?"

"Sure," Jeremy said. Nelson switched to a pop station. Then he grabbed hold of Jeremy's hand for the drive home.

As they pulled in front of his house, he announced, "I want you to meet my mom."

"You mean, now?" Jeremy peered nervously out the window.

"Yeah. She's dying to meet you. Besides, that way she won't yell at me for being out so late."

"Oh, great. She'll yell at me instead."

"No, she won't. I left her a note." Nelson squeezed Jeremy's shoulder. "Please?"

Jeremy stared at him. "Have you told her yet?"

Nelson knew what he meant: about the HIV. "I'm waiting for the right moment. Come on!" He opened the door.

Jeremy ran a hand through his hair. "Do I look all right?"

"You look great," Nelson said out loud, in his mind adding, *not the least bit HIV positive.*

As they walked up the sidewalk Atticus started barking. Nelson opened the front door and grabbed the dog by the collar to keep him from jumping all over Jeremy.

"I'm home!"

"I was about to phone you," his mom said, walking into the foyer.

"Mom, this is Jeremy. Atticus, leave him alone!"

Nelson yanked back the dog, which had discovered Jeremy's crotch.

"Um, hi, Mrs. Glassman," Jeremy said, awkwardly pushing Atticus away.

"You can call me Felicia." She extended her hand. "I see you've met Atticus."

"Nelson told me about his skin condition," Jeremy said, shaking her hand. "Is he better?"

"Much better, in spite of the fact that *somebody*—" she gave Nelson a hard look "—keeps forgetting to put medication on him. Did you remember today?"

"How can I remember if you don't remind me?" Nelson grinned.

"Wow!" Jeremy said. His gaze had fallen on the prints lining the walls. "Those are awesome."

"Mom made them," Nelson said. "She's a graphic artist. Tell Jeremy how you did them."

While Nelson spread cream on Atticus, his mom toured Jeremy around the first floor, telling him about her work. The lilt in her voice hinted that she liked him. Nelson had always imagined introducing his mom to a boy he liked—even though his dream had never included fretting because of HIV.

"Well," Jeremy said, after chatting for a time. "I better go. It was nice meeting you Mrs.—I mean—Felicia."

"It was nice meeting you, too." She reached out, clasping both her hands around his. "I hope to see more of you."

"I'll walk you out," Nelson told him.

When they got to the car, Jeremy leaned against it and heaved a sigh. "You think she likes me okay?"

"*Likes* you? I think she'd marry you if you were straight."

Jeremy raised an eyebrow. Nelson could tell what he was thinking. "Don't worry, I'll tell her." He leaned forward, wrapping his arms around Jeremy, and kissed him. "Thanks for the ride home."

As soon as he came back inside, his mom exclaimed, "I think he's wonderful! Why were you so scared of me meeting him? He seems very mature. How old is he?"

"Nineteen," Nelson said, closing the door behind him.

"Well, he definitely seems older. I think he'll be very good for you."

"Mom! You make it sound like we're getting married."

"No. I just think dating steady will be a very positive step for you."

Crap. Did she have to use the word "positive"?

"Good night, sweetie," she called to Nelson as he climbed the stairs to his room. "Remember you have to take Atticus to the vet tomorrow!"

Nelson curled up in bed, dialed Kyle, and told him about his evening.

"You asked for his underwear?" Kyle shrieked into the phone.

"Yeah," Nelson said. "Hey, can you help me take Atticus to the vet after school tomorrow?"

"I can't," Kyle said. "I have swim practice." The call-waiting signal beeped. "Can you hold on a sec?"

While Nelson waited, he brought Jeremy's jockeys to his cheek, inhaling the fresh detergent scent.

Kyle came back on. "You mind if I take the call?"

"Let me guess," Nelson said. "Does his name begin with a J?"

"Yeah," Kyle said in that wistful tone he got.

Nelson restrained himself from gagging. "Tell her I send a big, wet, sloppy kiss."

After hanging up, Nelson undressed for bed and slid beneath the sheets, hugging the briefs against his chest. *If only*, he wished, *their previous owner was inside them.*

jason kyle

nelson

Kyle tapped the flash button on his phone. "Jason? I'm back. Nelson says hi." He left out the big, wet, sloppy kiss part, and leaned back on the pillows in his bed. "We missed you at the GSA meeting. How was your day?"

"I totally zoned out at lunch. My whole day sucked. It totally blew."

"Why?" Kyle sat up. "What happened?"

"Where to begin? Well, I did talk to MacTraugh after school. She brought up the RM thing."

"RM? Oh, RM!" Kyle laughed and fell back on the bed, stroking his chest. "See? Everyone thinks you're a role model."

"Whatever," Jason grumbled. "Anyway, I was late for practice, so I had to do fifty push-ups."

"That sucks," Kyle agreed, even though the image of Jason in his satin uniform, arms pumping, wasn't the least bit sucky.

"Before all that," Jason continued, "at lunch I was sitting with Corey when Cindy and Debra came over and . . ." Jason paused, clearing his throat. "Um, in conversation it sort of came up . . . about you and me."

Kyle sat up again. "Was she angry? Debra, I mean?"

"Well . . ." Jason hesitated. "She was angry I hadn't told her. She said we need to talk, whatever that means."

"Oh," Kyle said, switching the phone receiver to his other hand so he could wipe the sweat from his palm. "At least now it's out in the open."

Jason didn't say anything for a moment, then he asked, "Are you angry?"

"No . . . I'm just . . . nervous. I guess I feel guilty."

"Guilty?" Jason asked. "Why should you feel guilty? You didn't do anything wrong."

Kyle switched the phone receiver again to wipe the sweat from his other palm. "Did she understand it happened after you and she broke up?"

"I told her that. Besides, she's the one who broke up with me. It wasn't your fault."

Kyle thought about Debra and Jason, his mind drifting to the whole HIV issue. "Um, since we're talking about you and Debra, there's something I want to ask you, but it's, um, kind of personal."

"What is it?" Jason said, his voice guarded.

Kyle gripped the phone receiver harder so it wouldn't slide out of his hand.

"When you were going out with Debra? Did you, um, use condoms? Or was she—you know—taking the pill?"

Kyle held his breath, waiting. It bothered him he couldn't see Jason's response, but he was also glad Jason couldn't see him practically sweating a puddle onto the bed.

"What makes you ask that?" Jason said.

The testiness in his voice made Kyle want to take back the question. He let out his breath, shimmying up the bed onto his pillows.

"Well, um, since you and I are involved, I just—you know—want to make sure we're safe, that's all."

He listened to the silence on the other end of the line and tapped his hand on the bedspread, waiting. Finally he heard Jason sigh.

"At first we used condoms, then after a while she started taking the pill."

Kyle thought that through. It meant Jason had had unprotected sex with Debra.

"I wonder," Jason continued, as though having a realization, "if maybe that's part of why she was so angry at me about all this. Know what I mean? Maybe she was scared she could've caught something from me. Of course she couldn't have, since I was never with anyone else."

"And are you sure *she* was never with someone else?" Kyle asked.

"Yep. I was her first and only. That's probably another part of why she's angry."

Kyle slid down on the pillows, feeling a little relieved.

"Listen," Jason said. "Promise you won't spread it around about her being on the pill, okay? She might not want people to know."

"I won't," Kyle reassured him. "Thanks for—you know—being honest with me about it."

"*No problema,*" Jason said, yawning. "It's getting late. I should get to sleep. See you tomorrow?"

"Okay," Kyle said, and added, "I love you."

It was the first time he'd said it since they'd made love. He could hear his heart thumping while he waited for a response.

"Love you back," came the voice from the other end. "Good night."

Kyle lay awake for a while, watching the neon tetras in his aquarium flit from side to side, and wondering: Would he ever get used to being in love with a boy who used to like girls?

The following day was fairly uneventful, with the exception of a calculus quiz for which Kyle wished he'd studied more. But he felt that way every test, even though he always ended up getting the highest grade in class.

After school he walked to the pool for swim team practice. In the locker room he changed into his swim briefs, trying to ignore the usual testosterone high jinks—burps resounding off the tile walls, lockers being slammed, and general horseplay.

"Hey, Meeks!" a teammate yelled, striding in late. "Coach Sweeney said she wants to see you."

"Thanks," Kyle said. He figured she probably wanted to talk about some doughnut sale or car wash, since Kyle helped to organize the team's fund-raising projects.

He finished tying his drawstring and started out the door, but not before Charlie Tuggs faked a cough, uttering "faggot" beneath his breath.

Kyle ignored it. Ever since he'd spray-painted his locker, a handful of teammates had started snubbing and harassing him. He felt like shouting "Grow up!" but figured that would only fuel them more.

Through the pool-office window, Coach Sweeney motioned him in. "Hi, Kyle. Have a seat."

She peered at him across the desk, pressing the palms of her thin, tanned hands together.

"Is something wrong?" Kyle asked.

"I don't know how to say this." Coach Sweeney took a deep breath. "I'll just say it. One of your teammates objects to having to shower in the same room as someone who proclaims he's gay." She lifted a sheet of paper off the desk. "His father sent a rather forceful note."

Kyle stared at the paper, speechless. Why was this happening to him? He'd never even remotely come on to any guy on the team. In fact, he went out of his way to avoid glancing at his teammates in the shower. They were the ones who yanked down each other's briefs, pretending they were joking.

"Kyle, I'm not sure how to ask you," Coach Sweeney was saying. "But I need to know. Is there any reason this boy should be concerned?"

"No!" Kyle snapped. How could she even think that?

"Okay." Coach Sweeney backed off. "I believe you. But I'm afraid this is uncharted territory for me. What do you think we should do?"

Kyle gazed out the office window at the boys walking onto the indoor pool deck, swim goggles in hand, laughing as they stretched. He wondered from whose dad the note had come. Maybe if he just reassured the guy . . . But why should he have to reassure anyone?

"I don't know," he said. He wanted to tell her she should rip the note up and tell the boy and his dad to go jump into a huge, bottomless lake. But Kyle liked Coach Sweeney, and obviously she was struggling with this.

"I can wait till I get home to shower." He gave a shrug of resignation. "It's no big deal."

Coach Sweeney pressed her lips into a smile. "Thanks, Kyle."

During practice he watched his teammates, trying to figure out who was responsible. And he outraced each of them, his times better than ever.

When Kyle arrived home, he opened the front door and picked up the mail on the floor. Crossing the foyer, he glanced through the pile, expecting the usual junk.

But an envelope from Tech caught his gaze. Tearing it open, he found a freshman housing form asking dorm preferences. It wasn't due for several weeks. Hopefully by then he'd have a more concrete idea where he and Jason would both be going.

He started to toss the rest of the pile on the side table when he noticed another envelope—this one from Princeton.

His heart jumped. A million thoughts sprang into his head. Could he actually have been accepted? But then what about Jason? Kyle had applied to Princeton in the fall, pre-Jason. Never in a million years had he imagined they'd become boyfriends.

Kyle turned the envelope over, half hoping for some hint of its contents. He held it up to the light. Nothing showed through. His heart was racing, his mind spinning.

He laid the envelope on the table and sat down, holding his head in his hands, trying to think. What should he do? He'd put off seriously considering he might actually get accepted to Princeton, till now.

Maybe he should throw the letter out, pretend he never got it. Yes, that's it. He got up, snatched the envelope, carried it into the kitchen, and opened the trash compacter.

The envelope dangled between his fingers. But shouldn't he at least find out whether he'd been accepted? He'd probably been rejected anyway. At least then his dad would get off his case. Besides, if he did simply throw out the letter, his dad would eventually call the admissions office anyway.

And even if Kyle had been accepted, that didn't mean he had to go. Being accepted would be a huge compliment, but wasn't it mainly an ego trip? After all, what really mattered was that he go to college, not necessarily which one. If Princeton had accepted him, he'd simply turn it down.

He wedged his index finger beneath the flap of the envelope, tearing it open. He unfolded the letter and quickly scanned the page. Halfway down, the words rose up at him.

We are pleased to inform you of your acceptance for admission.

Kyle slumped against the kitchen counter and stood there, stunned.

Then, like a volcano gaining momentum, his whole body began to shake. Erupting in excitement, he leaped into the air, screaming and hollering. "Yes! I did it! I actually got in! Yes!"

Of course, this absolutely screwed up his life. Hadn't he practically promised the love of his life to go with him to either Tech or community college?

Kyle raised the letter again and read back over it once more, just to make sure.

Yep, the words still read the same.

Kyle paced the kitchen. He had to tell someone, but whom? Someone who'd help him figure out what to do.

His dad? No way. He'd already made his bias clear. His mom? She'd probably agree with his dad. Jason? Not till Kyle could calm the thoughts running amok in his brain.

Nelson? Hmm. Nelson *was* his best friend. But what if he

went ka-bonkers, as usual? But who else could help Kyle sort out his mixed feelings?

He picked up the phone and dialed. "Hi, it's me."

As soon as Nelson heard Kyle's voice, he shouted, "Woo-hoo! Did you get your housing form?" His fingers snapped in the background. "Of course we're dorming together. We're going to have so freaking much fun!"

Oh, great, Kyle thought. Nelson was already going whackers.

"Nelson?" Kyle said firmly, trying to calm him down. "Something's happened."

"Omigod," Nelson said, his voice plunging. "What? Are you all right?"

"Um . . ." Kyle gripped the receiver, summoning his courage. "Remember last fall when I applied to Princeton?"

Nelson's end of the line went suddenly silent—an ominous sign. Nelson never went silent.

"Hello?" Kyle said, his voice quavering.

"You got accepted," Nelson replied in a sullen voice. "Didn't you?"

Kyle hesitated, his heart slipping down inside him. "Yeah."

"Kyle!" Nelson shouted. "I *told* you not to apply to Princeton, didn't I?"

"I know," Kyle squeaked. "But I didn't think I'd get in."

"I *told* you," Nelson repeated. "I said if you apply, you'll get in. But you wouldn't listen to me. You expect me to listen to you, but do you ever listen to me?"

"What was I supposed to do?" Kyle said. "You know my dad insisted."

"Stand up to him!" Nelson replied. "Have some *chutzpah.* Go where *you* want. You don't have to do everything he says."

Kyle bristled, the back of his neck growing tense. "I don't do everything he says. And if you wanted us to stay together so much, why didn't you apply to Princeton too?"

"Kyle, you and I both know they'd never accept me."

"You don't know that."

"Kyle? Yes, I do. I'm not smart enough and my dad's not an alumni."

"Alumnus."

"See?" Nelson huffed. "I am so totally pissed at you. We're talking about our college experience, Kyle. We always said we'd go to college together. Remember when we took that stupid test last year? We had to list colleges we wanted to go to—and you and I agreed wherever we went, we'd go together. Remember?"

"Yes, I remember."

"And you remember," Nelson railed on, "I didn't even *want* to apply to geeky Tech. I did it to be with you!"

Kyle sighed, feeling guiltier every minute. "I'm sorry, Nelson. I'm really sorry."

"Don't you dare try that puppy dog whimper. How could you do this?"

"Well, I haven't said I'm going to accept it yet."

"Yeah, right. You know what? I don't want to talk anymore."

"I said I'm sorry!" Kyle shouted.

"I can't deal with this," Nelson said. "I gotta go."

With that, the line clicked off. A moment later, the dial tone buzzed in Kyle's ear.

Kyle slid down into the kitchen chair, hating his life.

The front door sounded. "Kyle!" his mom called. "I'm home!"

Quickly Kyle grabbed the Princeton letter and shoved it into his pants pocket. He wasn't ready to discuss it with his mom and dad yet. First there was one other person with whom he needed to talk. But how on earth could Kyle tell him?

chapter 9

jason kyle

nelson

"Mr. Perez?" Principal Mueller's throaty voice blared out of the loudspeaker during the middle of algebra. "Is Jason Carrillo in your class?"

Jason sat up in his seat. He'd been dreading this moment ever since Coach had mentioned Mueller.

"Yes, sir," Mr. Perez shouted toward the speaker. "He's here."

Classmates turned to stare at Jason. Oh, great. Not only did he have to face Mueller, he'd have to deal with the whole school speculating about why the principal had called him down.

"Please instruct him," Mueller's voice squawked, "to report to my office immediately."

As the loudspeaker crackled off, a few of Jason's goofball classmates started teasing and hooting.

"Quiet!" Perez yelled. "Or I'll send you all down."

Boy, was that the wrong thing to say. The catcalls only got louder as Jason collected his books and headed out the door.

His footsteps echoed against the lockers in the empty hallway. A million questions ricocheted around in his head. What exactly had Coach told Mueller? And how had Mueller responded?

Passing the front doors to the school, Jason slowed and gazed out the window. Beneath a clear blue sky, rows of cars reflected brilliant sunshine. A couple of his teammates crossed the parking lot, heading off campus, enjoying senior year privileges.

Why not join them? Jason thought. Forget all this coming out crap. He'd tell Mueller and Coach he'd made a mistake—that he was stressed with senior year and the upcoming state championship. Impulsively Jason gripped the door handle, but stopped short.

From amid the clutter of graffiti scratched into the paint of the front door, a single word jumped out: FAG.

Jason stood staring. He clenched his eyes shut, wishing there were some way to get away from the ever present slurs. But he knew he couldn't. Opening his eyes again, he released the door handle and turned toward the main office.

Mueller sat behind his massive oak desk, pulling a rubber band between his fingers. Across from him sat Coach Cameron.

"Have a seat," Mueller told Jason, with a familiar tone of disappointment. Had he taken the news of Jason's coming out as badly as he took the basketball team's losses?

"Hi, Carrillo," Coach said, offering a tense smile. But his jaw remained set, like when he tried to force encouragement during a difficult game. "I've explained your situation to Mr. Mueller."

Jason slid into the hard-backed wooden chair, bracing himself.

"Jason," Mueller began, "I've seen a lot of boys and girls come through that door." He pointed, as if to leave no doubt which door he meant. "When a situation results in a student being called to my office, I take it very seriously."

Jason shuffled his shoes on the floor, wishing Mueller would get to the point.

"Quite frankly," Mueller continued, "I was surprised when Coach informed me what you'd confided in him. *Very* surprised. Have you thought about how your teammates might react to this?"

"Yeah."

"Really?" Mueller challenged. "Tell me. How do you think they'll react?"

"Well . . ." Jason felt his stomach grinding. "I'm not sure."

Mueller tossed the rubber band aside. "You think they'll be happy and congratulate you?"

Jason gritted his teeth, resisting the urge to volley back some equally sarcastic response. "They'll probably be upset," he said in a low voice.

"Yes. That's exactly right." Mueller gave a sigh. "Jason, what I'm trying to get at . . . This isn't just about you. It's about your team. Do you even care about your team?"

"Yeah, I care about them!" Jason answered so loud that Mueller reeled in response.

Jason sat up straight in his chair, trying to anticipate what might happen next.

It was Coach who spoke. "Jason cares a lot about the team. That's why he came to me with this."

Jason glanced at Coach. The mere sight of his steady, confident expression made Jason sit even taller.

Mueller's eyes darted between Coach and Jason, till he let out a breath. "I believe you do care about the team, Jason." His voice had switched tone again, now uncannily sincere. "You know why? Because I've seen you on the court. You're one of the best team players our school has ever had."

Then why'd you challenge me just now? Jason wondered.

"And you've made too great a contribution to this school to just toss it away like this."

Jason listened carefully, trying to guess where the principal was heading.

"I'm going to be blunt," Mueller said. "If you feel the need to jeopardize your future with this, that's one thing. But for you to risk upsetting your team as we head toward the state title . . ." He shook his head as if genuinely mystified. "I can't believe you'd do that, Jason."

At the words "state title," something clicked in Jason's mind. Was that why Mueller was concerned about him coming out? If it was, Mueller could take a hike.

"A lot of these boys look up to you, Jason. I see it in their eyes. I hear how fondly they speak of you."

Oh, no, Jason thought. *Not again.* Much as he tried to resist, the role model crud got to him every time.

"I know you've got a lot going on," Mueller said, bringing a hand to his forehead. "Between school and the state championships, it's no wonder you feel pressured to come out with this. But don't you agree it might make sense to wait a few more weeks? Let your teammates celebrate another winning season? Would you be willing to do that for them?"

Jason shifted his feet, trying to wade between the *BS* and the truth. He had to admit Mueller had a point. Would it hurt to wait?

He turned to Coach for guidance, but Coach gestured back to him.

"This one's up to you, Jason."

Jason glanced down at his chewed-up fingernails. He'd waited seventeen and a half years. What were a few more weeks? "Okay," he told Mueller.

"Great!" the principal exclaimed, extending his hand. "I know we'll win this title."

Jason shook Mueller's hand, though inside he was thinking, *We?*

As they left the meeting Coach patted Jason on the back. "I could tell that was a tough decision."

"Yeah," Jason said, his voice barely a whisper.

"Hey." Coach stopped and looked him square in the eye. "Stop by to talk if you need to. You have my home number. All right?"

Jason nodded as the bell started ringing. A second later students began pouring into the hall.

For the rest of the day Jason tried to reconcile what he'd done. Had it been the right thing? Or a wimp-out?

He needed to talk to someone about it. But whom?

Not his best friend, Corey. He'd be relieved that Jason had put off coming out. He'd told Jason he thought this whole thing was a big career mistake.

Not his ex-girlfriend, Debra. She was still *PO*'d at him for not having told her about Kyle.

Not his mom. She had enough to worry about. Besides, she was still in denial about his being gay.

The obvious choice was Kyle. But would he be disappointed in Jason for bagging out?

After the last bell, Jason meandered to Kyle's locker. "Wha's up?"

"Um, hi," Kyle mumbled.

"You okay?" Jason asked.

"Yeah . . ." Kyle muttered, not very convincingly. "I was going to call you tonight. It's about . . . Tech."

"What happened?" Jason asked impatiently, casting aside his own problems.

"Um, remember back in the fall," Kyle said, fidgeting with his backpack zipper. "I told you I'd applied to Princeton?"

Jason vaguely recalled the mention of it.

Kyle reached into his backpack, pulled out an envelope, and handed it to Jason. The return address was Princeton. A knot formed in Jason's stomach as he unfolded the letter.

Halfway down the page, he stopped reading, too stunned to continue. What about their plans to go to Tech together? What about Kyle's willingness to stay and go to community college so they wouldn't be separated? What about their being "boyfriends"? Had Kyle forgotten all that?

"Congratulations." Jason shoved the letter back. "That's great."

"Is it?" Kyle said, his hazel eyes gazing up.

Jason wasn't certain what he meant.

"Can I come over later?" Kyle asked. "So we can talk about it?"

"Yeah." Jason nodded. "Sure."

At practice Jason had trouble getting into stride. With his thoughts bouncing between Kyle one instant and Mueller the next, he could hardly score a basket.

But then Corey positioned him for a layup and Jason made a hook shot he'd long been practicing.

"Good one," said Andre, clapping him on the shoulder.

rainbow high

Jason was in sync again, his mind focused on the one thing in his world that always made sense.

It turned out to be one of their best practices ever. At least it seemed that way, with each teammate knowing the others' moves, as if playing in perfect harmony. And afterward, in the locker room, everyone laughed together—even Dwayne.

Mueller's right, Jason thought. How could he let the team down now, before the state finals?

That evening, as Jason was finishing dinner, Kyle arrived. Melissa ran to greet him at the door.

"Just in time for dessert," said Jason's mom. When Kyle sat down at the table, she served him a dish of flan.

"It's like custard," Jason said, in response to Kyle's crinkled expression. "Try it. It's really good."

Kyle tasted a spoonful. "It's great," he told Jason's mom. "How do you make it?"

She explained how she'd learned to make it from Jason's grand mom on his dad's side.

As she spoke Jason wondered if she understood that he and Kyle were not just friends. He'd told her Kyle was gay, but that was all.

"We're going to study awhile," Jason said when they finished their desserts.

Melissa clung to Kyle's hand. "I want to go too!"

"Let them study," Jason's mom said, holding her back.

"She's really gotten insecure since my dad left," Jason told Kyle on the way back to his room.

From atop the bed, Jason's cat glanced up sleepily as Kyle sat down beside it and began scratching its chin. "Hey, Rex. How's it going?"

Jason closed the door and sat on the desk chair across from Kyle. He crossed his arms, eager to talk out everything going on.

Kyle glanced up from petting the cat. "I don't know what to do about Princeton. How can I accept it?"

"Is it expensive?" Jason asked.

"Yeah, but it's not that. It's because . . ." Kyle's hazel eyes peered up at Jason. "It's because of us. It's because of you."

Jason's leg started jiggling. Would Kyle seriously consider passing up Princeton because of him?

"Kyle, you're crazy. You can't pass this up. No one passes up Princeton. Have you told your mom and dad?"

"Not yet. I know they'll tell me Princeton's a better school. But Tech's a good school. And it's closer to home and cheaper, too."

Jason listened skeptically. He *wanted* Kyle to go to college with him. But . . .

"Kyle, you know Princeton's better. If you don't go there, your mom and dad will hate me."

"No, they won't."

"Oh, yes, they will. And what if I lose the scholarship? You'd be passing up Princeton for a community college?"

Kyle shrugged silently, his eyes filled with trust, making Jason no longer want to sit apart from him. He moved over to the bed, beside Kyle.

Kyle turned to him, his mouth open. In an instant the two of them fell back on the bed, their arms encircling, as the cat sprang away meowing.

"Oops." Kyle laughed and Jason kissed him more deeply, then said, "I like your chlorine smell."

"I'm sorry," Kyle told him. "Some jerk on the team told Coach Sweeney he doesn't feel safe showering with me."

Jason pulled away. "Are you serious?"

"I'm so ticked," Kyle said. "But I don't know what to do about it. And Sweeney's no help."

Jason's anxiety about his own team came flooding back. Would they react like that? How would Coach Cameron handle it, if they did?

He sat up. "Mueller called me down to his office today."

Kyle sat up beside Jason, listening as Jason told him what Mueller had said.

"Do you *want* to put off coming out?" Kyle asked.

"No. But I don't want to screw up our chances for the championship."

Kyle hung his head, staring down at the carpet.

"Are you disappointed in me?" Jason asked.

"Of course not!" Kyle looked up. "In fact, I was thinking. If you win the state championship, they're less likely to take your scholarship away, don't you think?"

Jason guessed where Kyle was going with this. "Kyle, you can't count on that. I don't want you to do something that you'll end up resenting me for."

"I won't," Kyle said, and leaned forward, pressing his lips onto Jason's.

Jason kissed him back, wanting more than anything for them to go to Tech together—except if that meant Kyle had to pass up Princeton.

His turmoil wasn't helped much after Kyle left, when his mom asked, "Does Kyle have a girlfriend?"

"Ma!" Jason shouted. "I've told you Kyle's gay. When are you going to stop being in denial?"

He stormed back to his room and cranked his stereo, trying to stop the doubts pummeling his head.

chapter 10

jason   kyle

nelson

Nelson dodged Kyle at lunch, still furious at him for getting accepted to Princeton. But Kyle nabbed him in the hall.

"Nelson! I haven't even decided if I'm going!"

"You're going to reject Princeton? I don't think so," Nelson scoffed, though secretly he hoped Kyle would.

After school Nelson sat at his computer, ignoring Kyle's instant messages. Across the desk lay his own acceptance letter to Tech—the only school to which he'd applied. His mom and counselors had told him he should target at least three universities, blah, blah, blah. . . . But what for? He wanted to go to college with Kyle. And Tech was the only one of Kyle's choices he'd stood a chance of getting into.

But if Kyle isn't going there, Nelson thought, *why should I?*

Besides, going to Tech would mean leaving Jeremy . . .

Suddenly a new idea popped into Nelson's brain. Why

not go to community college with Jeremy?

Of course, he'd have to convince his mom. She was so puk-ingly proud of him getting into Tech. But she also really liked Jeremy. Except, Nelson still hadn't confided the teeny little HIV detail.

That evening was the weekly supermarket night. Out of boredom Nelson accompanied his mom. While waiting for her to select between sour or sweet pickles, he combed through the greeting cards. Why not get one for Jeremy?

Nelson flipped through them for something romantic but not intense, sweet but not syrupy, cute but not silly.

He finally found the perfect one—a chimpanzee on the cover, with the inside caption: WANT TO MONKEY AROUND?

Somehow his mom knew whom it was for. "Is it his birthday?"

"Um, no."

His mom gave him a look, then her mouth curved into a drippy smile that made Nelson turn away, blushing.

"Why don't you invite him over for dinner?" she asked.

Nelson nearly tripped over a pyramid of lima bean cans. "You mean the three of us?"

"It would be fun," his mom replied.

"No, you mean weird. Severely weird. Get a life, Mom."

Her mouth fell in a wounded look, the kind that struck Nelson instantly guilt ridden.

"I'm sorry." He put his arm around her. "Okay, I'll invite him to dinner." He tried to sound enthusiastic, though his heart was fluttering with anxiety.

"Dinner with your mom?" Jeremy asked, when Nelson phoned.

"I know it sounds kinky," Nelson told him. "You can say no if you want."

"Well, um . . ." Jeremy hesitated. "Have you told her yet?"

Nelson knew what he meant.

"I will," he answered, trying to sound convincing.

"Okay," Jeremy agreed, and they set a time for Saturday.

Before going to bed, Nelson pulled out the card he'd bought. He wanted to write a personal note, but everything he came up with sounded either too chummy ("Hoping we'll always be friends"); or like a marriage proposal ("Wishing we can be together forever"); or like a needy plea ("I hope you like me as much as I like you").

Yuck.

Why not simply sign his name? But that seemed so indifferent, like something his dear old dad would do. He should at least write a personal closing: "Best regards" or "Warmest wishes" or—his heart gave a lurch—"Love."

He stared at the card. Did he really have the nerve to write the *L* word? He'd never done that, except with relatives and Kyle.

He raised the pen to his lips and bit into it, wondering. *Was* he in love with Jeremy? And if so, was he ready to admit it?

For the rest of the week, the only thought on his mind was Jeremy's visit.

When Saturday evening arrived, Nelson went through six shirts, four pairs of jeans, two belts, three pairs of shoes, five neck chains, two bracelets, and three brands of briefs, before finally settling on what to wear.

In the living room his mom arranged trays of hors d'oeuvres on the side tables.

"Mom," Nelson yelled, bounding down the stairs. "That's enough to feed an army!" He pulled the curtain back, peering out the window just as a car door slammed outside. Immediately Atticus started barking.

"He's here!" Nelson screamed in a whisper.

"How do I look?" his mom said, puffing her hair.

"Hey, he's *my* date," Nelson said, crowding her away from the mirror. "How do *I* look?"

She laughed and brushed off his shoulders. "You look great."

Nelson grabbed Atticus by the collar and swung the front door open. Jeremy was carrying a bouquet up the front steps.

"Omigod!" Nelson yelled. "Irises are my favorite." Leaning toward Jeremy in plain view of his mom, he made a point of kissing him full on the lips.

"Um . . ." Jeremy blushed. "These are actually for your mom."

"I know. Just kidding." Nelson laughed, though he felt a little disappointed.

"Um, hi, Mrs. Glassman," Jeremy said, wiping his feet as Atticus pawed him.

"I told you to call me Felicia. Atticus, calm down!" She pulled the dog back. "Thanks for the flowers. Come on in. Let me take your coat."

"I'll take it," Nelson offered.

While his mom finished preparing dinner, Nelson got Jeremy a Coke and came to sit with him.

Jeremy asked in a low voice, "Did you tell her?"

"Um, I meant to," Nelson said, offering a smile. "But the right moment never came up."

"Dude, you said you'd tell her." Jeremy's voice was tense.

"Sorry." Nelson took hold of Jeremy's hand. "I'll tell her. I promise."

Jeremy gave an exasperated sigh.

"Dinner's ready!" Nelson's mom called from the dining room.

The meal turned out better than any boyfriend-and-mom fantasy Nelson could've dreamed of.

She coddled and pampered Jeremy, encouraging him to "Eat more!" and keeping his Coke glass full. For his part, Jeremy was the perfect guest: polite (always "please" and "thanks"); flattering Nelson's mom ("Those are cool earrings . . ."); and funny ("Can I borrow them sometime?").

Even Atticus fell in love with Jeremy, insistently attempting to woo his leg.

"Atticus!" Nelson's mom squawked. "Nelson, please put him outside."

Jeremy completed winning her heart after dinner. "Let Nelson and me clean up."

For the first time ever, Nelson delighted in rinsing plates, standing side by side with his boyfriend. Giggling and bumping hips, they loaded the dishwasher.

Afterward, his mom merrily suggested, "Let's play Monopoly."

"No way, Mom." Nelson crossed his arms, glaring at her. "We—*Jeremy and I*—are going to hang out in my room." He felt a little guilty being so stern, but with parents sometimes you just had to draw the line.

It was Nelson's first time having Jeremy in his room and he'd spent most of the day cleaning. He'd arranged his CDs—pop, rock, dance, and show tunes. He'd gathered his videos from around the TV and lined them neatly on a single shelf. He'd wiped his dresser clean of zit cream tubes and other gross junk. Gobs of stuff got tossed beneath the bed or chucked in the closet.

"I'm impressed," his mom had commented, seeing the

neat room. "We should invite Jeremy over more often."

When Nelson led him in, the first thing Jeremy noticed was the floor-to-ceiling plush banana in the corner.

"Kyle gave me that my last birthday," Nelson grinned. "We always give each other a gag gift along with a real one. I'm so pissed at him about Princeton. He never should've applied. I told him, 'If you apply, you'll get accepted.'"

As Nelson talked Jeremy flipped through CDs, picking out the latest Pet Shop Boys. Nelson put it on, then bounced onto the bed—the only place to sit since he'd cleverly removed his desk chair, side chair, and every other sittable surface.

Jeremy sat down beside Nelson and put his arm around him. Nelson inhaled deeply, taking in the moment.

"What's this?" Jeremy asked as Nelson handed him the card from the supermarket.

"Open it."

Nelson had to sit on his hands to keep still, waiting for Jeremy to read the closing.

Jeremy stared at the card for what seemed like forever, then he folded it into the envelope. "Thanks." His brown eyes gazed up. "Nelson, you've got to tell your mom, okay?"

Nelson turned away, frustrated. That wasn't the reaction he'd expected to someone reading "Love" in writing.

He took a deep breath to collect himself. "I told you I'll tell her."

"I know. You keep saying that," Jeremy protested. "But I mean it. I feel like I'm lying to her."

"Okay," Nelson said. "I heard you already."

They stared at each other a moment, till Jeremy whispered, "Thanks for the card. I like you a lot too."

That wasn't exactly the same as "love," but it was enough

to make Nelson fold himself into Jeremy's arms.

Nelson *wanted* to tell his mom, but the way she kept raving about how much she liked Jeremy only made it harder.

One night later the next week, Nelson was in the kitchen, sharing brownies with Atticus, when his mom returned home from her PFLAG meeting.

"Honey!" his mom scolded. "You know that upsets his stomach."

While she turned to hang her coat in the closet, Nelson tossed one last chunk and watched Atticus leap for it. "Did Kyle's parents show up?"

"I didn't see them, but it was a pretty large crowd. We discussed starting an HIV-AIDS support group."

Nelson abruptly stopped chewing. Could he have asked for a better opportunity to confide about Jeremy?

Instead he jumped off the kitchen stool. "I need to put the cream on Atticus. Come on, boy. Let's go find your cream."

"Here." His mom held the tube out. "Honey, I want to ask you something. Has Jeremy been tested?"

Nelson's heart pounded so hard he was certain his mom could hear it. "Mom, that's pretty personal."

"Nelson . . ." Her voice took on an annoying parental tone. "I'm not about to repeat what we just went through."

"*We?*" Nelson shook his head in disbelief.

"Yes, *we.* I assumed you were being safe, and look what happened."

"I tested negative, didn't I?" Nelson tossed the tube of cream onto the counter. "See? This is exactly why I don't talk to you about stuff. Any time I tell you something, you end up throwing it back at me."

His mom clenched her jaw. "Okay, let's start over. Have you and Jeremy at least talked about HIV?"

Nelson sat back down on the counter stool, fidgeting with an earring, and let out a long, tortured sigh. "Yeah, we've talked about it."

"Good," his mom said, as though trying to reassure herself. "That's good." She took in a breath. "And has he been tested?"

Nelson rubbed his forehead, debating what to say. He could lie, but that would only complicate things later.

"Yes," he admitted, trying to keep his voice steady. "He's been tested."

His mom stared at him, her face taut. She gripped the counter as if bracing herself. "And?" Her voice trembled as she spoke.

"And . . ." Nelson replied, giving a feeble shrug. "He's . . . positive."

Staring open-mouthed, his mom crumpled onto the other counter stool.

Oh, crap. Nelson thought. What had he done?

"Wha . . .?" his mom asked, as if lost for words. "Wh-When did he tell you?"

Nelson shifted in place. "He told the whole youth group, when I first met him."

His mom peered back at him, a blank look on her face. "And you went out with him?" Her voice cracked with disbelief. "Why?"

"Because . . ." Nelson said. "I like him. A lot. Same as you do."

His mom closed her eyes, gave her head a little shake, and opened them again. "Nelson, you haven't had sex with him, have you?"

"Mom!" He sat up straight in his stool. "I'm not going to tell you every time I have sex. I promised you I'd be safe from now on. I know what I'm doing."

"Nelson!" His mom stood up. "This is completely unacceptable. You're too young to be risking your life. I don't want you going out with him."

"You can't tell me who to go out with." Nelson stood facing her. "What's unacceptable is your prying into my sex life. You yourself said how wonderful he is."

"This is nothing against him. You can be friends. That's one thing. But you didn't tell me he was positive. I don't want you dating him. That's final."

"Oh, yeah?" Nelson turned, stormed into the hall, and grabbed his jacket from the front closet as Atticus followed.

"Nelson, come back here!" his mom called after him. "We're not through talking about this. Where are you going?"

"Out!" Nelson yelled over Atticus's barking.

"I'm calling your father," his mom threatened.

"That's supposed to scare me?" Nelson pulled Atticus out of the way and slammed out the front door.

Trudging down the street, he pulled out a cigarette. Inside his jacket pocket his cell phone rang. He yanked it out and glanced at his mom's number on the screen. Did she really think he'd answer? He let the call go to voice mail and lit his cigarette.

Halfway down the block, he realized he'd automatically started walking toward Kyle's. Did he really want to go there? He was still *PO*'d at him. But where else could he go?

rainbow high

jason **kyle**

nelson

Kyle sat at his computer, doing calculus homework between instant messages and glancing at his onscreen buddy list, hoping Nelson would come online.

Downstairs the doorbell rang. "Kyle," his mom called. "It's Nelson!"

Kyle leaped up from his chair, tipping it over. He rocketed down the stairs. At the sight of the blue hair and leather jacket, he threw his arms around Nelson and breathed in the sweetly familiar scent of cologne and cigarettes.

"How can you be sure," Nelson muttered, "I'm not here to yell at you?"

"You can yell if you want."

Leaning back, Nelson cracked a half smile. "I'll take a rain check."

In Kyle's room Nelson crashed onto the bed. "I just had a

nuclear meltdown with my mom. I told her about Jeremy."

Kyle righted the desk chair from the floor and sat across from Nelson, dying to tell him, "I told you so." Maybe Nelson's mom would be able to drive some sense into him, though Kyle doubted it.

"I'm not going to let her police my love life," Nelson continued. "I'm of legally consenting age. She's got no right telling me who I can go out with. She says she's going to call my dad. Big whoop."

Kyle clasped his hands behind his head. "Well, at least everything's out in the open now."

Nelson's cell phone rang. He glanced at the number and turned the ringer off. "It's her again. Do you know she invited Jeremy over for dinner last Saturday? She couldn't shut up about how much she liked him."

"Have you told Jeremy what happened?"

"No way! He'll freak out about her freaking out." Nelson groaned and rolled over, covering his head with a pillow. "I hate my life."

"Join the club," Kyle said. He stood up and closed the door, so his parents wouldn't hear, and sat down again. "I told Jason about Princeton."

Nelson pulled the pillow off his head. "What did he say?"

"He says I'd be crazy not to go. But I can tell he's upset."

"So you've decided not to go?"

"I don't know. I know I don't want to leave either of you."

"Well," Nelson said, "I'm not sure I'm going to Tech anymore."

Kyle leaned forward. "What do you mean?"

"The only reason I was going to that geeky school was because of you. If you don't go there, it's kind of pointless.

rainbow high

Plus, I'd have to leave Jeremy. I'd rather go with him to community college."

Abruptly Nelson sat up on the edge of the bed. "Hey, isn't that what you said Jason might do? Can you imagine him and me and Jeremy in class together? You come too! Let's all go!"

Kyle imagined the four of them at the local campus. Hadn't he told Jason he might stay with him and go there? Yeah, but that was before.

"Pass up Princeton for a community college? My dad would love that."

He slumped down in his chair, envisioning his three friends sharing their college adventure, while he was stuck with a bunch of strangers.

"Yeah," Nelson said. "You know I don't want you to go away, but Jason's right. You'd be stupid to pass it up."

The faint sound of the phone ringing drifted upstairs. Kyle leaned back in his chair, relieved that Nelson had stopped being angry with him. "Well, I still haven't decided yet."

"Nelson?" Kyle's mom tapped on the door. "Your mom's on the phone."

"Oh, crap," Nelson moaned, covering his head with the pillow again.

Kyle opened the door and took the cordless as his mom peered in. "Thanks, Mom." He closed the door again.

Nelson yanked the pillow off his head. Frantically he flailed his hands, signaling Kyle to say he wasn't there.

"Hi, Mrs. Glassman," Kyle said into the phone. He could never bring himself to call her "Felicia," even though she asked him to. "I'll put Nelson on." He held the receiver out.

"No!" Nelson shouted in a stage whisper. "Tell her I'm not talking to her."

Kyle slid his palm over the mouthpiece. "Nelson!"

Nelson balked, shoving his hands beneath his armpits.

"Nel-son!" Kyle hissed. "If you don't want to talk to her, *you* tell her."

Nelson gave Kyle an evil look. Finally he took the phone.

For about five minutes he argued with his mom, saying things like, "No! I don't care. Oh, yeah? You do that, see what happens." In between, he rolled his eyes, sputtered, sighed, moaned, and made faces, till at last, he hung up and hissed, "Dragon lady!"

Kyle knew there was no point arguing. It was best just to let Nelson rant, which he did for about half an hour, till he finally went home.

After he'd left, Kyle's mom stopped by. "Is everything all right?" she asked. "Nelson's mom sounded pretty upset."

"Everything's fine," Kyle said, not wanting to go into all the Jeremy stuff.

But his mom sat down on the bed across from him. "What's going on, honey?"

"Nothing!" Hoping to put her off, he added, "Just boyfriend stuff."

That was the wrong thing to say. "Oh?" Her brow piqued with interest. "Does Nelson have a boyfriend now?"

"Yeah, sort of. I guess." Kyle *really* did not want to go into this with his mom.

But she did. "You and Nelson should invite him over sometime." Her voice brimmed with congeniality. "I'd like to meet him."

Oh, peachy, Kyle thought. He could just imagine her freaking out once she learned why Nelson's mom had freaked.

"Um, Mom? I'm not quite done with my homework." He gestured to his book.

"All right," she said, standing up. "But if you or Nelson ever need to talk about 'boyfriend stuff,' as you call it . . . " She gave Kyle's shoulder an affectionate tug. "I want you to let me know. Okay?"

Kyle nodded, managing a smile.

His mom bent over and kissed him good night. He watched her leave, wondering: Would she be able to understand his "boyfriend stuff," like why he couldn't bear to leave Jason for Princeton?

The following evening, while Kyle finished setting the table, his dad sorted through the day's mail.

"I don't understand why you haven't heard from Princeton yet." He tossed the stack aside. "You want me to call tomorrow and find out when the letters are being sent?"

Kyle bit into his lip, debating whether to come forth. His mom sat down opposite him, setting a dish of steaming green beans on the table. Kyle drew a deep breath, looked down at his own plate, and said in a low voice, "Um, I already got my letter."

It took a moment for him to summon the nerve to look back up. His dad's brow was furrowed, either in anger or confusion, while his mom's eyes were wide with surprise.

She spoke first. "You got your letter from Princeton?"

The enthusiasm in her tone made Kyle want to crawl beneath the table. He swallowed the lump in his throat and nodded.

"Honey!" his mom exclaimed. "When? Today?"

"Um . . ." Kyle's fingers nervously clinked his knife and fork together, fidgeting. "Um, actually, a few days ago."

His mom glanced across the table at his dad. His dad blinked, obviously baffled.

"Why didn't you tell us, son? Didn't you get accepted? You should've told us."

Kyle hesitated. Should he let them believe that? It would solve everything. But he couldn't deceive them.

"No," he admitted. "I was accepted."

His dad leaned forward. "You were accepted?"

"Yeah."

"Well, Kyle!" His dad shook his head, his brow wrinkling with agitation. "When were you going to tell us?"

"Um, now. I guess."

"Honey!" his mom spoke up. "What's going on? Why didn't you mention it?"

"I'm, um . . ." He gulped a sip of water, trying to get the words out, and noticed his hand trembling. "I'm not sure I want to go to Princeton."

"Not go to Princeton?" his dad boomed. "Kyle, what's the problem?"

"Um, I'm thinking of going to Tech."

His dad pushed his chair back from the table, like he needed more breathing room, then he leaned forward again. "I thought Tech was your fallback school. Isn't that what we agreed?"

"Yeah, but um, I've decided I want to go to Tech." Kyle was trying to keep his voice calm, but his dad's rising pitch wasn't helping.

"Kyle, this is not your decision alone."

"I'm the one going to school!" Kyle's voice grew louder.

"Yeah," his dad growled. "But *we're* the ones paying for it."

"Then you should be happy," Kyle was nearly shouting. "Tech is cheaper."

His dad narrowed his eyes. "It's Nelson. He's behind this, isn't he?"

"No!" Kyle snapped back, definitely shouting. It made him furious the way his dad always blamed everything on Nelson. He turned to his mom. "Can I be excused?"

"We're not through talking," his dad bellowed, his face muscles straining. "I want to know what's behind this."

"It's my decision," Kyle shouted, his voice choking. "That's all there is to it. You can't tell me where to go. Or I won't go anywhere!"

His mom chimed her fork against her glass, the family signal for a time-out.

"Can I be excused?" Kyle repeated.

"You haven't touched your food, honey. How about if we all calmly finish eating and have a family council after dinner, okay?"

"I don't want to eat anything." Kyle crossed his arms.

His mom gave him a stern look and passed him the string beans. "I'd like you to eat something."

He glared back at her, then uncrossed his arms and took the dish of beans, but only because he was a little hungry.

Family council was a parenting thing his mom had begun when Kyle was in grade school. It was supposed to be a discussion but it was actually more like being summoned before the Supreme Court. His dad sat in his massive leather recliner on one side of the living room. His mom sat on the crimson velvet wingchair opposite. Kyle slouched on the sofa facing them, ready for his family's own version of the Spanish Inquisition.

His mom smoothed her pleated dress. "Now, honey, what's going on? Why didn't you tell us you'd received your acceptance to Princeton?"

"Because . . ." Kyle said, sitting up. "I'm not sure I want to go there. Everyone I know is going to Tech."

His dad's mouth opened to say something, but Kyle cut him off. "Not just Nelson! Other friends too, and . . . Jason."

His dad adjusted his glasses. "Jason's going there? Is that what's swaying you?"

Kyle wasn't sure how to answer. His dad might like for him to go to Tech with Jason. On the other hand, he might dislike Jason for taking him away from Princeton. "That's part of it," Kyle said.

"Jason is a fine boy," his mom said. "You know Dad and I both like him. We understand he's special to you. But what you need to consider now is academics, the quality of your education. A school like Princeton will open a lot of doors for you."

"Tech's a good school," Kyle argued.

His dad shook his head. "We're not saying it isn't. We're just saying that since you're fortunate enough to be able to choose between a good university and an *extraordinary* university, the choice is obvious."

Not to Kyle it wasn't. "I don't want to leave my friends."

His dad gripped the arms of the recliner. "We're not paying for you to hang out with your friends."

"I'm not going just to *hang out with my friends*," Kyle mimicked his dad. "I'll go to school—just not the school *you* want."

"Well, *you* applied there," his dad yelled. "If you were going to turn it down, then why'd you apply in the first place?"

Kyle's head was burning, his breath coming hard. How could he *not* have applied there, when for seventeen years, every other word out of his dad's mouth was "Princeton-this" or "Tigers-that." Kyle had wanted to please him. And he'd always dreamed of going into their math program. But he'd never imagined he'd become boyfriends with Jason. It wasn't fair.

"Fine," Kyle said. "If you don't want to pay for college, then I'll pay for it myself."

"Yeah?" his dad leaned forward. "How?"

"I'll . . ." Kyle thought for a moment. He hated having to depend on his parents. He wished he had the money to do whatever he wanted. ". . . I'll get loans!" He kicked his feet onto the coffee table, pleased with his reply.

"Oh, that's really smart." His dad smirked. "Borrow thousands a year and compile massive debt, just so you can hang out with your friends! That's brilliant."

"Guys?" his mom intervened. She turned to Kyle. "Honey, I'm sure not *all* of your friends are going to Tech. People go to different schools, but they manage to keep in touch. You'll still get together during breaks and in the summer. It's not like you'll never see them again."

Kyle knew she was right. He could get by seeing his other friends during vacations. But it was hard to imagine life without Nelson's daily wheedling and cajoling. As for being separated from Jason—his parents may as well stretch him out on the coffee table and rip his heart out right now.

"Besides," his mom purred on, like some hypnotist. "Wherever you go, you're going to be plenty occupied with your coursework, believe you me. College is a lot tougher than high school. You need to think about this decision very carefully. The school you go to can make a big difference in whatever you decide to do in life."

Yeah, sure. As if he had the foggiest idea what he was going to do with his life. The future seemed so vast and uncertain, whereas the present—his friendship with Nelson and his love for Jason—were so immediate, so essential. Couldn't his parents see that?

"You don't understand."

"Honey, we do understand. We know Jason and your friends are important to you. But you've been accepted to one of the finest schools in the country. Opportunities like this take sacrifices. If they're really your friends, they'll appreciate that. And they'll stay your friends throughout the course of your life, regardless of where you go."

But would Nelson stay his *best* friend? And would Jason stay his *boy*friend?

"When do you need to let them know your decision?" his dad asked.

"Next week."

"Honey . . ." His mom let out a deep breath. "You know we both love you. We only want what's best for you."

Kyle waited to see if she'd finished. "Am I free to go now?"

His dad replied with a disapproving frown. His mom sighed and nodded. Kyle stood and trudged up the stairs.

In his room, he cast himself atop the bed. After staring at the ceiling for a while, he pulled out the Princeton letter from his nightstand. He'd carefully hidden it between the pages of his yearbook, opposite his favorite photo of Jason, at last year's basketball championships.

His gaze shifted back and forth between the letter and Jason's photo. How could he leave Jason? And how could he pass up Princeton?

jason   kyle

nelson

Next day when the lunch bell rang, Jason pressed his way through the tide of students waving and high-fiving.

As he entered the cafeteria he spotted Corey and some teammates. He was about to join them when he saw Dwayne.

Never mind, Jason decided. Turning in the opposite direction, he noticed Nelson, wearing a blinding pink shirt, exiting the food line.

Instantly Jason's mind flashed forward. As if watching two cars approach, about to collide, he knew he was powerless to stop what was about to transpire.

Dwayne put his foot out and simultaneously bumped Nelson's shoulder. Nelson lost his balance, tumbling to the floor, his tray crashing beside him.

The lunch crowd turned toward the commotion, whistling and jeering.

As Nelson picked himself up from the floor Dwayne shouted, "Why'd you bump me, faggot?"

Nelson yelled back, "You bumped into me, jackass!"

At that, Dwayne grabbed him by the collar.

In an instant Jason was beside them. "Let him go, Dwayne."

Dwayne glared back at him. "Stay out of it."

Meanwhile Nelson, wedged between them, wore an almost beatific smile, as though brimming with unwavering faith in Jason.

"I saw what you did," Jason told Dwayne. "Now leave him alone."

Dwayne's mouth opened to snarl something, but Corey stepped in, nudging them apart. "Come on, guys. You're both going to get in trouble." He gestured to a cafeteria monitor marching toward them.

Dwayne released his grip on Nelson, shoving him away. "You know," Dwayne sneered at Jason, "people are starting to think *you're* a fag."

Jason's stomach clenched. A month prior he might've winced or lashed out at the remark, but he'd been through too much since then. "What if I am?" he volleyed back.

As soon as the words leaped out of his mouth, he remembered his promise to Mueller. *Oh, crap.*

Corey and his other teammates darted glances between one another, Jason, and Nelson.

"No, you're not!" Andre said, with a hollow laugh. Odell and Wang joined in.

"What's going on, boys?" the cafeteria monitor asked.

"Nothing," Corey said and gently tugged Jason's arm. "Come on, guys. Lunch is already half over."

Dwayne shot Jason one last scowl and spun toward the food line, followed by the others.

"Go ahead," Jason told Corey. "I've got something to do."

Hurrying out the lunchroom door, Jason thought he heard Nelson yell, "Thanks," but he didn't take time to look back.

"Coach, can I talk—" Only after Jason had tapped on the doorway did he realize Coach was on the phone.

"Sorry," Jason whispered and leaned back out to the hall. While Coach growled into the receiver, Jason bit his nails and tried to gather his thoughts.

"Carrillo?" Coach bellowed, hanging up.

Steeling himself, Jason walked into the office. "Sorry, Coach. I didn't mean to—"

"Take a seat," Coach interrupted, glancing up from a bowlful of soup. "What the hell's so important?" He blew to cool his spoonful.

Jason eased into the familiar vinyl chair and took a breath. "I think I said something I shouldn't have."

His voice quivering, he told Coach what had happened.

Coach listened till Jason finished. Then he wiped a paper napkin across his mouth and crumpled it onto the desk. "Damn it, Carrillo!"

Jason had expected a rebuke and felt relieved to get it.

Coach leaned back in his swivel chair and crossed his arms. His clear gray eyes peered through his glasses. "So, what do you want to do?"

Jason glanced away, thinking. Could he really say what he wanted?

"I guess I want to get it over with. But I don't want to upset the team."

jason   nelson   kyle   123

"I've been giving this a lot of thought." Coach rubbed a hand across the back of his neck. "What if you came out to the team in a special meeting before practice?"

"Today?" Jason's voice came out in a squeak. He envisioned himself standing before his teammates, admitting Dwayne had been right. "But—I mean—what about what I promised Mr. Mueller?"

Coach gave a shrug. "You tried it his way. It didn't work. We've just got to make sure we win the championship."

He made it sound so simple. Jason sat speechless. He'd never expected things to move this quickly. Was he really prepared to stand before his peers? "What would I say?"

Coach leveled his gaze at him. "The same things you've told me."

"But . . ." Jason's leg started jiggling. "How do you think the guys'll react?"

"That I don't know." Coach brought his hands together and interlaced his fingers. "It's definitely going to impact them and all the teams that follow. It could be a major upset." He let his hands spread apart and laid them on the desk. "I think most boys—and their parents—will look to see how *I* react."

As Jason listened it dawned on him how much this man was putting himself on the line for him—more than his dad had ever done.

"Coach? Can I ask you something?"

"Yeah?"

Jason hesitated, suddenly unsure what to say. "Why are you doing this?"

Coach's lip squiggled up, like at practice when someone asked a dumb question. "For the same reason I sent you on the court all those games." He gazed at Jason steadily. "Because I believe in you."

Jason stared back and felt his throat choke up. "Thanks," he told Coach and wiped his nose, embarrassed.

As Jason returned toward the lunchroom he recognized the girl ahead of him, carrying a load of books.

He'd avoided Debra since the day when he'd let it slip about dating Kyle. Although she'd said she wanted to talk, how could he talk about dating a guy with his ex-girlfriend?

Even now he considered hanging back, except . . . If he was going to come out to the team that afternoon, shouldn't he let Debra know? After all, she was his ex. No doubt she'd get flak about it.

Jason ran a hand through his curls, walking up behind her. "Wha's up?" he said cheerily.

She stopped, obviously surprised. "Where did you come from?"

"I was talking to Coach." Jason shoved his hands into his pockets. "I—um, I've been meaning to call you."

"Well . . ." Her blue eyes peered at him, full of questioning. "Right now I need to get these back to Ms. Darsie." She started to leave.

"Let me help you," Jason said, taking half the load. As they walked he glanced at the clock. In a minute the bell would ring, flooding the hall with students.

"I need to tell you something," he said in a hushed voice. "Coach decided I should come out to the team this afternoon."

Debra stopped. She turned to face him, staring silently. "O . . . kay . . ." she said slowly, as if letting the information sink in. "Thanks for giving me plenty of warning."

Jason adjusted his grip on the books. "He just decided. Are you angry?"

Debra raised an eyebrow, shook her head, and started walking again. "Yes—no—Jason, I don't know." She stopped again, rolling her eyes as though exasperated. "I just wish you'd call me rather than dump things like this on me."

"I'm sorry," Jason protested. "It's just hard talking about this stuff."

"It's hard for me too," Debra said, her voice gentler.

The bell rang. Doors slammed open. Students poured into the hall. "Can we talk later?" Jason asked.

"Sure," Debra said, still sounding upset.

Jason helped her carry the books through the crowd, then he hurried to class.

Jason was glad he hadn't eaten lunch. All afternoon he felt about to be sick. He was totally unable to concentrate—chewing his nails, his leg jiggling as if it were spastic. In algebra his pencil lead broke from pressing down so hard.

He desperately wanted all this over with. But what if he wasn't able to go through with it? Or what if he *did* go through with it? What then?

There was one more person he wanted to talk to even though there was barely time. As soon as the last bell rang, he bolted to Kyle's locker.

"Did Nelson tell you what happened at lunch?" Jason whispered, out of breath.

"Yeah." Kyle smiled. "He said you're his hero. He wants to build you a monument."

"This isn't funny." Jason wiped the sweat from his brow, and told Kyle about his decision with Coach. "I'm really nervous. What should I say?"

"Well . . ." Kyle said calmly, his expression serious. "Tell the team how much they mean to you. Say you want to be up-front with them."

"Yeah, that's good," Jason said. But would he remember it?

Kyle gazed into his eyes. "You'll do great. I'll be thinking of you."

Jason glanced away. "Um, I better go." He headed toward the gym, wishing Kyle could come with him.

In the locker room teammates were clowning and talking trash, as usual. In the thick of it, Dwayne gloated about some girl supposedly begging to go down on him. His boasting somehow led Wang to make a stupid gay joke.

Jason changed into his practice uniform, trying to stay focused.

"You okay?" Corey asked as the other guys laughed at Wang's punch line.

"Yeah," Jason said. He'd decided not to tell Corey what he was up to, lest Corey try to talk him out of it.

"Hurry it up!" Coach barked, marching between the boys. He glanced at Jason. "All set?"

Jason nodded and followed him out to the gym. Several boys were already warming up—dribbling and shooting. The pounding of balls reverberated on the lacquered wood floor.

Andre made a pass, but Jason's mind was so out of it, he missed the ball.

Coach blew his whistle. "Gather up, everyone. Team meeting!" He waved them over with his clipboard.

The balls stopped thumping as one boy followed another to the bleachers. Jason perched on the front bench, followed by two of the squad's juniors. Tim clasped Jason a handshake and sprawled on one side. Tom deposited himself on the other.

"Listen up!" Coach growled. "We're now counting days to finals. That means I want *no* missed practices, understand? I don't care if your granny gets pneumonia, or if your dog eats your sneakers, or if Miss Teen America calls you for a date. . . . No excuses. Got it?"

The team laughed and answered, "Yes, Coach."

He made a couple more announcements, but Jason didn't hear. All he could think about was summoning the nerve to stand up in front of everyone.

"Next item," Coach bellowed. "Carrillo's got an announcement. It's something he and I have talked about. I want you all to pay attention. He's got my respect and I expect you to give him yours. We'll discuss it afterward. Go ahead, Carrillo."

Knees trembling, Jason stood. He turned to face the Whitman High School varsity basketball squad. All eyes were on him. He blanked for a moment, his thoughts spinning.

"Um . . ." He started to speak, but no words came. His mouth felt dry as wood.

Coach nodded to him, his face filled with expectation.

"Um . . ." Jason cleared his throat. "There's something I want to tell you." His voice quavered. "Because . . ."

He scanned the faces of his teammates. After this moment, they would never see him the same way again.

"Because during these past four years you guys have been like family to me."

Odell nodded in agreement. Skip smiled. Then Dwayne roared a yawn that sent everyone turning toward him.

Jason faltered, unsettled by the interruption.

Dwayne gave a diabolical smile, and a flame of anger flared through Jason, emboldening him.

rainbow high

"I want to be up-front with you. And put to rest any rumors. I want to let you know . . ."

He took a breath, trying to make his heart slow down. "I'm not only your teammate. I'm also gay. And . . . I'm proud to be both."

Wang's jaw dropped. Odell bolted upright. Dwayne's eyes bulged.

To Jason, it felt as though all the oxygen had been sucked out of the room. *Breathe,* he told himself.

Several boys turned to Coach, but he gestured them to keep their attention on Jason.

Tim and Tom leaned forward. Seeing their earnest glances, Jason continued.

"This doesn't change anything between us. I'm still the same person I've always been. I'm still your friend. And I hope you're still mine."

Corey glanced back at him, nodding.

Jason paused. What else did he want to tell them? He recalled Kyle's experience with his swim teammates.

"Some of you may be worried about me coming on to you. If you are, well, don't flatter yourselves, because I'm not interested."

He didn't mean it to be funny, but several guys burst out laughing—probably from nerves, but at least it broke the tension.

"All right." Coach stood up and patted Jason's shoulder. "Any questions or problems with this? Get it out now."

The team sat speechless.

A couple of guys shrugged, Skip coughed, and almost everyone else stared at their sneakers. Jason glanced around nervously, hoping this would end soon.

Coach scanned the reticent group. "One other thing. From now on, I don't want to hear any more homophobic slurs. That means no 'fag,' 'homo,' 'pansy,' 'fairy,' none of that crap."

He tapped his clipboard against his leg. "I know I've used them. But will I from now on? No. If I can change, you can change. First time, you get a warning. Second time, suspension. Is that clear?"

A low laugh came from Dwayne. Coach whirled toward him. "Something to say, Smith?"

Dwayne shifted. "You're not serious, Coach. I mean, you wouldn't suspend us right before championship?"

Coach walked directly over to him. "Go ahead," he told Dwayne, staring him square in the eye. "Try me."

Dwayne stared back, then lowered his gaze.

"That goes for all of you," Coach bellowed. "I don't care if you're gay, or blue, or what you are, you're a team. I expect you to act like one. Any differences between you, put them aside. Anyone who can't, is off the team. Understood?"

When no one answered, he cupped a hand around his ear and yelled, "I said, *understood*?"

"Yes, Coach!" the team answered in unison.

"All right." Coach clapped his hands. "Let's play."

With that, the boys bounded off the bleachers, shoes pounding the aluminum. Jason hung back, absorbing what had happened.

No one had heckled him. Or stormed out. Or croaked from shock.

"Carrillo?" Coach barked. "What are you waiting for? You're still part of this team, aren't you? Get out there!"

Even though Jason felt more wiped out than ever in his life, he complied. For the next two hours, he tried to concentrate on the game. Coach was right, he kept telling himself, what did it matter if he was gay?

But it did matter, gauging by his teammates' plays. Everyone except Corey seemed thrown off balance.

Jason kept watching the clock, eager for practice to end.

"All right," Coach finally announced. "Go shower!"

Jason's stomach gave a lurch. Slowly he walked to the locker room.

Should he skip his shower, like Kyle? Except, Kyle *swam.* He didn't finish his practices stinking from sweat.

"Hey, Jason!" Wang extended his hand. "I feel bad about the joke I made before practice. I didn't know, man."

"That's okay." Jason shook hands. Encouraged, he cautiously peeled off his shirt and shoes. He stepped out of his shorts. Taking a breath, he strode toward the shower room, eyes averted from his teammates.

Amid the spray of water, Corey was talking about some TV show with Skip, while Andre discussed cars with Odell. As Jason entered, everyone became quiet.

Jason began soaping himself down as rapidly as possible.

"So, Jason!" Andre's voice boomed across the tile.

Jason braced himself, expecting his first challenge. "Yeah?"

"So if none of us handsome studs is your type—" Andre laughed. "—who is?"

"Yeah, Jason," Odell chimed in. "What kind of insult is that?"

Jason shook the water from his ears. Was he hearing things? Were they actually *joking* with him?

"You know, my cousin's gay," Andre crooned on. "I'll introduce you, but don't get your hopes up. He's nowhere near as good-looking as me."

Jason knew their kidding was a cover-up for the awkward-
ness. And yet he was grateful. He laughed along, aiming his face
into the shower spray, hoping no one would notice the tears of
relief streaming down his face.

chapter 13

jason   kyle

nelson

After school Nelson's friend Amy dropped him off at the mall's music store. He wanted to buy Jeremy a CD—to help smooth things over when Nelson related his mom's going mental over the HIV.

He was flipping through country music discs when his cell phone rang, displaying Kyle's number. "Whoa, dude," Nelson answered. "Some of these cowboys are severely cute."

"He did it," Kyle responded. "Jason came out to the team. He just called to tell me."

"Omigod!" Nelson shouted, snapping his fingers. "I've got to congratulate him. What's his number?"

When Jason answered the phone, Nelson yelled, "Woo-hoo! Congrats, girl! How's it feel?"

"Um . . ." Jason gave a nervous laugh. "Okay, I guess."

They talked for several minutes. Actually Nelson did most of the talking, until Jason's call waiting clicked and he said he had to go.

When Nelson arrived home, his mom had already set the table for dinner. Next to his place setting lay a newspaper clipping headlined: HALF OF ALL NEW AMERICAN HIV INFECTIONS OCCUR IN YOUNG PEOPLE AGES 13-24.

Slowly Nelson lifted his gaze from the paper. "Mom?" he uttered through clenched teeth. "Are you whacked?"

"Are you?" she retorted, and carefully spread her napkin on her lap.

Not another word passed Nelson's lips during dinner. Under his breath he swore he'd never speak to her again.

When the phone rang during dessert, Nelson leaped for it, grateful for the distraction. "City Loony Bin."

"Nelson?" It was his father's voice. Great. Just what Nelson didn't need.

"Hold on." He extended the receiver out to his mom.

"Who is it?" she asked.

Instead of answering, Nelson started clearing the table.

"Hello?" his mom said, taking the phone. She talked with his dad for a minute, then said, "Nelson! He wants to talk to *you*."

"As if," Nelson replied. Nevertheless, he took the receiver back. "Yeah?"

"Your mother called me about this boy you're seeing. Why do you have to upset her like this?"

As usual, his dad never bothered to ask Nelson's side of it.

"I'm not doing this to upset her," Nelson protested.

"Well," his dad retorted, "that's what you're doing, whether you mean to or not."

"Yeah?" Nelson glared at his mom. "Did she also tell you

rainbow high

how much she enjoyed meeting him? How she said she thinks he's 'wonderful'? Her exact words. 'Very mature.' Thinks he's going to be very good for me."

His mom frowned, even though every word he'd said was true.

"She told me the boy's sick," Nelson's dad growled.

"He has HIV," Nelson corrected. "That doesn't mean he's sick. He's healthier than I am."

His mom crossed her arms, her jaw clenched.

"She wants you to stop going out with him," his dad insisted. "I want you to listen to her."

"Like *you* ever listened to her," Nelson snapped back. He wasn't sure what prompted him to say that. Divorce residue, no doubt. He tossed the receiver back to his mom. "I'm going out."

"Going out *where*?" his mom demanded. "Nelson, wait!"

But he'd already grabbed his jacket and was out the front door, CD in hand.

As he walked toward the metro, he lit up a cigarette, pulled his cell phone from his pocket, and dialed.

"I need to talk to you," he said when Jeremy answered. "Can I come over?"

"Yeah, sure. What's the matter?"

Nelson exhaled a stream of smoke. "I really, really want to see you."

"You're fading out," Jeremy said.

"I want!" Nelson shouted. "To! See! You!" But the line had cut off.

The moment Jeremy answered the door, Nelson wedged himself into Jeremy's arms.

"I hate her," Nelson groaned. "She's an evil witch."

"Your mom?" Jeremy's voice rose in disbelief. He looked a little pale. Was something troubling him?

"Here." Nelson pulled the CD out from his jacket. "I got you this. You don't have it, do you? It just came out."

"Awesome!" Jeremy yelped. "I was going to get it! Thanks." He pecked Nelson a kiss and turned to the stereo. "Let me put it on. Have a seat. My brother's out."

"Can I get us something to drink?" Nelson asked. "Do you want anything?"

He got them each a ginger ale while Jeremy put the music on. When he returned to join Jeremy on the loveseat, a thrill tingled through him. They were alone. But when he took hold of Jeremy's hand, he again noticed Jeremy didn't look quite right.

"Are you feeling okay?"

"Um, not really." Jeremy rested his free hand on his stomach. "My stomach's been upset all day. But never mind. I want to hear what happened with your mom."

"Well . . ." Nelson took a sip of some soda, but it went down the wrong way. "I told her about—" cough "—you know—" cough "about you. And we got into—" cough "a sort of fight."

"I knew this was going to happen." Jeremy sat up, patting Nelson's back. "Now what are we supposed to do?"

"Would you please not yell?" Nelson took another sip of ginger ale. "She's not going to stop me from seeing you."

"I told you to tell her, didn't I?" Jeremy lowered his voice. "This whole time I felt like I was keeping something from her."

"She's not going to control me," Nelson insisted. "I'll be eighteen soon. She can't rule my life."

Suddenly Jeremy made a pained face and clasped his stomach. He looked so odd that Nelson thought it was a joke. Then

rainbow high

he realized Jeremy might be really sick. "Are you all right?"

"I feel like . . ." Jeremy flinched. "Oh, no!" He leaped up from the loveseat and bolted to the bathroom, slamming the door.

A second later came the echoes of barfing—*so* not romantic. Nelson fiddled with an earring. He'd never had a date get sick. Should he excuse himself and leave? But this was all part of liking—or loving—someone, wasn't it?

He walked to the bathroom and gently tapped on the door. "You okay?"

"I'll be out in a minute," Jeremy moaned.

Nelson adjusted another earring. What to do? Glancing toward a shelf, he noticed his "love"-inscribed card to Jeremy proudly displayed. Nelson's heart melted. He couldn't bail now, even if Jeremy's cookie tossing totally grossed him out.

Beneath the chords of the country CD, the toilet flushed, followed by the sound of the sink faucet, then gargling.

Jeremy staggered from the bathroom. "I'm sorry." He collapsed into the loveseat. "I'm so embarrassed."

"Don't be silly," Nelson said, sitting beside him. "Have some ginger ale. It'll soothe your stomach." He raised the glass to Jeremy's lips.

"Thanks," Jeremy whispered and took a sip. "I think it's the meds. They're so toxic. My doctor put me on a new regimen. But I'm scared of getting 'The Look.' You know—the caved in face, Skelctor cheeks . . ."

Nelson recalled one of the adult facilitators of the downtown youth group, whose face *did* look caved in. But the guy was old already—at least in his thirties.

"Don't be crazy," Nelson said. "You're too young for that."

"Unfortunately . . ." Jeremy sighed, taking hold of Nelson's hand. "I'm not."

"Oh, you'll be fine." Nelson leaned over, following the scent of fresh mouthwash, to softly plant a kiss on Jeremy's cheek.

They sat quietly after that, listening to the CD cowboy croon a sad ballad.

Nelson had never really thought of Jeremy as sick before. He'd always seemed so hunky and healthy. What if something really serious happened to him? Who would take care of him?

Nelson interlaced his fingers between Jeremy's. He was feeling something new, something different from what he'd felt with other guys. He felt like Jeremy needed him. He wanted to take care of Jeremy. He wanted to be there for him. No matter what his mom said.

The CD changed to an up-tempo track. "Do you really know how to dance this stuff?" Nelson asked.

"Two-step?" Jeremy's face lit up. "Yeah. Want to learn?"

"Aren't you sick?" Nelson said.

"I think I'm okay now. Let's try." Jeremy rose, followed by Nelson. "First," he instructed, "give me your right hand. Now put your left on my shoulder. That's it."

He slipped his arm around Nelson's waist, resting his palm on Nelson's back.

Nelson's skin tingled. He'd never danced close with anyone, not even Kyle.

"Now, I'm going to start with my left foot." Jeremy slid his thigh between Nelson's legs.

Nelson gulped. Country music was quickly becoming his favorite.

"And you slide your right foot back," Jeremy continued. "Now your left foot. That's basically it—two quick, short steps and two long, slow ones. Quick-quick, slow . . . slow."

Awkwardly at first, he moved Nelson around the parquet

floor, whispering, "Quick-quick, slow . . . slow."

Nelson tried to keep up, but how could he concentrate with Jeremy's lips brushing his ear and his thigh pressing against him? "Crap. I can't do this."

"You're doing great." Jeremy led him across the room. "Just close your eyes. Relax. Feel the signals my body gives you."

I'm feeling the signals loud and clear, Nelson thought. Everything seemed so right, so perfect.

"You okay?" Jeremy asked.

"I'm doing great." Nelson grinned as the song twanged to a conclusion. Jeremy raised Nelson's hand in the air and spun him in a final twirl. Then he bowed and Nelson leaned onto him, out of breath. "Except I've got to quit smoking."

"Nelson, let go!" Jeremy gasped, the blood draining from his face.

He clamped a hand over his mouth and pushed Nelson aside. This time Jeremy only reached the kitchen sink before starting to upchuck.

Following after him, Nelson held Jeremy's forehead, to keep it from hitting the faucet—majorly not romantic.

After Jeremy finished, he turned away, grabbing a paper towel to wipe his face.

"Whoa dude," Nelson said. "Are you crying?"

"I'm sorry," Jeremy said in a raspy voice. "I shouldn't have danced. You must be so grossed out."

"No, I'm not," Nelson lied, putting his arm around him. "I don't mind."

"Yeah, right." Jeremy blew his nose in the paper towel. "I better get to bed. And you better get home."

Nelson didn't budge. "I can spend the night if you want . . . in case you need anything."

Jeremy gave him a skeptical look. "That would be cozy. You, me, and my brother. Besides, what about your mom? Does she even know where you are?"

"It's none of her business," Nelson mumbled. "I'm not a baby anymore."

"But she's still your mom."

Nelson cradled his head on Jeremy's shoulder. "Whose side are you on?"

"I'm trying to help you see her side of it."

Through Jeremy's chest, Nelson could hear his heartbeat. "How about if I call and tell her I'm with you?"

"Yeah, then she'll *really* like me." Jeremy pulled away, gently prying Nelson's hands off him. "Come on. I need to get to bed and you need to get home."

It took another fifteen minutes of persuasion before Nelson finally left.

On his walk to the subway he tried to sort out the evening. It had kind of creeped him out seeing Jeremy sick. And his mom and dad weren't helping matters. Between her having joined the sex police and the old goat phoning in a guest appearance, it was worse than a daytime talk show.

But then he remembered gliding across the floor in Jeremy's arms, laying his head softly on Jeremy's beautiful shoulder, feeling the tender thump of his heartbeat. He recalled the card he'd given Jeremy displayed on the shelf. He thought of how Jeremy needed him. Wasn't it all part of loving someone?

Sure it pissed him off that Jeremy was sick, but there was nothing Nelson could do about that. So why waste time thinking about it?

When he arrived home, the lights were on. Atticus met him at the door. His mom was reading *Newsweek,* no doubt scouring the pages for a newly alarming HIV article.

With dramatic flair she glanced at her watch. "You know this is a school night."

"It slipped my mind," Nelson replied, deadpan. "Did anyone call?"

She fired him her Wicked Witch of the West look. "Kyle did. You know, Nelson, your dad was very upset by your ignoring his phone call."

"Oh, yeah, right. Like he gives a crap?"

"He does!"

"He does not!" Nelson turned toward the stairway.

"Nelson!" She tossed her magazine down. "We're not through discussing this."

"I'm going to bed," he called over his shoulder. "It's a school night, you know."

When he got to his room, he slammed the door. Plopping onto the bed, he pulled out his cell phone to call Kyle.

chapter 14

jason   **kyle**

nelson

Kyle sat at his computer, absorbed in proudly e-mailing the GSA and everyone else he knew about Jason's coming out. He didn't even hear the phone ring.

"Kyle!" his mom called. "It's Nelson!"

Kyle snatched up the receiver. "Where were you?"

"Jeremy's. Omigod, he got really sick. It totally traumatized me—at least a little. It made me think. You know?"

Kyle leaned away from his computer screen. Was Nelson finally getting some sense about dating Jeremy?

"But everyone gets sick sometimes," Nelson said in the next breath. "He thinks it's the meds. He taught me to two-step. Kyle? I think I'm totally in love with him."

Kyle clamped down on his bottom lip, wanting to shout, "Nelson, he's HIV positive!" But he knew it would be no use.

"I want to ask you something," Nelson continued. "With

    rainbow high

Jason, do you ever feel like he really *needs* you? You know what I mean? Like, you sort of feel you want to take care of him? Like you want to make him realize how special he is and be there for him?"

Kyle thought about Jason's brooding times, when his eyes turned stormy and he withdrew into himself—times when Kyle wanted to take him in his arms and soothe him.

"Yeah," he told Nelson. "I know what you mean."

"That's how I felt tonight," Nelson said. "Like he needs me. And I need him."

Kyle listened patiently, wanting to feel happy for Nelson finding someone special. Except, why did it have to be someone *positive*?

Better to change the subject, Kyle decided, before all this made him nuts.

"I've been EM-ing everyone about Jason."

"Oh, yeah." Nelson yawned. "It should be an interesting day tomorrow."

They talked for a while, till Nelson yawned even louder. "Whoa! I think it's time for my beauty sleep."

After hanging up, Kyle stared at his life-size screensaver of Jason's face, wondering if Jason's coming out would change things between them.

He sent one more e-mail, then shut down his computer and climbed into bed.

When Kyle opened the door to school next morning, it felt as though a *Star Trek* force field had energetically charged the entire building. In doorways and hallways kids buzzed like crazy about one thing: Jason.

"Did you hear? Oh, my God! No way. I think it's great.

What a waste. Can you imagine? So bizarre. But he's so cute. I don't know, man. Can you believe he really said that? It's creeping me out. I want to see him."

Kyle felt like an electron, bouncing from one overheard conversation to another, propelled toward Jason's locker. Unfortunately, once he got near, he could only glimpse the top of Jason's curly brown hair. The rest of him was mobbed by chattering girls.

"When are you going shopping with us?" A girl with braces laughed, while another mentioned two boy bands, asking, "Which do you think is cuter?"

This wasn't exactly what Kyle had expected, even though most of his own female friends had become closer after *he* came out.

All during morning classes, every time Kyle heard a girl gossip about Jason, he longed to whisper back, "I'm his boyfriend. Yep, out of all the guys in the world, he chose me."

But he knew Jason wasn't ready to let the whole world know about them. He understood that Jason needed to come out at his own pace. Nevertheless it was killing him to sit by invisible. Maybe at lunch they'd have a chance to talk.

But even in the cafeteria crowds of girls surrounded Jason.

"Don't they have anything better to do?" Kyle grumbled to Nelson.

Nelson gave a mischievous grin. "A little jealous, are we?"

"No!" Kyle said, stabbing his spoon into his chocolate pudding.

He watched as two of the school's biggest, loudest homophobes approached Jason's table. *Uh-oh.* Kyle dropped his spoon. Was there going to be a fight?

He stared in disbelief as the guys actually shook Jason's

hand, wedging themselves into the packed harem of a table.

"Am I seeing things?" Kyle asked.

"Hmm . . ." Nelson scratched his chin. "I've got it! Where are the chicks?"

"With Jason."

"So . . . where are the guys who want the chicks heading?"

"But those guys hate gays!"

"Jason's still a jock." Nelson shrugged. "Being a jock trumps being gay."

"What about me?" Kyle protested. "I'm a jock."

"Nah, swimming's different. Besides—nothing personal, but you just don't have that whole spit-and-scratch-your-nuts charisma."

Kyle watched as Jason laughed with the homophobes. He handed Nelson his pudding spoon. "Just gouge my eyes out, please?"

The GSA meeting that afternoon totally focused on Jason and how wonderful his announcement would be for the group.

As Ms. MacTraugh guided the discussion, Kyle sat silent, chomping on his lip.

He hadn't yet told her about Jason and him being boyfriends. When the meeting ended and she asked him to stay, he wondered if she suspected.

"How are you doing?" she asked. "You look a little troubled. How are things with the swim team going?"

"Fine. I just shower when I get home. It's no big deal. I'm okay."

She raised an eyebrow. "Just okay?"

Kyle averted his gaze, unwilling to confide about Jason. "Yeah. I got my acceptance letters—you know—to college."

"That's great news! Congratulations. Where to?"

"Well," Kyle said, "to Tech . . ."

"That's a good school." Ms. MacTraugh smiled, then her brow scrunched up. "And any word from Princeton?"

By her tone, Kyle could tell she was prepared to console him.

"Um," he mumbled, "I got accepted."

"Kyle!" Ms. MacTraugh beamed. "That's fantastic! Why didn't you come and tell me?" She grabbed his hand, shaking it vigorously. "How exciting! Your parents must be so proud. *You* should feel so proud!"

"I do." He smiled uneasily. "Except, um . . . I have a boyfriend now."

"Oh?" Ms. MacTraugh's expression transformed from glee to surprise. "I see. . . ."

Kyle glanced down, blushing. His legs were swinging nervously off the side of the desk. "The problem is . . . he's going to Tech."

"That *is* a problem," Ms. MacTraugh nodded. *Finally,* an adult understood him.

"The thing is . . ." Kyle sat up. "I really, really like him. Mom says I can see him at breaks, but I don't want to see him only at breaks. I want to be with him. Did you ever feel that way? Like you'd burst if you couldn't be with someone?"

"Oh, yes." She nodded and added softly, "It sounds as though you like him a lot."

"Yeah!" Kyle nearly shouted.

"And what's he say about your going to Princeton?" Ms. MacTraugh asked.

"He thinks I'd be crazy not to go. But what if he forgets about me?" The words surprised Kyle, even as he spoke them.

rainbow high

He'd never voiced his fear aloud. "What if he meets someone else?"

"Well," Ms. MacTraugh said, "that might happen even if you both went to the same college. If you love someone, you have to trust them."

"I trust him," Kyle said quickly.

But as he walked home, he kept thinking about what Ms. MacTraugh had said. *Did* he trust Jason?

All during dinner Kyle watched the clock, calculating what time the late bus would've gotten Jason home from practice. Not only had Jason not looked for him the entire day at school, but he hadn't phoned when he got home either.

As Kyle shoveled down sweet potatoes, his dad asked, "How are classes going?"

"Fine," Kyle said, not wanting to talk. In order to pre-empt another question, he added, "And no I haven't decided about college yet. I'll let you know when I do."

His dad gave an exasperated glance at Kyle's mom, who merely sighed.

After dinner Kyle grabbed the cordless to take to his room.

"Oh, Kyle?" his mom said. "I need to make a call before you use it."

"But Jason might phone."

"Don't worry." His mom smiled. "I'll let you know if he does."

Kyle tramped up the stairs. In his room he dropped a stack of books onto his desk and turned on the computer. It was just as well if Jason *didn't* call. He had a load of homework to do anyway.

But instead of sitting at the desk, Kyle rolled his chair in front of the aquarium. He sprinkled some flakes onto the bubbling surface and watched his fish crowd around the food. The image of Jason surrounded by girls popped into his mind.

Jason's popularity had never bothered Kyle before. That was one of the things Kyle liked about him. But he'd never expected Jason to become the god of freshman girls.

Jason's whole bisexuality thing worried Kyle. He could understand it intellectually, but in practical terms, it simply wasn't part of his experience.

In the aquarium, one of the fish hung apart from the group, not eating. Kyle hoped he wasn't sick.

His dad tapped on the doorway. "Mom's off the phone. She said to tell you Jason didn't call."

"Thanks," Kyle grumbled, still watching his fish.

"By the way," his dad asked, "how's he doing?"

"Jason? Fine."

Kyle should've left it at that. But for some reason he swiveled his chair around. "He came out to the team. Within about sixty seconds the whole school found out."

"Oh?" Kyle's dad tossed the cordless onto the bed. "What's been the reaction?"

"All the girls seem to love him for it."

His dad scrunched up his face, like he didn't understand.

Kyle considered explaining it, but decided his dad probably *still* wouldn't get it.

"It's a big step for him," Kyle continued. "A big risk, too, since he might lose his scholarship."

His dad adjusted his glasses. "So he might not go to Tech?"

"Yeah," Kyle said.

His dad stared blankly at him. "Kyle, you're too smart *not* to

rainbow high

go to Princeton. Especially when you don't even know if Jason will end up going to Tech."

"Dad, I don't want to talk about it." He turned back toward his aquarium and stared at his fish.

"Don't pass this up," his dad insisted. He walked up behind him and laid his hand on Kyle's shoulder. "You have such a tremendous opportunity," he said softly. "Don't toss it aside."

"Are you through?" Kyle asked. "I need to study."

His dad's hand lifted. Kyle heard him sigh. Then he watched his dad's reflection in the aquarium glass as he left the room.

Just when Kyle finally cracked open his books, the phone rang. Kyle jumped for the receiver. His heart thumped wildly, but—

Better to let it ring a second time. He didn't want Jason to think he was sitting around waiting for him to call.

The instant the phone stopped ringing, Kyle pushed the "answer" button. "Hello!"

"Wha's up?" Jason said.

"Oh, hi," Kyle said nonchalantly, trying to slow his breath down. "How'd it go today? You were like a rock star with the babes all over you."

"I know." Jason laughed. "Where were they when I was straight?"

Uh-oh. Was Jason reconsidering?

"I had a good talk with Debra, too," Jason continued. "This whole thing has been awesome. I just wish I hadn't waited so long. I never thought I'd be able to stand in front of a group of people and tell them. I was sure I'd never be able to show my face in school again."

Kyle had never heard Jason talk so excitedly about himself—not even about basketball.

"Can you believe," Jason continued, "I've gotten notes shoved through the slats of my locker from people telling me I've given *them* courage?"

Kyle swiveled back and forth in his chair, listening. He felt buoyed by Jason's exuberance and yet, at the same time, increasingly agitated.

"Can I ask you something?" he said.

"Sure."

"Are you still attracted to girls?"

After a moment Jason answered, "I guess so. Why?"

Kyle braced his foot against the bed, so that his chair stopped swiveling. "Do you think you might ever, you know? . . ."

Kyle wasn't sure how to finish. And did he really want to hear the answer?

"Might what?" Jason asked, his voice serious.

"You know." Kyle swiveled in his chair. Did Jason really not know what Kyle wanted to ask? "That you might ever want to be with a girl again?"

"Kyle . . ." Jason heaved a long, loud sigh. "I think I've got enough to deal with right now. Why are you even asking that?"

"I'm sorry," Kyle said, even though the lack of reassurance only served to unsettle him further.

"That's okay," Jason told him, and geared back into exuberant mode. "I'm still worried what Mueller will say, though. All day long I kept expecting him to call me down to his office. But you know what? I don't care. I feel like a lot of good is going to come from this. You know? I feel like, whatever happens, I've made a difference. Did I tell you I talked to Debra? Oh, yeah, I told you already. Here I am babbling. Tell me, what about you?"

"Um . . ." Kyle thought about his day. "I talked to

MacTraugh. You know, about everything going on. Then I got into an argument with my dad tonight. He won't let up about Princeton. He says I'm too smart not to go there."

"That's what I told you!" Jason said.

That wasn't what Kyle wanted to hear. He'd hoped Jason would sympathize with him, not with his dad. For the first time ever in their relationship, Kyle wanted to get off the phone with Jason. "I better get back to my homework," he said.

"Yeah," Jason agreed. "I need to get to bed soon too."

After hanging up, Kyle stared at the phone, trying to understand what he was feeling. Something was changing. Jason was changing. They were both changing.

He thought about what Nelson had asked—about needing someone and feeling needed. As Jason came out would he still need Kyle?

Kyle slunk down in his chair, feeling the hollow ache in his stomach. He had no desire to study. All he wanted was to crawl into bed.

He turned to shut off the aquarium light. But what he saw made him want to cry. That lone fish was floating on the surface, belly up. "Oh, great."

chapter 15

jason

kyle

nelson

Jason hung up the phone, a little baffled. Why was Kyle acting so weird, asking him if he was still attracted to girls? Why was *everyone* acting so goofy?

First his teammates kidded him in the showers because he wasn't interested in them. Then all those curious girls fussed and fawned over him in the halls.

Then there was Debra, whom he'd called the night he'd come out. He'd expected her to be angry again, but instead her voice rose with concern.

"You okay? Can I come over?" She arrived within minutes. "How did the team take it? Did anyone say anything? What about Dwayne?"

"I'm not scared of Dwayne," Jason assured her. "I can take care of myself. Besides, everyone was fine."

He related the entire story and she calmed down. Then he

told her about Andre and Odell kidding him. Somehow, that led her to ask, "How's it going with you and Kyle?"

Jason shifted uneasily. Was he ready to talk to her about that?

Debra's brow knitted up. "Jason, I'm afraid something's going to happen to you."

"Like what?"

"I don't know. AIDS!"

From whom? Virgin Kyle, who'd confessed to never even having made out with anyone else in his life? Not likely.

"Kyle does *not* have AIDS," Jason said firmly.

"You don't know that," Debra insisted.

"Yes, I do. Trust me. Kyle does not have AIDS."

Debra gave him a hard look, her blue eyes glistening. "I swear, Jason. If anything happens to you . . ."

Her concern made Jason wish he *could* talk to her about Kyle—about how it felt when Kyle wrapped his arms around him, giving him a strength he could never admit he felt himself lacking; or about the night he cried with Kyle, wiping each other's tears, and how he felt a closeness he'd always yearned for with another guy; or about how they laughed over stupid guy stuff, like each other's stinky sneakers.

Maybe one day he'd be able to tell Debra all that. But for now the best he could manage was, "I like him a lot." With those words, a wave of sadness overcame him. "I don't know what's going to happen though, if I go to Tech and he goes to Princeton."

Debra sat up in surprise. "Kyle got accepted to Princeton?"

"Yeah. But he hasn't decided if he's going."

"Why wouldn't he?" she asked.

It embarrassed Jason to admit it was because of him. "Because he's being dopey."

Debra gave Jason a knowing look.

He averted his gaze, blushing. "What about you?" he asked, trying to change the subject. "Are you dating anyone?"

"Not for now," Debra said matter-of-factly. "Lance Lanier asked me out, but I'm not sure I'm ready yet."

Jason hardly knew Lance, a tall, blond guy on the tennis team, but he seemed nice enough.

"Maybe I'll be ready by the time prom comes up," Debra added. A smile sneaked onto her face. "Are you going?"

"Yeah, right. Like I don't have enough to think about?"

The more they talked, the more relaxed he felt. When it came time for her to leave, they both stood awkwardly by the door. Tentatively he reached his arms out. She embraced him in return, her rose perfume bringing back so many memories. He held her tight, and thought how small and delicate she felt compared to tall, lanky Kyle.

No sooner had Debra said good-bye than Jason's mom started her weirdness again.

"I miss her," she said with a sigh. "Such a nice girl. Maybe you and she could work things out."

"Ma!" Jason shouted. "There's nothing to work out. I came out to the team. The whole school knows I'm gay. I'm not getting back together with Debra."

He stormed to his room, cursing in disbelief.

The following morning Jason entered the school through a side door, hoping to avoid being mobbed by another crowd of swarming girls. But even though the halls were buzzing, only a handful of students came up to him.

Was his coming out no longer breaking news? That was a relief, but also a little disappointing. He'd enjoyed the rush of attention. It was kind of a high.

rainbow high

During algebra, Principal Mueller's voice crackled out of the loudspeaker. "Mr. Perez?"

Jason slunk down in his seat, covering his face. Intuitively he knew what was coming.

"Is Jason Carrillo in class?" Mueller growled wearily.

Jason peered between his fingers. Mr. Perez was waving him forward. "Yes, sir. I'll send him down."

While crossing the lobby to the main office, Jason casually glanced out the window and noticed a truck from the local news channel pulling out of the driveway. *What's that about?* he wondered.

As before, Mr. Mueller sat behind his fat desk, twisting a rubber band between his fingers. Coach Cameron sat across from him.

"Jason," Mueller said sternly, "I thought we had an agreement. I've told Coach how disappointed I am with you. *Very* disappointed."

Jason glanced over at Coach, who sat calmly, his face impassive.

"Coach has reassured me the team doesn't seem too disconcerted by your . . ." He struggled for the word. ". . . your revelation. And I hope that's the case."

He tossed his rubber band aside. "In any event, a new matter has come up, about which I'm concerned. *Very* concerned." He swept a hand across his desk. "I want to make one thing absolutely clear. Under no circumstances will I allow this school to become some sort of media carnival."

What the heck was Mueller talking about? Jason's face must have registered his confusion because Coach intervened. "Channel Seven wants to do an interview with you about your coming out."

An unexpected lump appeared in Jason's throat. A TV

interview? He'd spoken to reporters before, but only about sports, never about anything *personal*.

He ran a hand through his hair. What would they ask? What would he say?

"Given the nature of the interview," Coach continued, "they'll need your parents' permission."

Mueller stood up and traveled around the desk to Jason. "I've told the station to come back after school. I'm not going to try telling you what to do again. If you decide to do it, I'm counting on you to make us look good."

He patted Jason's shoulder. "Don't let me down again, Jason."

Make *us* look good? Had his coming out become a reflection on the school?

"You okay?" Coach asked as they exited Mueller's office.

Jason looked up to see Coach peering into his face. "Um, yeah, I just—I hadn't expected this. What if they ask me stuff I don't want to talk about?"

"Then just say you don't want to talk about that. You don't have to answer every question. Play offense. Determine what you want to say and say it."

Coach made it sound so simple. Jason stared back at him. "Do you think I should do it?"

"That's up to you. It'll definitely give you a higher profile. If Tech hasn't heard anything yet, they definitely will now. That might be a good thing . . . or it might hurt."

Jason bit into a fingernail. Should he do it?

"Take some time to think about it," Coach said reassuringly. "Whatever you decide, I'll back you up. Good luck, Carrillo." He clapped Jason on the back. "And don't be too late for practice."

Jason watched him leave, not sure what to do. Did he really want the whole world to know he was gay?

rainbow high

"Can I make a call?" he asked the secretary.

"You're becoming quite the celebrity," she said, gesturing toward the phone.

Lucky me, Jason thought. His hand trembled a little as he picked up the receiver.

His mom was in a meeting with one of the attorneys at the firm where she worked as a paralegal, but an assistant called her to the phone.

"What's the matter?" his mom asked. "Is everything okay?"

He told her about the interview. "I need your permission to do it."

The line was silent a moment. "Jason, I'm not sure about this. What if it hurts your chances for college? What if you lose your scholarship?"

Her anxiety only confused him even more. "I'm not sure either, but Coach said it might help."

Jason didn't mention Coach also saying it might hurt.

The line went quiet again. At last his mom responded. "It's your decision. I'll give my permission. But I don't think you should do it."

"Thanks," Jason mumbled, and scribbled down her fax number, though he still wasn't certain whether to go through with it.

At lunch Debra was sitting with Lance. Jason knew he needed to tell her about the interview. Anyone who'd known Debra and him as a couple and hadn't heard about his coming out was bound to hear about it now.

"Wha's up?" Jason said, carrying his tray over. "Can I talk to you?" He felt kind of awkward barging in on her and Lance, but Debra didn't seem to mind.

"Hi, Jason. Sit down. Do you know Lance?"

Jason extended his hand and the three of them made small talk as Jason gathered his nerve. What if she didn't want him to do the interview? In that case, he wouldn't do it.

When the chitchat hit a lull, he brought it up. To his surprise, Debra took it a lot better than he'd expected. "That's awesome!"

"Tell me if you don't want me to do it," Jason warned her. "You realize a lot of people will see it?"

"I know. And I think you should do it."

Lance nodded in agreement.

Jason bit into a thumbnail. Was no one going to stop him from doing this?

There was one other person with whom he needed to talk. As he exited the cafeteria he spotted him.

"Kyle, guess what?" Jason ran up, whispering. "Channel Seven wants to interview me. You think I should do it?"

"On TV?" Kyle gasped. "Wow! You realize how many people will see it?"

No doubt he was thinking "role model" again.

Jason noticed a couple of guys looking over. Were people starting to gossip about Kyle and him? Why couldn't they mind their own business?

"I think I'm going to do it," Jason said. "It'll be after school. Will you come?"

"I wouldn't miss it for anything," Kyle told him.

All during afternoon classes Jason could hardly sit still. As last period ended he watched the clock, his books stacked and ready. The instant the bell sounded, he bolted down the hall.

The TV reporter was waiting in the main office. Jason

rainbow high

recognized her from the news—a petite African-American woman. She seemed a lot taller on TV.

"The crew is setting up outside," she told Jason. "Let's talk a few minutes first. Have you ever been on TV before?"

"Yeah," Jason said, trying to keep his voice steady. "I've gotten interviewed a couple of times after games."

"So you know to just relax?"

"I know," he told her, biting into a nail.

"Okay." She gave him a skeptical look. For several minutes she asked background questions about school and family. "All right," she said. "Ready?"

"Sure," his voice piped out.

They walked out to the front steps, where a crowd of students had gathered by the camerawoman. At the forefront, the GSA students cheered. Jason waved sheepishly

"Just relax," the reporter told him again. "Breathe and be yourself."

A moment later tape began rolling as she spoke toward the camera. "We're here today at Walt Whitman High School. This week senior athlete Jason Carrillo, who plays varsity basketball, made a shocking announcement to his teammates. He told them he's gay."

Jason felt his legs tremble beneath him. Did she actually say *shocking*?

"What prompted you to come out?" she asked.

"Um, I was sick of hiding . . . and I thought maybe I could help other people who are going through what I've gone through."

The reporter nodded sympathetically. "And what did your parents say when you told them?"

"Well, my dad . . . we've never gotten along anyway."

"So he didn't take it well? What happened?"

Jason hesitated, recalling what Coach had told him. "I'd rather not talk about it."

"It must have been difficult," the reporter filled in for him. "And your mom?"

Jason wasn't sure what to say. "She loves me," he replied vaguely.

"And how have your schoolmates reacted?" the reporter pressed on.

"With me, they've been great. But there's always been a lot of name-calling in the halls. You know—'that's so gay,' stuff like that. A lot of homophobia. I think the GSA is helping make things better."

The GSA students burst into applause and cheers.

The reporter smiled. "It looks like you have some fans."

Jason blushed.

"What plans do you have for after graduation?" the reporter asked. "I understand you got a scholarship to Tech. Do they know you're gay?"

Jason took a breath. "Now they do."

"And what do you think they'll say?"

"Well, the scholarship is for playing ball. I don't see why this should change anything. I'm still the same ball player I was before. I hope they realize that."

"So will you be taking a date to your senior prom?"

Jason faltered. Why was everyone so fixated on prom already? "I hadn't thought about it yet."

The reporter leaned toward him as if she were a confidant. "And do you have a boyfriend?"

Jason froze. Where had *that* question come from? She hadn't said anything about asking that. What could he answer? He wasn't ready to deal with the whole school yakking about him

rainbow high

and Kyle. But if he said he didn't want to talk about it, everyone would surely take that to mean he *did* have a boyfriend. They'd hound him to death.

Jason scanned the crowd for Kyle, hoping for help. Maybe Kyle was behind him, but Jason couldn't exactly turn away from the camera to look for him.

The reporter moved the microphone closer, her face eager for Jason's response.

There was only one answer he felt capable of giving. "Um, no."

The reporter gave him a cordial smile. "Well, thank you very much Jason, and good luck!"

She said a few more words to close the interview, but Jason had stopped listening. The moment the camera switched off, he turned around and saw Kyle. His eyes were like wells, deep and wounded. Nelson gestured something from behind him, as if trying to signal Jason.

As Jason approached them, shaking hands with the dispersing crowd, Kyle glared over his shoulder and Nelson said, "Um, I'll wait for you by the flagpole."

Jason shoved his hands into his pockets. After Nelson left he told Kyle in a low voice, "I looked for you. I didn't know how to answer when she asked that."

Kyle's eyebrows rode up. "You could've answered it honestly."

"Well," Jason protested, "I didn't know if you wanted the whole school to start talking about us."

"Like they're not talking about you already?" Kyle crossed his arms. "Are you embarrassed about me?"

"No! Kyle, don't make this a bigger deal than it is. I didn't mean it personally."

"Well," Kyle said, "I am taking it personally, because I *am* a person. And I am your boyfriend, I *think*—although you just negated that in front of the whole world. That's a pretty big deal to me."

Jason glanced around. People were staring. "I don't have time for this," he muttered. "I've got to get to practice."

With that, he turned and strode away, wondering: Why was Kyle acting so goofy again? Didn't he realize how much pressure the interview had put him under?

At practice the team played totally out of sync. Everyone was stressed because the quarterfinals were set to start the following day. Even Coach yelled more than usual, or at least it seemed that way.

That evening, as Jason waited for the eleven o'clock news broadcast, he kept telling himself he was glad he'd said he didn't have a boyfriend, because he wasn't certain he could deal with one right now.

Yet every time the phone rang, he jumped for it, hoping it was Kyle.

jason kyle

nelson

"Excuse me!" Nelson ranted at passing cars as he walked home with Kyle. "I'm queer too! Where's *my* TV debut? And what was that hideous green shirt about? If he's going to represent gay youth, he needs to get some fashion sense."

Kyle ambled alongside him, shaking his head. "I can't believe he told the entire world he doesn't have a boyfriend. Maybe he really doesn't think of me as his boyfriend."

"Kyle!" Nelson snapped his fingers. "That's like a ten on the stupid-meter. Of course he thinks you're his boyfriend."

"Then why did he say that?"

"Honey, not to put a stain on your party dress, but the guy's human. Humans say stupid things. He probably just didn't want the whole school blabbing about it. Let it go!"

But Kyle couldn't let it go. "I can't believe I'd pass up Princeton for him and—"

"Hold it right there!" Nelson thrust his arms out, blocking Kyle's path. "You are *not* passing up Princeton."

Kyle pursed his lips, as if thinking. "I haven't decided yet."

"Is that why you want to be angry at him? To help you decide?"

"No," Kyle grumbled. "I don't *want* to be angry with him."

"Well . . ." Nelson brought down his arms. "Whatever you decide, I told you *I'm* not going to Tech."

Kyle peered at him. "Are you just saying that so I'll go to Princeton?"

"No. I told you I never wanted to go to Tech in the first place. I don't know what I'm going to do. I haven't decided."

When they got to his house, Nelson continued trying to get Kyle out of his mopiness—by making brownies, listening to CDs, playing with Atticus—until at last Kyle started cheering up. But that night, after Jason's interview played on TV, Kyle phoned, dejected again.

The following day at lunch Nelson continued consoling him. "Hey, you want to come with me to meet some of Jeremy's friends tonight?"

"No thanks," Kyle replied. "I've got to get to bed early for that swim meet trip tomorrow."

"In that case—" Nelson smiled as charmingly as possible "—can you cover for me if my mom calls you? Please, please, please?"

He knew Kyle hated lying, but with his mom so set against his dating Jeremy, what choice was there?

That evening Nelson told her, "I'm going to Kyle's!" and slammed out the door before she could question him. He metroed downtown to the gay coffee shop, trying his hardest to be on time. But even so, he was late.

"I'm sorry," he told Jeremy, kissing him in front of the entire café. "Where are your friends?"

rainbow high

"Not here yet." Jeremy sighed. "The late gene must be linked to the gay gene."

"Do I look all right?" Nelson checked himself in the mirror. "I hate my hair. I wish I'd worn something else. I bet your friends are all buff, aren't they? Will I be the only skinny one? What if they think I'm a dweeb? What did you tell them about me?"

"I told them you're a skinny dweeb with bad hair who doesn't know how to dress."

Nelson swatted him. "You are so evil."

"Dude, you look great," Jeremy assured him. "They're going to like you just fine." He rested a hand on Nelson's shoulder and gave it a squeeze. "What would you like to—"

"Are they all positive?" Nelson interrupted.

Jeremy replied with a cross look, frowning.

"Sorry," Nelson mumbled. But could he help being curious?

Jeremy ordered chai. Nelson asked for an extra-tall double espresso. He may as well have mainlined caffeine, especially since he practically guzzled down the drink.

They sat at a table, and half an hour later Jeremy's friends trickled in.

First there was flawless-faced, perfect-posture, every-hair-in-place, zero-body-fat Reed, wearing creased khakis and a pressed white shirt. *Probably irons his underwear too,* Nelson thought. Merely looking at him made Nelson want to go shopping.

After Reed, Bob showed up. He was cute in a nerdy sort of way. His nose was a little big, and his ears stuck out a tad much, but Nelson liked that. At least he felt more at ease with Bob than with cover model Reed.

Then there was hunky, blond spiky-haired Matt, with superhero pecs and biceps as thick as Nelson's neck. *Put "Go to Gym" on To-Do list,* Nelson thought.

None of the guys looked positive. When they went to order their drinks, Nelson leaned close to Jeremy and whispered, "They hate me. I can tell."

Jeremy grabbed Nelson's hand reassuringly. "No, they don't. Relax."

As the group of friends returned from the counter, Bob asked, "So where did you and Nelson meet?"

"That group," Jeremy told him.

"You're in the HIV group?" Matt asked eagerly. "I've never seen you there."

Nelson leaned back, surprised. Matt was *positive*? No way!

"Not that group," Jeremy clarified. "The youth group."

Bob's cell phone alarm rang. He shut it off and pulled out a pill case. "Cocktail hour," he told the group in a low voice. "It's the only way I remember to take them."

"I can't believe you're doing that in public," Reed told him.

"I should probably take mine, too." Matt pulled out a pill case with a dozen little compartments. "I keep forgetting."

"Can I have one?" Nelson asked, joking of course, though he did feel a little left out. "Just kidding," he added in response to Jeremy's scowl.

"What happened to that new guy you were dating?" Jeremy said, turning to Matt.

"The jerk. He told me I was getting fat, so I dumped him. Do you think I'm getting fat? I think it's the drugs."

"You look fine," Reed told him, and turned to Bob. "What about that red-haired guy you went out with?"

Bob made a glum face. "He couldn't deal with—" Bob raised his fingers to signal quotation marks "—The Issue."

"I stopped dating anyone negative," Reed said. "It's too much work—not to mention the whole condom crap. I've got enough to deal with. The least I can do is enjoy sex."

Jeremy raised an eyebrow. "You're continuing to re-infect yourself, you know."

A sly grin crossed Reed's lips. "Not often enough."

As the group joked and laughed, Nelson only understood half of what they talked about. But clearly, they all shared a common bond. One that he didn't.

After about an hour, the group began disbanding and saying good-bye.

"They didn't like me," Nelson said as Jeremy and he walked outside.

"Yes, they did." Jeremy laid his arm around Nelson. "How could they *not* like you?"

"Because I'm negative."

He didn't mean to say it—or maybe he did.

Jeremy stopped, turned to him, and let his arm slide off Nelson's shoulder.

"I mean . . ." Nelson stared across the sidewalk at Jeremy. "All of you are positive and I'm not. Maybe if I was . . ."

"You're talking crazy," Jeremy said, shaking his head.

"Everyone has it but me," Nelson protested.

"No, they don't! Everyone doesn't have it."

"You all do. Everyone you guys talked about does."

"Let me get this right." Jeremy's eyes grew wide with disbelief. "You want to get a life-threatening illness that makes you totally dependent on toxic drugs forever, just because you think everyone else has it?"

Nelson gave an unabashed shrug. "I'll probably get it eventually anyway. Besides, I heard then you can get steroids legally."

"I can't believe you!" Jeremy threw his hands in the air. "Not a day goes by that I wish I didn't have this stupid thing, and you're telling me you wish you had it?"

Nelson fidgeted with an earring. "At least I wouldn't worry all the time about when I'm going to get it."

Jeremy became quiet. His forehead wrinkled, then his brow smoothed.

"What?" Nelson asked.

"I was remembering when I got it," Jeremy replied. "I felt this awesome sense of relief. At least I didn't have to worry anymore if I was going to get it."

"See?" Nelson asserted. "That's exactly what I mean."

"Yeah." Jeremy heaved a deep sigh. "But take my word for it, the worrying doesn't stop. You just trade the old worries for new ones." He laid his arm across Nelson's shoulder again. "Believe me, babe. You don't want it."

It was the first time Jeremy—or anyone—had ever called Nelson "babe." He wrapped his arm around Jeremy's waist, not wanting to think about all this crap anymore.

As they approached the metro station, Nelson asked, "Can we go to your place?"

When they got to the apartment, Jeremy said, "My brother's away for the weekend."

Nelson's heart took off at a gallop. They had the place to themselves.

"Want something to drink?" Jeremy asked. "Water, Coke, Sprite?"

"Water's fine." Nelson pulled his jacket off. "Can I put some music on?" He chose the cowboy's CD again. It was starting to grow on him.

Sitting down on the loveseat, he kicked off his shoes and

started peeling off his socks. He paused to make sure Jeremy wasn't looking and sneaked a sniff of his feet. Good thing they were okay.

Jeremy brought their drinks and sat beside Nelson. He brought a foot up to pull off his boot, but Nelson said, "Here," and pulled it off for him, then helped with the other.

"You'll spoil me." Jeremy grinned.

Nelson gazed into those imploring, espresso-colored eyes, and next thing he knew, his tongue was slipping between Jeremy's lips, rolling across his Sprite-sweet tongue.

While the cowboy sang about having to choose between fishing and his wife, Nelson folded himself into Jeremy. Their hands feverishly grasped each other—pressing, holding, caressing, clutching. He plucked at Jeremy's shirttail and, encountering no resistance, slid his fingers beneath.

The touch of skin made his hormones do a quick cancan. In a flash he'd yanked Jeremy's shirt off and in awed silence beheld the spectacular sculptured pecs he'd merely imagined in bedtime fantasies.

"What's the matter?" Jeremy said, peering at Nelson.

"I'm in love." Nelson sighed, unable to stop staring.

"You're a nut." Jeremy laughed. But Nelson ignored him, bending down to paste a tribute of kisses on the beautiful chest.

"Yours too," Jeremy said, tugging at Nelson's shirt, but Nelson drew back, embarrassed by his scrawny chest compared to Jeremy's. "Can we turn off the light?"

Too late. Jeremy had pulled the shirt off. His hands slid across Nelson's bare chest, triggering an explosion of goose bumps. Ever since he was a kid Nelson had been prone to gooseflesh.

"Cool." Jeremy grinned.

Nelson buried his face in the valley of Jeremy's chest, blushing.

"We better talk about this," Jeremy whispered.

"My goose bumps?"

"No, silly. What we're going to do."

"Not again!" Nelson groaned. They'd already talked to death about safe sex. Instead, he started laying tiny kisses along the Happy Trail of downy hairs leading toward Jeremy's belt buckle.

"You're making this very hard." Jeremy moaned beneath him.

"I noticed," Nelson replied.

"Dude!" Jeremy's tone grew stern. "First you have to promise we'll be really safe." He hauled Nelson back up to where he could face him, gently holding his chin and peering into his eyes. "Promise?"

"Yes," Nelson whispered. "I promise."

Thirsty from kissing, he reached over and gulped his water down, setting the glass back on the coffee table. Then he brushed his lips softly across Jeremy's goatee, pasting a tiny kiss to the right of Jeremy's lips, then to the left, then below.

Jeremy opened his mouth, beckoning, and reciprocated the kisses. Each grew more fervent as their hands tugged and fumbled with belt buckles.

Unable to control himself a second longer, Nelson sat up to yank his jeans off. In the process, his foot accidentally kicked the coffee table.

His empty glass wobbled. Jeremy grabbed for it, but the glass toppled off the tabletop.

Nelson winced as it shattered onto the parquet floor.

He raised a hand to his face, covering it in disbelief. Just once, couldn't he get laid without some mishap?

"Crap," Jeremy said, propping himself up. "I better get the broom."

"Can't you leave it for later?"

But Jeremy was already leaning over the side of the loveseat, picking up a glass shard. "I don't want you to step on—!"

He gasped, dropped the glass, and yanked his hand up.

"You okay?" Nelson reached out. "Let me see."

The finger had a slight cut with one droplet of blood.

"What a wuss," Nelson kidded him, and leaned toward the finger, making a kiss-kiss sound.

Jeremy's arm darted out, shoving Nelson across the narrow loveseat. Although the push wasn't hard, Nelson careened off balance.

Jeremy reached to grab him, but too late. Nelson crashed off the side, his butt banging onto the floor.

"Are you crazy?" Jeremy yelled, leaning over the loveseat.

Nelson peered up at him, dazed, his butt throbbing. "Why'd you push me like that?"

"You saw the blood!" Jeremy waved his finger like a loaded gun or something.

"I was just kidding," Nelson argued back. "I wasn't really going to kiss it!" Did Jeremy think he was stupid?

Nelson pushed himself off the floor and onto his feet, examining his rear end to make sure it was still intact. "Stop yelling at me."

It was bad enough that his mom and dad yelled at him. He wasn't going to take it from his prospective boyfriend, too.

"How can you kid like that?" Jeremy shouted. "You promised we'd be safe."

"If you don't stop shouting," Nelson warned him, "I'm leaving."

"Watch where you put your feet!" Jeremy yelled. "There's glass all over!"

That did it. Nelson reached for his socks, pulling them on.

Jeremy's expression softened. "Hey, wait. I'm sorry I pushed you."

Nelson slid into his shoes, wavering. Was Jeremy *really* sorry?

"But you shouldn't have done that." He started shouting again. "I'm bleeding!"

Nelson tugged his shirt over his head and grabbed his leather jacket. "I'm out of here."

"Nelson!" Jeremy called after him. "I said I'm sorry."

"Later," Nelson said and was out the door.

When he arrived home, Atticus ran into the foyer to greet him, leaping up and wagging his tail. In contrast, his mom sat rigidly by the living-room window, glaring at him with arms crossed.

"I called Kyle's," her voice strained angrily. "I know you weren't there."

"So?" Nelson shot back, in no mood to get chewed out even more.

"Nelson, I phoned your dad. He's very upset. He's coming down next weekend."

Nelson pulled off his jacket and tossed it onto the hall table. "I'm *so* scared."

He stomped upstairs, slammed the door to his room, and dialed Kyle.

"Sorry," Kyle said, "about blowing your cover. My mom answered the phone while I was in the bathroom. She told your mom you weren't here. I tried calling your cell—"

"I had it turned off," Nelson interrupted. "Don't worry about it."

rainbow high

He told Kyle about the whole evening—meeting Jeremy's friends, going back to his place, how Jeremy and he came so close to finally boinking, and then disaster.

"I can't believe he pushed me like that."

"But he was trying to protect you," Kyle said softly.

"By shoving me on the floor?" Nelson reached for a cigarette, annoyed he wasn't getting sympathy. "I can accept him being positive, I can tolerate his liking country music, but I can't deal with his being so freaking paranoid about infecting me!"

Kyle was silent on the other end. "So are you breaking up with him?" he said at last.

"I don't know." Nelson lit up and tossed the match aside. "I know you want me to."

"Well . . . I just don't want you to get infected."

"Men are such twits," Nelson groused, summarizing his current worldview. "Did Jason call you?"

"No." Kyle gave a sigh. "Quarterfinals started tonight. Oh, my gosh! I should check the news to see if we won. I'll call you Sunday, when I get back from the swim meet."

"Can I go with you?" Nelson asked, joking.

"I wish you could."

"Break a leg or whatever," Nelson told him.

After hanging up, he pulled back his top sheets, uncovering the pair of briefs from Jeremy, neatly folded where Nelson had left them. Snatching them up, he hurled them aside. "Jerk!"

He kicked off his shoes and removed his clothes. Every few moments he glanced over at the briefs in the corner, till finally he climbed into bed and turned off the light.

chapter 17

jason **kyle**

nelson

After Kyle hung up from Nelson's call, he let out a sigh. Although he liked Jeremy, the ongoing possibility of Nelson becoming infected was getting way too nerve-racking. Better to return his thoughts to their usual subject: Jason.

Kyle leaped out of bed and tiptoed past his parents' bedroom, then he raced downstairs and turned the TV on just in time to catch the eleven o'clock sports recap.

He hoped there might be a shot of Jason but only glimpsed an elbow that looked vaguely familiar. Anyway, the important thing was Whitman had won their game, moving the team on toward semifinals.

Kyle stood to go upstairs but then . . . He returned to the TV and popped in the videotape he'd made of the school interview. Nestling into the sofa, Kyle hugged a cushion to his chest and for the millionth time watched Jason appear on the screen.

The lush curly hair, imploring brown eyes, and breathtaking lips made him look like the star of some TV teen drama. Even though Kyle wanted to hurl the remote at the tube each time Jason told the reporter he didn't have a boyfriend, he couldn't stop watching and rewatching.

He didn't even hear his mom come downstairs in her robe and slippers, till she brushed her fingers through his hair. "Honey, don't you have to get up early for your swim meet?"

"Oh, yeah." Kyle blinked up at her. "I'll go to bed in a minute."

But he didn't. He fell asleep on the couch, dreaming of the dark-eyed boy on the TV screen.

"Hey, sleepyhead." His dad jostled him awake. Sunlight was streaming in through the window slats. "You're going to miss your bus."

Kyle hustled to gather his swimsuit and pack his stuff, then his dad drove him to the school parking lot, where the bus waited, idling.

"You're the last one," Coach Sweeney said, herding Kyle onto the crowded bus.

"Sorry." Kyle bounced down the swaying aisle toward the back where the boys sat, and spotted an empty place beside Charlie Tuggs, the team's champion 'fly swimmer. He was one of the guys who had shaken Jason's hand in the lunchroom. But when Kyle approached now, Charlie kicked his feet onto the seat.

"Don't even think about it, fag."

Kyle stopped and braced himself on the seat handle. *That's a great start,* he thought, glancing around for another seat.

A girl called, "Hi, Kyle!"

It was Cindy, Corey's girlfriend. Even though Kyle had known her for years, they'd never had a conversation beyond "Hi." Now, like a heaven-sent angel, she said, "Have a seat," and moved her bag aside.

"I was late too," she confided as Kyle slid in beside her. "Overslept." Then she leaned over and whispered, "Jason told me about you and him dating."

"He did?" Kyle whispered back.

"He said not to tell anyone." Cindy glanced over her shoulder to make sure no one was listening. "He's a great guy. You are so lucky."

Maybe Nelson's right, Kyle thought, *about Jason simply not wanting the whole school blabbing about us.* For the remainder of the morning's drive, Kyle turned over in his mind Nelson's comment about him wanting to be angry with Jason so he could make a decision for Princeton. Was Nelson right about that, too?

Halfway into the trip the bus stopped for a lunch break. While Kyle was in the restroom, Charlie and another boy made a big show of refusing to go in.

"Hurry up, pervert!" Charlie yelled.

Coach Sweeney had to have heard him, but she did nothing.

For lunch Kyle sat at Cindy's table, with a couple of other girls. During the last half of the bus trip, he fell asleep, waking to find Cindy and he had conked out on each other's shoulders.

"Sorry," he told her, blushing.

"Don't worry." She wiped her eyes. "I just hope I didn't drool on you."

Kyle laughed, wishing they'd become friends long before.

When the bus reached the motel, everyone piled out and gathered in the lobby. The chatter of the team rumbled through the room as Coach Sweeney started distributing keys.

rainbow high

"Room three-thirteen!" She held up a key and read from her clipboard. "Charlie, Vin, Frank, and Kyle."

"I'm not sleeping in the same room with no fag," Charlie hissed.

Immediately the entire lobby turned silent. All eyes turned to Kyle. Blood surged into his face, burning with shame.

Charlie nudged an elbow at Vin, who shifted his glance from Kyle to Coach Sweeney. "Um, I'm not rooming with him either."

At that, everyone looked to see what Frank would say. He nervously glanced away from Kyle and echoed, "Um, me neither."

The team turned to Coach Sweeney. Her gaze skipped between Kyle and the other three boys, an irritated look on her face. "All of you, stop being silly."

Kyle's embarrassment turned to outrage. Coach Sweeney thought making him feel like a leper was "silly"? Had she ever heard the word "harassment"?

Doubtless trying to be helpful, Cindy said, "He can stay with us." The other girls giggled.

"Yeah," Charlie quickly chimed in. "He can stay with the *girls!*"

Kyle's eyes began clouding. His chin started quivering. As the first tear trickled down his cheek, he whirled around. No way would he let Charlie and those creeps see him cry.

He stormed out the door to the parking lot, with no idea where he was heading. He'd walk all the way home if he had to.

"Kyle!" Coach Sweeney yelled, running after him. "Where are you going?" She grabbed his sleeve.

"Let go of me!" He yanked his arm away, spinning around.

Coach Sweeney stepped back, startled. Now teammates were

filing out of the motel, gathering in the parking lot to watch.

"Calm down!" Coach Sweeney's voice shook, either out of fear, or anger, or both. "You're being disrespectful."

"No, *you* are!" Kyle snapped back, wiping his face with his sleeve.

She glowered at him. "Lower your voice and come inside. We'll discuss this after everyone's in their rooms."

"I'm not staying with those jerks." Kyle glared across the lot at Charlie. "And I'm not staying with the girls, either."

Coach Sweeney rolled her eyes. "Of course you're not."

"Then where am I going to stay?"

Her brow furrowed in thought. "You can have my room. *I'll* stay with the girls."

She was caving in to them again. Couldn't she see that?

From the crowd, Charlie sneered and said, "Now he's getting his own special room."

"Charlie!" Coach Sweeney spun around. "Everyone go back inside! I mean it. Now!"

Slowly the team shuffled back into the lobby, only to stare out from behind the plateglass windows.

Coach Sweeney turned to Kyle, her eyes burning with anger. "I've had enough, Kyle. You brought this on yourself. If you hadn't started this whole coming out business, none of this would've happened."

True enough. When he'd been the quiet, shy kid, no one had picked on him. But why should he have to go through school invisible?

Things might never have come to this if she'd said something the times those jerks made stupid comments, and if she'd stood up to the dad who wrote that note about the shower.

"No," he said. "*You're* the one who brought this on. None of

rainbow high

this would've happened if you'd stopped them in the first place. You're the coach, aren't you?"

"That's enough!" Coach Sweeney snapped. "You're barred from swimming tomorrow."

What? He'd come all this way, endured all this, only to be barred from swimming?

Kyle stared at her in disbelief then turned toward the roadway.

"Kyle!" Coach Sweeney shouted, running in front of him to block his path. "You do *not* have permission to leave. I'm phoning your father." She pulled her cell phone from her jacket. "What's your number?"

Kyle considered stepping around her. It would've been funny if he weren't so furious. Instead he told her his number.

She punched her keypad. "Hello? Mr. Meeks? This is Coach Sweeney. Fine, thank you. I'm calling because Kyle tried to leave the group without permission. . . . No, he's here with me. But he's been extremely disrespectful. His attitude has been completely out of line."

She told Kyle's dad her side of what had happened.

"I'll put him on," she said when she'd finished.

Kyle took the phone and turned away. "Hi, Dad."

"What happened, son?"

Kyle wasn't sure where to start. Should he go back to the note about the showers? The taunts in the locker room? The bus ride? The restaurant? There was so much Sweeney had left out. He decided to begin with the hotel. "Those jerks said they weren't going to room with me."

That came out sounding whiny, not what he intended.

"What did Ms. Sweeney say?" his dad asked.

Kyle glanced over his shoulder. Coach Sweeney was peering at him hawklike, listening to his every word.

"She said they were being silly. Now she says I can have her room and she'll sleep with the girls."

"And what's wrong with that?" his dad asked.

"Dad!" Kyle's voice rose. "That's not the point."

"Kyle, what *is* the point?" His dad's tone was sharp. "You can't just take off in some strange town because some other boys are being jerks. Where were you going?"

"I don't know," Kyle said, his mind spinning. Couldn't his dad understand how it felt being made fun of in front of everyone? And Coach Sweeney not stopping it?

"You knew," his dad continued, "you weren't supposed to leave the group, didn't you?"

Kyle bit the inside of his cheek, exasperated. "I couldn't stay, Dad."

"In that case, you shouldn't have gone in the first place. I'm very concerned about this, Kyle. Your mother and I gave our permission assuming we could trust you."

"Can you come get me?" Kyle pleaded, cupping his hand around the mouthpiece. "I don't want to stay."

His dad was silent, as though considering. "What about your swim meet?"

Kyle glanced at Coach Sweeney and gave a sputter. "She said I'm barred from swimming."

Over his shoulder he could see Coach Sweeney staring back at him, hands on her hips.

"I'll talk with her about that," his dad said. "What time is your first event? I'll drive down in the morning and bring you back. It'll give us time to talk. For now I want you to apologize to Ms. Sweeney."

"What for?" Kyle cried out.

"For leaving without permission. You knew better. Now tell

rainbow high

me you're not going to do anything else foolish. Can you promise me that?"

Kyle gave a groan. "Yes."

"If you have any other problem call your mother and me collect, okay? Put Ms. Sweeney back on the phone. We love you, son."

Kyle didn't feel like echoing that, but forced himself. "I love you too," he mumbled. Turning back to Coach Sweeney, he shoved the phone at her. "Here."

"Yes?" she said, placing the receiver to her ear. "That's correct. He's barred from—"

She became quiet, her expression shifting from anger to intimidation to capitulation. Kyle would've given anything to hear what his dad was saying.

"Only if he apologizes," Coach Sweeney agreed. "We can set up a meeting next week, but he has to promise to behave. Yes, I'll do that. I have your number. Yes, you too. Good-bye."

She flipped the phone closed and stared at Kyle. "You wish to tell me something?"

Quite a few things, Kyle thought. But he restrained himself, taking a long, measured breath. "I'm sorry I walked out like that. I promise I won't do it again."

Shoving his hands into his pockets, he followed Coach Sweeney back inside.

"You okay?" Cindy asked.

"Yeah." Kyle nodded. "Thanks."

Nothing else terrible happened the rest of the day. Kyle stayed as far away from Charlie as possible. His other team members seemed like they actually felt sorry for him. Even Vin and Frank looked guilt ridden and averted their eyes.

As it turned out, having his own room wasn't so bad. In fact, it ruled. He'd never had a hotel room to himself before. After dinner with Cindy, Kyle sprawled across the king-size bed, watching TV. Almost immediately, he fell asleep.

After breakfast next morning, Kyle browsed through the hotel gift shop, then the team headed to the university pool.

As they warmed up, Kyle kept glancing at the crowd gathering in the stands. Where was his dad? It wasn't usually such a big deal for him when his dad came to meets. But for some reason, today it was.

The meet started—and still no dad.

The team lined up for the 200 individual medley relay: Charlie first; Kyle behind him. The air between them almost crackled with tension.

One last time Kyle gazed up at the stands. A familiar face waved to him. His dad had made it.

The starting gun went off. As Charlie dove into the pool Kyle watched his powerful arms thrash the water. Charlie was a great 'fly swimmer, but at everything else, Kyle could pummel him. And today, Kyle decided, he would do exactly that.

The instant Charlie touched the wall, Kyle flew into the water. The team placed first. But Kyle's even bigger win was the 100-meter freestyle. Not only did he win, he set a team record.

Afterward in the locker room, the other boys joked and laughed. Kyle yanked his suit's drawstring, intending to towel dry.

But inside him something had shifted. He no longer cared if some nameless jerk didn't want to shower with him. Kyle dropped his suit and stepped toward the showers.

Across the spray of water, Charlie spotted him and muttered, "Fag."

rainbow high

Kyle stopped and drew himself up. "Does that threaten you?" he answered back. "Feel free to leave."

Charlie wiped the water from his eyes, his face red from heat—or anger.

Oh, crud. Kyle braced himself. *Did I really just tell him that?* In an attempt to hide his trembling, he turned the shower handle on beside him.

To his relief, Frank called out. "Hey, Kyle! Congrats on the team record."

Kyle nodded back, his throat too tight to speak. Out of the corner of his eye, he could see the steam rising off Charlie. Vin clasped his arm to hold him back, telling him, "Let it go, man."

Charlie shook him off. After a moment, he let his shoulders relax. "Fag," he grunted at Kyle again, and turned away.

Kyle ignored it this time. Instead he let the warmth of the locker room shower wash over him for the first time in weeks.

Before starting the drive home, his dad took him to lunch. Kyle ravenously chomped down two double burgers, large fries, and a sundae.

Once on the road, Kyle waited for the inevitable lecture.

After only a few miles his dad said, "I'd like to hear what exactly happened yesterday."

Kyle told him everything—going back to when his locker had been graffitied with the word QUEER and Kyle had spray-painted AND PROUD!

His dad listened calmly. Only occasionally, when Kyle got ahead of himself, would his dad ask a question.

He isn't such a bad guy, Kyle thought. *If only he'd learn to stop getting so worked up every time I want to do something that doesn't match his expectations.*

As the rolling hills passed by, Kyle kept expecting his dad to bring up the whole Princeton-Tech thing again. But he didn't.

And with that absence of pressure, Kyle was able to admit that apart from his dad, mom, Jason, Nelson, Ms. MacTraugh, and everyone else on the planet who wanted him to go to Princeton . . . he did too.

Coming to that conclusion, he sat up straighter in his seat.

Not only that, he no longer felt angry at Jason. But would he be able to tell Jason his decision? He should probably wait till after the basketball championships.

But that didn't mean he couldn't call Jason as soon as he got home. He glanced at the speedometer, wishing his dad would hurry up, except . . . A new worry suddenly entered Kyle's mind: Even though he was no longer angry at Jason, would Jason still be angry at him?

rainbow high

jason
kyle
nelson

Jason had spent most of the weekend at home, hanging out with friends, basking in the triumph of his team's semifinal win, playing little-girl video games with his sister, and overhearing his mom's phone conversations with friends and relatives about his TV interview.

The broadcast had forced his mom to finally deal with his being gay.

After each call, she'd ask him a new question like, "What about ex-gay groups? Have you heard of those?"

"Ma," he said angrily. "It's taken me this long to accept who I am. I'm not going to let some fanatics try to confuse me. They should mind their own business."

He returned to the video game with his sister, most of the time letting her win, much to her delight—but not always, so she wouldn't catch on.

The phone rang again.

"It's Kyle," his mom called.

Jason faltered with the controller, causing his player to wipe out on the screen.

"My turn!" Melissa squealed happily, taking the controller from him.

Slowly Jason walked toward the phone. All weekend he'd hoped Kyle would call. Even though he still felt a little hurt and angry about how Kyle had acted after the TV interview, he also felt bad about the way he'd reacted in response.

He ran a hand through his hair and picked up the phone receiver. "Wha's up?"

"Hi," Kyle said. "Congratulations on your win."

"Thanks," Jason said, wrapping the phone cord around his finger. "Um, how'd your swim meet go?"

As Kyle told him about it, Jason relaxed a little, unraveling the phone cord.

"That's great," he told Kyle. "Congrats back at you."

"Thanks. Um . . ." Kyle cleared his throat. "Can I come over?"

Jason wound the phone cord around his finger again. "All right."

Kyle arrived at the door with a plastic bag wedged under his arm.

"Kyle!" Melissa ran over, nearly tackling him as she threw her arms around his legs, making him drop the bag. "What's inside?" she asked.

"Nosy," Jason scolded her and picked the bag up for Kyle.

"Want to play my new video game?" she asked Kyle, grabbing him by the hand.

The three of them played a dorky game in which you scored points for choosing dress patterns. Jason's mom offered Kyle a

Coke. After three games, Jason decided Kyle had been tortured enough.

"Kyle and I are going to my room now," he told Melissa.

"I'm going too!" she announced.

"Oh, no, you're not." He stretched out his arms, blocking her path. "Ma!"

When they got to Jason's room, Kyle opened the bag he'd brought, pulling out a navy blue T-shirt. "It's for you. I got it at the gift shop where we stayed. I know it's your favorite color."

Jason smiled at the unexpected gift. "Thanks. It's great. How was the hotel?"

When they sat down, Kyle told Jason about what had happened with Charlie and the boys not wanting to share a room, about his argument with Coach Sweeney, and about finally taking a shower. "I don't care if those creeps like it or not."

Jason extended his hand, wanting to say, *It's about time.*

"Thanks," Kyle shook his hand. "See? You *are* a role model."

Jason bit into his lip, for the first time not challenging Kyle about that.

"Anyway . . ." Kyle shifted on the bed. "I'm sorry about— you know—" his head bowed slightly "—that I got so upset after your interview."

Jason leaned back in the desk chair, wondering. Should he feel vindicated or should he apologize too?

"I had no idea the reporter was going to ask that," he said at last. "She totally caught me off guard. I didn't want everyone blabbing about us, you know?"

Kyle nodded and Jason said softly, "I'm sorry too. I didn't mean to snap at you like I did."

Kyle gazed up from beneath the sandy brown hair hanging across his forehead. "I understand."

Jason grinned, his warm feelings toward Kyle returning as he considered what he was about to say.

"Well, um, I think people are starting to kind of blab anyway. Maybe once the championship is over—" he gave a nervous shrug "—I can deal with telling people about us. Just not right now, okay?"

Kyle smiled from ear to ear, as if he'd just received a present. "Okay."

Jason let out a sigh. "By the way, everyone on the team gets a couple of tickets for the section down front. My mom and sister are coming, but I think I can get an extra if you want."

"Sure!" Kyle nodded eagerly. His bright hazel eyes glowed with such enthusiasm that Jason felt ashamed for ever having gotten angry at him.

A little awkwardly he moved over to the bed, wrapping his arms around Kyle. He parted his lips, thinking it had been way too long since they'd kissed.

In the middle of making out, Kyle pulled away, whispering, "What's that sound?"

"Huh?" Jason, lost in rapture, hadn't heard it. He cocked his head to listen, and groaned.

His cat was meowing at the door. If it wasn't one interruption, it was another.

At school on Monday the excitement over Jason's coming out had all but been replaced by students' collective fervor over the upcoming basketball finals.

The sense of anticipation increased each day. Students put up banners and posters in the halls. Cheerleaders led pep sessions in the cafeteria. Teachers gave up on calming down hyper students and postponed exams.

And every afternoon the basketball team drilled and

rainbow high

practiced. Under Coach Cameron's watchful instruction, their moves grew more fine tuned as their rhythm became nearly flawless.

With regard to Jason's coming out, the team's hardest adjustment had been to watch their language—like when Odell called Andre, "You quee—"

Coach whirled round. "What did you say?"

"Nothing, Coach!" Odell shook his head vigorously, looking terrified at the thought of suspension. Quickly, he turned to Jason. "Sorry, Jason."

Jason clapped Odell on the back, feeling a little guilty about the fuss. But at the same time, the constant talk about role models was making him realize this wasn't only about him. It was about all those players who would come after him, no longer having to endure homophobic slurs.

The team had gotten through Jason's coming out and the school would be the better for it—thanks most of all to Coach. By handling the whole thing the way he had, Coach had shown the team *they* could handle it.

Something else occurred as a result of the TV interview. Jason started receiving mail—initially from students at other schools, then from adults—applauding his courage for coming out.

Jason wasn't sure how they got his address—probably from the phone book—but each day his family's mailbox grew more packed with envelopes.

At first it felt weird getting letters from strangers saying they admired him. Then he reminded himself how hard coming out had been.

He cleared a desk drawer and after reading each letter, carefully saved it.

Wednesday night, as Jason headed to the kitchen for something to eat, he overheard his mom on the phone with his dad. Jason's skin prickled, as it did every time they talked. With each call her voice lost more of its edge, becoming increasingly softer.

Jason searched the fridge, listening attentively, and the moment she hung up asked, "What did he want?"

His mom began clearing the kitchen counter. "To talk about things. He wants to see Melissa."

"Of course he wants to see *her*." Jason let the fridge door slam.

His sister had always been the favorite, spared of their dad's abuse.

"We discussed your championship," his mom continued. "I asked if he's coming."

"I don't want him to come," Jason shouted. "He's trying to weasel his way back, isn't he?"

His mom moved the toaster aside. "We haven't discussed that."

"What's to discuss? Have you forgotten what it was like with him? You never wanted to face his drinking, just like you don't want to face the fact I'm gay! If he comes back, I'm not staying."

His mom stopped cleaning the counter. "Do you think it's because of him that you're—" the skin around her mouth wrinkled as she struggled with the word "—gay?"

"Oh, right! A drunk dad who used to beat up on me makes me like guys? That makes a lot of sense."

"I don't know, Jason." She brought her fingertips to her forehead. "I'm trying to understand."

"Then try listening to me. There's no *why* about it, Ma. Accept that I just *am*." Halfway out the door, Jason paused. "And tell him I don't want him coming to the game!"

Almost to his bedroom Jason realized he hadn't gotten anything from the fridge. It didn't matter. He'd lost his appetite anyway.

Saturday night nine busloads of Whitman students made the trip to the university field house, eager to see if Whitman could defend its state title.

Spectators, blowing horns and carrying placards, jammed the stadium. Whitman got off to an awesome start, scoring 7 points against Northside in the first five minutes.

Every once in a while Jason would catch a glimpse of his mom and Melissa and Kyle. But he didn't let it distract him. Simply knowing they were there was good enough.

At the end of the second quarter the game was tied at 29. In the locker room Coach huddled with the team.

"You're doing great, but we need a little more offense." He shifted several positions, including Jason, having him cover the center.

As the team trotted back out to the stadium, the crowd roared. When the buzzer sounded Jason was all over the Northside center—a big-shouldered guy, six inches taller than Jason, with blond hair, a thick brow, and deep-set eyes.

As he turned his back on Jason to protect the ball, he glowered over his shoulder. "You the famous fag player?"

Jason made a misstep, rattled by the comment, but only for an instant. After all, if his coach and team accepted him, who cared what some jerk from the opposing team thought?

"That's right!" Jason grinned, regaining his stride. "So you better watch your backside."

The center whirled around. Did he think Jason was serious? In that moment Jason stole the ball, quickly passing it to Corey, who made a perfect bank shot. Jason couldn't stop beaming.

As the final minutes counted down, the game turned more defensive, the score remaining close—Whitman would get ahead by 2 or 3, then Northside would advance or tie.

The crowd grew louder, more frantic. At fifteen seconds, the score was tied at 78, then Northside was fouled, but missed one of their two free throws.

Whitman took possession of the ball. Corey and Odell made a series of rapid passes, trying to find a shot. Then Corey passed to Jason—in perfect line for a throw. Jason knew what he had to do. He raised the ball but—

The Northside's center slammed into him, and the ball fumbled from his hands. He spun around, furious, as the referee blew his whistle.

"Foul!"

The center lumbered away, hands on hips, sneering. Jason wanted to kill the jerk.

The crowd booed—half at Northside, the other half at the referee.

Jason bent over to catch his breath. The game was now up to him.

The stadium turned quiet as Jason stepped up to the free throw line. The ref tossed him the ball. Jason took a breath. *I'm going to make them,* he told himself. *I have to make them.*

He brought his feet up to the foul line, dribbled a couple of times, aimed at the basket and shot. The ball flew through the air and sank through the net.

The crowd roared as the scoreboard marked the point. The teams were tied at 79.

The ref tossed Jason the ball again. The state championship had come down to this: one shot, one person. Jason.

rainbow high

He glanced over toward the bench, recalling other games when the outcome had hinged on him. But this time was different. It wasn't just about winning a championship. It was about a team and a coach who'd accepted him. How could he let them down now?

Coach was signaling him with the palm of his hand, as if to say, "Easy. Take your time. Don't get cocky."

Jason wanted to look over at his mom and Kyle, but didn't dare. *Focus,* he told himself. *Relax.* He gazed at the basket. *You can do it.*

Jason lifted the ball and threw. The ball arced silently through the air. The stadium crowd watched, absolutely still—not a cough or a cheer. Jason watched the ball sail over the court, sink toward the hoop, and . . . whisk through the net!

The crowd exploded in thunderous applause, stomping, cheering, and shouting.

Jason whooped with excitement as the clock counted down to zero, sounding the buzzer. The entire Whitman team ran onto the court, jumping and hugging. The crowd was screaming. And then his mom was there, carrying his little sister. Everyone had their arms around each other. And there was Kyle, grinning from ear to ear. Jason put his arm around him, too, totally uncaring who saw them.

Several reporters appeared, shoving microphones in Jason's face, asking about the game. Even a camera from Channel Seven was there. A reporter glanced at Kyle and asked Jason, "Is this your boyfriend?"

High with excitement, Jason didn't think twice. "Yeah," he replied.

And then he did something he'd never have imagined in his wildest dreams. In front of hundreds of stadium viewers and the TV camera, he turned to Kyle—and kissed him.

chapter 19

jason   kyle

nelson

For the first time in his life, Nelson watched the eleven o'clock sports recap that evening, leaping off the sofa when he heard the results of the championship.

The sports anchor made a brief reference to Jason as "the senior defensive guard seen here on Channel Seven after announcing to his school he's gay."

A clip from the school interview came on, then the sportscaster continued with other game scores.

Nelson clicked the TV off, muttering, "Jason, Jason, Jason." Why did everyone keep making such a big whoop about him? As if he was the first high school student to ever come out? So what if he was a sports champ? Did that make him superior?

Nelson wandered into the kitchen for some ice cream to cool his irritation. As he was piling up a bowl the phone rang.

rainbow high

He darted a glance at the microwave clock. Who'd be calling at this hour? He grabbed the receiver. "Hello?"

"Did you see it?" Kyle asked. "Did they actually show it?"

"Show *what*?" Nelson asked. "That tired old interview again?"

"Us *kissing*!" Kyle shouted into the phone.

Nelson dropped his ice-cream spoon, dumbstruck.

"Were you watching Channel Seven?" Kyle's breath raced. "After the game they interviewed Jason. I was standing with him and the reporter asked if I was his boyfriend. Jason looked at me and this time he said *yes*! Then he kissed me!"

"No way! He *kissed* you?"

"They didn't show it?"

"No! He *kissed* you? *In front of everyone*?" With every word Nelson's voice became more excited.

"Yep," Kyle said proudly. "And he said I was his boyfriend. Are you sure you didn't miss it?"

"Kyle!" Nelson jabbed the spoon into his ice cream. "I *told* you I'm sure. The station probably wussed. Shootings and gore they'll show, but teenage boys kissing? That would scare people too much."

"Oh," Kyle mumbled.

Nelson could hear his disappointment. "So tell me about it," he said, in spite of being sick of hearing about Jason.

Kyle perked up, at least a little, and gave him the details.

After hanging up, Nelson chowed down his ice cream. On one hand he felt happy for Kyle, but on the other hand, why couldn't *he* find a boyfriend like that?

The following morning Nelson was still asleep when his cell phone rang. He stretched a hand out from beneath the covers, groping on the nightstand, knocking over his cigarettes, a Vaseline jar, and a ketchup bottle.

"Hello?" he croaked out, his fingers fumbling to pry the receiver open.

"Hey, it's Jeremy."

Nelson strained to pull himself from his sleep haze. "Jeremy?"

"Yeah, you know, the guy whose calls you don't return?"

They hadn't spoken since the night Nelson got knocked on his butt. Each time Jeremy had called, Nelson screened his number on the caller ID and let it go to voicemail. He was still too *PO*'d to talk to him.

"Oh, yeah," Nelson said, elbowing himself up onto his pillows. "Um, sorry. I've been—you know—kind of busy."

Ugh. Lame-o!

"Well," Jeremy said, "now that I got hold of you, I want to see if we could get together this afternoon? For coffee? So we can talk?"

Nelson scratched a hand through his hair, his anger dissipating, being replaced by a different feeling—one Nelson couldn't yet identify.

After agreeing on a time to meet, they hung up. Nelson stared at the phone, wondering how he could feel so weirdly ambivalent about seeing a guy he used to die to be with.

He dialed Kyle, lit a cigarette, and told him about Jeremy's call. "So, what am I going to say when I see him?"

"What do you *want* to say?" Kyle asked.

"I don't know. In spite of everything, I still like him. And it would be a monumental waste to dump him *sans* first doing him. After all this stress, I should at least get something out of it, but . . ."

rainbow high

He took a long drag from his cigarette and exhaled a deep sigh. "I'm just not sure it's going to work out with him. You know?"

"I know," Kyle acknowledged, sounding almost jubilant with relief. "But you've learned a lot from this, haven't you?"

"Oh, Kyle! You sound like a forty-year-old schoolteacher." He watched the smoke curling up from his cigarette. "Yeah, I guess I've learned a lot. I'm not sure what, though. Maybe I should just tell him it's not going to work."

Abruptly, a wave of panic overcame him. "Omigod!" He sat up in bed. "What if he's planning to dump *me*?"

"Well . . .," Kyle said calmly. "So? Didn't you just say—"

"Yeah, but I don't want him to dump me first." Nelson snubbed out his cigarette. "Oh, crap! Who will I take to prom?"

"Nelson, that's weeks away."

"Yeah! Like I'm going to meet a dozen gorgeous guys dying to go with me between now and then?"

"Can't he still go with you?" Kyle asked. "Even if you're not dating?"

"Oh, yeah, right. I'll tell him, 'Jeremy, I'm dumping you but will you still go to the prom with me?'" Nelson tossed a pillow aside. "I better get dressed. I'll call you when I get back—and before I slit my wrists. Remember, at my memorial service I want them to play 'Like a Virgin.' And I want to wear the Doc Marten boots you gave me. And I expect lots of tears and testimonials. I'm counting on you."

After showering and dressing, Nelson headed downstairs. His mom sat at the computer. She and he still weren't speaking to each other—at least nothing more than shouts and grumbles.

"I'm going out," he told her, grabbing his jacket from the closet.

She turned toward him, scowling. "No, you're not. Your dad's coming today, remember? I'm waiting to hear what flight he'll be on."

Oops. Nelson had forgotten all about it. Not that it made any difference. He wasn't going to sit around waiting for something he knew wasn't going to happen.

"Get real," he told his mom. "I'll be back in a couple of hours."

"Nelson!" his mom yelled as he closed the door behind him.

The aroma of fresh-ground coffee filled the coffee shop where Nelson had met Jeremy's friends. Jeremy was waiting, as usual, except this time he didn't look mad.

Uh-oh, Nelson thought. *Is he trying to hide that he's about to dump me?*

But Jeremy pecked him a kiss so tender it had to be genuine.

Crap. Suddenly Nelson no longer wanted to break up.

Once again Jeremy ordered a chai and Nelson a double espresso. Nelson had wanted to treat, but Jeremy beat him to it. Nelson shoved his money back into his pocket, worried sick there might be some rule—whoever pays gets to dump.

The table where they sat last time was occupied by a guy-girl couple that looked disgustingly happy—laughing, gazing into each other's eyes, displaying public affection all over each other.

Proceeding to a different table, Nelson sat across from Jeremy.

"So, how's it going?" Jeremy pursed his lips as he blew into his steaming cup.

"Fine." Nelson sipped his coffee, scalding his tongue as he tried to figure out what to say to Jeremy. Maybe he should just

rainbow high

forgive him for knocking him on his *tuches*. But was that really what this was about?

"Dude, you're trembling," Jeremy whispered.

Nelson tried to steady his cup with both hands.

"I really am sorry about the other night," Jeremy said. From his tone, there was no doubt he meant it.

Maybe he's not going to dump me, Nelson thought. But how could he be sure? This whole thing was making him crazy. He had to make a decision fast. The longer he delayed, the more difficult it would be to say anything. He took another jolt of coffee and dropped the cup to the table.

"Okay, listen! We both like each other, right? But we know this isn't going to work. You're sorry, I'm sorry. So, why don't we just agree to dump each other? Mutual consent. No one gets hurt."

Jeremy reared back in his seat, eyebrows raised in surprise—not the expression of someone who'd been planning to dump.

Omigod, Nelson thought. *What did I just do?* Blood surged into his face.

"I mean . . ." Nelson stammered. "Do you think we can work it out? Look, forget what I said before. I'm sorry. I didn't mean it. What do you think we should do?"

Now what am I saying? Nelson thought. He took a gulp of coffee, searing his tongue again. "I must sound like such a flake."

Jeremy peered at him, his mouth half-open, and didn't argue. He merely breathed a deep sigh. "You sound confused, babe. I think if I were you, I would be too."

Nelson slunk down in his seat, feeling like a skank. Why couldn't he have kept his mouth shut?

"So what should we do?" he asked in a meek voice.

Jeremy reached out and laid his fingers lightly on Nelson's

hand. "I like you a lot. But the fact is, I've got HIV. Nothing's going to change that. Maybe one day there'll be a cure, but for now . . . this is a lot to deal with. Maybe you're right. Maybe we should break up."

The response hit Nelson like a car smashed through the plate-glass window. He sat stunned, feeling like his heart was shattering into a million pieces. But why? Hadn't he braced himself?

He turned his hand over, grabbing tightly onto Jeremy's, trying to figure out his mixed-up feelings. But the longer he remained sitting, the more screwed up he felt.

"I better go," he finally said. "I promised Kyle to go shopping with him."

It was a lie, but the truth was too confusing. When they stood to say bye, Jeremy encircled his arms around him.

"I still want to be friends," he whispered.

Nelson nodded silently, fearing if he opened his mouth, he might start sobbing. Without letting Jeremy see his face, he turned away.

He managed to hold it in for three blocks, making it to a little park with a fountain. There he found an empty bench and pulled out his cell phone.

Kyle answered, "Hello?" and Nelson let loose.

For what seemed like hours he sobbed into the phone, rocking on the bench, clutching his stomach.

"It hurts so much," he was saying, when the phone abruptly lost reception. Nelson wanted to smash the stupid thing. But when Kyle called back a minute later, Nelson had caught his breath. "Will I ever find *anyone* to love me?"

"Hey, come on. I love you."

"You know what I mean," Nelson wailed. "A *boyfriend*."

rainbow high

"Of course you will," Kyle assured him. "You have your whole life ahead of you."

Nelson sputtered into the phone. "I don't want to wait my whole loveless life."

"It'll happen," Kyle insisted.

"Oh, yeah? How do you know?"

"Because . . . you're a wonderful guy."

"Yeah, yeah, yeah," Nelson whined. "Then why doesn't wonderful me have a boyfriend?"

"Be patient," Kyle said with confidence. "It'll happen."

Nelson wished he could believe him.

When he arrived home, his mom was sitting by the phone, drumming her fingers on the arm of the chair, looking ticked off.

Crap. Nelson realized he'd forgotten about his dad.

"Did he come?" Nelson asked, a little startled by his own excitement.

His mom stopped drumming her fingers. "He called and said he had a crisis at work."

Nelson's heart plummeted faster than a cartoon anvil. How could he have gotten even momentarily excited about the old coot showing up?

"Mom, that's crap!" Nelson threw his keys onto the table. "Why can't you just accept the fact that he doesn't care?"

She glanced around the room, averting her eyes. "That's not true."

"It *is* true! Why do you keep calling him? It's like you do it just to hurt me—to remind me how worthless I am."

"Nelson, how can you say that? I don't do it to hurt you. But if you don't listen to me, what am I supposed to do?"

"Try *trusting* me. Stop treating me like a kid. I'm almost eighteen." His chin began to quiver. "If I make mistakes, then I make mistakes, okay?"

"Not with your health," his mom protested. "I won't simply keep quiet."

"Fine, then yell at me. Just stop trying to bring Dad into it."

She tapped the arms of her chair, taking a deep breath. "Nelson, I don't want you dating Jeremy. I can't go on living this way."

"You don't have to," Nelson answered. "He dumped me."

"What do you mean?" She gave him a slant-eyed look.

"*D-u-m-p*," he mumbled, feeling too drained to explain it. "Look it up."

In his room, he collapsed into bed. Out of the corner of his eye he spotted Jeremy's bright white briefs still lying by the wall where he'd hurled them.

He stared at them, thinking. Should he throw them out?

He hauled himself out of bed and picked them up. On impulse he brought them to his face, inhaling. They still smelled laundry fresh. How could he toss them? They'd been a gift.

He carefully folded the briefs, laid them in his dresser, and closed the drawer as Atticus wandered in.

Nelson climbed onto his bed and Atticus jumped up after him. Within minutes they were both asleep.

rainbow high

jason kyle

nelson

The following morning Kyle dressed for school, buttoning his shirt. On his desk the Princeton and Tech reply cards lay waiting. His eyes darted between them as he vacillated.

Hadn't he made his decision? But that was before Jason had kissed him in front of TV cameras—or at least *one* camera—and declared to the entire planet they were boyfriends. How could he abandon him now?

"Kyle!" his mom called from the doorway. "You're going to be late." She peered at his shirt. "Honey, your buttons!"

Kyle glanced down at his misbuttoned shirt.

When he got downstairs, his mom handed him a Pop-Tart. He shoved it into his backpack, too nervous to eat anything. "Thanks!"

He'd walked halfway down the block before he realized he'd forgotten the Princeton and Tech cards. Crud. Maybe he should put the whole thing aside till the afternoon . . . or till never.

He turned around and hurried back home, raced past his mom ("Forgot something!"), grabbed the cards and envelopes, and once more trotted down the street.

Beneath a weeping willow at the corner, the neighborhood mailbox loomed like an ominous four-legged creature.

Kyle slowed as he approached. From his jacket, he pulled out the reply cards—one for Princeton and one for Tech. One to be marked "Accept," the other "Decline."

His heart racing, he groped inside his pocket for a pen. With fingers trembling, he marked one decision, then the other, sealing them into their respective envelopes.

The iron box waited. Kyle wiped his brow and pulled the door handle. The blue mouth gaped open. Kyle's heart pounded. Taking a deep gulp of air, he dropped the envelopes onto the metal panel, and closing his eyes, let go. The door squealed, slamming with a bang.

Kyle let out his breath and opened his eyes again, an ache in the pit of his stomach.

Hurriedly he turned, running from the box, afraid to look back.

At school, prechampionship banners and posters still plastered the walls and bulletin boards. Students ran through the halls, laughing and shouting in celebration.

But when they saw Kyle, they looked at him in a funny way.

Two girls he vaguely knew pushed one another toward him. "Kyle?" asked one with glitter cheeks, while her friend giggled next to her. "Is it true you're Jason's boyfriend?"

Kyle felt the blood rush into his face. Obviously the word

had spread. Kyle had barely opened his mouth before another three girls crowded in, eager to hear his answer.

"Um, yeah," he said, certain he'd turned red as ketchup. Though it felt neat getting the attention, it went totally against his shyness.

"Oh, my God!" shrieked the glitter girl.

"I think that's *so* cool," said a girl with multilayered beads.

But then another girl scrunched her nose. "What do you two *do* together, like in bed?" She sounded both repulsed and intrigued.

"Yeah!" the shrieker jumped in. "Which one of you is the girl?"

"That's so disgusting," said scrunch-nose.

Kyle shifted his feet. This was getting way too bizarre. "I've got to go," he told them, and quickly scurried away.

During morning classes he slunk down in his seat, trying to hide behind his books.

In the hall between classes, he got the usual 'phobe slurs, but now new taunts were added.

"Hi, Mrs. Carrillo!" a group of boys jeered as Kyle walked past. "Jason and you going to run for prom king and queen?"

Kyle wanted to fold himself into a locker and lock himself in. Maybe Jason had been right not wanting to tell the whole world about their being boyfriends.

"What did you expect?" Nelson asked at lunch.

"Not this," Kyle murmured, just as a boy swooped past with his tray.

"Hey, Meeks, I'm going to tell Jason you're cheating on him!"

Kyle spun around. "Mind your own business!"

"Oh, yeah," Nelson bit into his veggie burger. "That'll stop them."

"Well, what am I supposed to say?"

"It's like this. . . ." Nelson put his burger down. "If you can't think up a good comeback, then just smile and wave. But don't let them get a rise out of you. That just eggs them on."

Kyle picked a pepperoni off his pizza slice, tossing it aside. "Nothing ever turns out like you expect, does it?"

"Tell me about it." Nelson began fussing with an earring. "So . . . Did you mail your Princeton acceptance?"

Kyle nodded silently, trying to swallow his bite of pizza.

"Oh," Nelson said.

After that, neither of them said much more.

Kyle's afternoon sucked as much as his morning, thanks to even more incredibly obnoxious comments.

Then as he was leaving calculus, he ran into Debra.

"Are you getting as much crap as I am?" she asked.

"Um . . . ," he stammered, trying to figure out if she was angry at him or at the harassment—or both. "Yeah, I'm getting a lot."

She groaned, dropping her forehead onto his shoulder. "This is *so* not the senior year I imagined."

Kyle froze, uncertain how to respond to her. *Please don't let her start crying,* he thought.

"Um . . ." He awkwardly patted her shoulder. "I'm really sorry."

"Thanks." She lifted her face up, her eyes tearless, thank God.

Adding to Kyle's gratitude, Lance Lanier walked up. Jason had told Kyle about Lance and Debra. He was glad to see them together now. At least it helped him feel less guilty about Jason's breakup with her.

When the day's final bell rang, Kyle let out a whimper of jubilation. It was over, except for one thing. He needed to tell Jason he'd sent in his Princeton reply.

Did he dare walk over to Jason's locker? He could imagine the taunts people would make at seeing them together. But it was bound to happen eventually. May as well get it over with.

"I'll be there in a few," Jason was telling Corey.

Corey turned and saw Kyle. "How's it going, man?" he said, and walked past.

"Hi," Kyle replied. He wondered how the team was dealing with all this.

"Wha's up?" Jason greeted him, snapping his lock shut.

Kyle leaned onto the neighboring locker and let out a breath, exhausted. "Your day suck as much as mine?"

"Not really." Jason smiled. "Mostly a lot of handshakes and celebrations."

Kyle stared at him, incredulous. "No one's hassled you about? . . ." He glanced over his shoulder and whispered, "About saying we're boyfriends? About our kiss?"

Jason gave a shrug. "Coach said it hadn't been the brightest thing to do. The guys on the team kind of hooted and whistled when I walked into the locker room. But they do that with everyone. It's no big deal."

Kyle listened, flabbergasted, shaking his head.

"Why?" Jason's eyebrows rode up in concern. "What did they say to you?"

Kyle hesitated, feeling a little weird about repeating some of the stuff guys had said, feeling weirder about the fact that they'd said it to him and not to Jason, and feeling most weird that he hadn't been able to do anything to stop them.

"Just stupid stuff," Kyle finally said.

"Like what?" Jason insisted.

"Like calling me—" Kyle forced himself to say it "—your bitch."

Jason's eyes clouded an instant, then he squared his shoulders. "If anyone said that to me, I'd beat the crap out of them."

Though Kyle knew that was true, it made him feel like a wimp in comparison. He'd hoped for a little more sympathy.

"Well," Kyle hissed, "that's probably why they *didn't* say it to you. Besides the fact that you're school hero." He rolled his eyes.

Jason leaned back, studying him. "Hey, don't take this out on me, Kyle. You're the one who wanted to tell people about us."

"And you didn't?" Kyle retorted.

Jason clenched his jaw, his eyes darkening.

Kyle took a breath, trying to calm down before this whole stupid conversation escalated out of control. "Never mind," Kyle said, holding his palms up. "I'm sorry. You're right." He tried to focus on what he wanted to say. "I came here to tell you . . . this morning I sent in my acceptance to Princeton."

As Kyle spoke he watched Jason's jaw go slack and his shoulders fall.

"Today was the deadline," Kyle explained softly. "I had to send it in. You told me I should go there, right?"

Jason nodded silently, his eyes downcast.

Kyle swallowed the knot in his throat. "It was really hard to do, Jason."

"You did what you had to do, man." Jason's voice came out distant and hoarse. "Um, listen, I better go. The team's having another celebration."

Kyle wanted to shout, "Who cares about another stupid

rainbow high

celebration?" But as Jason turned away, he saw the shimmer of pools forming at the rim of Jason's eyes.

As Jason disappeared down the hall, Kyle wanted to run after him and . . . Do what? Shake Jason? Or wrap his arms around him? Unable to decide, Kyle turned and walked home alone.

At dinner he picked at his chipped beef and parted his peas and carrots into distinct piles.

"Honey, what's the matter?" his mom asked, exchanging worried glances with his dad.

"Nothing. You'll be glad to know I sent in my Princeton acceptance today."

"That's a relief." His dad smiled, lifting his wineglass. "You made the right decision, son."

"That's wonderful, honey," his mom agreed.

"Can I be excused?" Kyle asked. "I'm not hungry."

In his room he lay in bed, clutching a pillow to his chest, thinking about Princeton and what it would be like to leave Jason. He barely noticed his mom come in and sit beside him.

"That was a big decision you made today." She brought a hand to his forehead and gently stroked his hair.

Kyle nodded. "Mom? Did you always know Dad was 'The One'?"

She cocked her head in a quizzical look. "Yes . . . and no. Only as I got to know him, over time. That's really the only way you get to know people."

Kyle thought how he'd known Jason since freshman year. Four years was a long time . . . except they hadn't actually become friends until this past year, really just a few months ago—not very long at all.

"Did you and Dad ever have to spend time apart before you got married?"

Kyle knew she must be guessing that he was thinking about Jason.

She nodded. " I didn't see him for two years when he went to grad school."

Kyle had known that, but he'd forgotten. "Were you ever afraid you might—you know—lose him?"

"Yes . . . and it hurt." She glanced back at Kyle. "But that's all part of trusting life. I think if two people are meant for each other, they'll end up together eventually."

Kyle studied her expression. Had she said that just to make him feel better? Or . . . could it possibly be true?

chapter 21

jason   kyle
nelson

At the recognition dinner that Coach Cameron threw for the basketball team, Jason put on a winning front. But behind the smile, his heart rampaged big-time.

He knew it was because of Kyle. But hadn't he encouraged him to accept Princeton?

The following day Jason trudged from one class to the other, barely able to pay attention. During government he didn't even notice an office aide knock on the door and hand his teacher a note.

"Jason?" Mr. Porter signaled him forward. "Coach wants to see you."

As Jason stepped down the tiled hall, he tried to imagine why Coach had called him out of class. *Probably nothing important,* he tried to assure himself, hoping to calm the grinding in his stomach.

Coach was working at his desk as Jason tapped on the office doorway. Amid a stack of papers was an overnight mail envelope similar to the one in which his scholarship letter had arrived.

Coach glanced up. "Close the door, Carrillo. Have a seat."

Jason dropped into the vinyl chair, wiping the sweat from his hands.

Coach stared silently at him, his mouth somewhat open, and scratched his chin.

"What's the matter?" Jason asked. "Is something wrong?"

Coach exhaled loudly. "This came for you." He handed Jason the overnight envelope.

Jason slowly tore it open, his hand shaking a little. He pulled out a letter from Tech. His heart began racing as he read down the page.

We regret to inform you that the scholarship previously offered to you has been rescinded, on the basis of the altercation in which you were involved . . .

Wait a minute. *What* altercation? He'd never gotten into a fight with another team. Was this a mistake?

Then he remembered . . . the scuffle with Dwayne on the court during the game with Chesapeake High.

The letter fell from his fingers onto his lap, as his heart slipped down inside him.

"But . . ." His voice came out faint and disoriented. "Dwayne started that fight." He leaned toward Coach, edging off the chair. "Can you talk to them? Can you tell them that?"

Coach pulled his glasses off and dropped them onto his desk. "I already called. I figured what the letter was about. They said their decision's made."

A swell of anger rose from Jason's chest up into his throat. "But that's not fair!"

"No, it's not."

rainbow high

"But I don't understand. If it's not fair, why can't we do something?"

"Jason . . ." Coach rubbed a hand across the back of his neck. "Maybe it's not really about that."

Jason stared across the desk at Coach, trying to understand. "You mean . . . it's really because . . . I'm gay."

Coach nodded, his eyes weary. "Maybe."

"But didn't you say there was that NCAA thing against discriminating?"

"Yes." Coach shook his head. "But they're not admitting it's about that. On the basis of what they're saying—"

Jason slammed back into his chair. "I'm screwed."

Dwayne had screwed him. Now Tech was screwing him.

"Take it easy." Coach waved him to settle down. "You're still a good player, Carrillo. It just means we need to find you another school."

But Jason couldn't simmer down. The blood was pounding in his temples. "Oh, right! Some rinky-dink college that's so hard up they won't give a crap." He threw the letter onto Coach's desk. "Forget it!"

Coach leaned back in his swivel chair. "Carrillo, we knew the risk."

"Then why didn't you stop me?" He stood, his whole body shaking. "I don't want another school! I'm not going anywhere. This is all crap!"

He yanked the door open, feeling like he was about to explode. Cursing, he stormed down the hall, kicking a locker, not knowing where he was headed. Where could he go? He wasn't going back to class. Besides, he'd left his books in Coach's office. He couldn't go back there. He'd never walked out on Coach before.

He slammed open the side door of the building, crossed the parking lot, and kept walking, muttering and trying to make sense of what had happened.

He should never have come out. That's what this boiled down to. Corey had been right all along. He should've just kept his mouth shut and never told anyone.

Jason punched a fist into his leg. How could he have been so *stupid*? He'd known Tech would take away his scholarship if he came out. So why had he done it? Why had Coach, MacTraugh, Kyle let him go through with it? Why hadn't someone stopped him?

"Arrgh!" he screamed, and kept walking. In his mind he retraced the events of the past few weeks over and over, trying to understand. Why had he risked his future like this?

Pausing to cross the street, he saw he'd reached Bluemont Park. That was ironic. It's where he'd always gone to get away from his dad and the yelling at home, where he'd learned to shoot baskets, where he'd spent hours trying to make sense of the world and all his feelings about girls . . . and about boys.

He sat down on the bench and hung his head in his hands, staring down at the names scratched into the weathered wood. Among them was his, dated ten years earlier.

He rubbed his thumb across the roughly gouged letters, thinking back to how he used to sit there between games, watching the older boys, wanting to play like them, wanting to be them, and wanting to be with them.

Jason wasn't certain for how long he now sat on the bench, but a school bus drove past, full of students. Classes must have let out. He got up and started walking. This time he knew exactly where he was heading.

From the outside Kyle's house was quiet, the driveway

empty, as though no one was home. Jason rang the doorbell, just to be sure. Then he hunkered down on the stoop, bringing his knees to his chest and wrapping his arms around them to keep warm. He wished he hadn't left his jacket in his locker.

A short while later Kyle appeared, walking from the direction of school, his backpack slung over his shoulder.

"Wha's up?" Jason said from the stoop.

"Hi." Kyle squinted a little, as if confused. "I looked for you at your locker. How'd you get here so fast?"

"I skipped last period," Jason said, rocking on the stoop. "I got a letter from Tech. They've withdrawn my scholarship."

Kyle slipped his backpack from his shoulder, letting it drop to the sidewalk. "Well . . ." He pressed his lips together a moment, as if determined. "We'll fight it."

"There's no fighting it." Jason spit on the ground beside him and told Kyle what the letter had said, concluding, "At least *you* didn't turn down Princeton. At least *you* get to go where *you* want."

He knew he was being spiteful and hated himself for it. He wouldn't blame Kyle for telling him, "Screw off!"

But Kyle merely stared, quietly studying him. "You look cold," he finally said.

"I don't care." Jason hunched his shoulders, starting to shiver.

Kyle gave a sigh. Pulling his keys out, he opened the door. "Want to come in?"

Jason rocked on the stoop a moment longer before deciding it was dumb to keep sitting on the cold brick.

Inside the house he followed the sound of tinkling glasses into the kitchen, where Kyle was pouring Cokes.

Wordlessly Kyle handed Jason a glass and leaned back against the counter, sipping his own drink. Every time he swallowed, his Adam's apple bobbed up, then down.

Jason guzzled his Coke, recalling the tenderness of Kyle's neck against his lips.

Kyle's gaze drifted up toward the clock above the cabinets. It's ticking reverberated through the silence. They were alone in the house—no parents, no little sister, no cat—just the two of them.

Kyle's gaze moved back to Jason. "What do you want to do?"

Jason hesitated, his chest stirring. Did Kyle mean right now? Or did he mean in terms of college plans?

As if in response, Kyle set his glass down and stepped toward him. His arms encircled Jason, warming him. His fine, thin hair brushed Jason's cheek, smelling sweetly of shampoo as his chin came firmly to rest on Jason's shoulder.

Jason felt his anger melting as Kyle's heart beat against his.

Then Kyle lifted his face, his breath warm on Jason's cheek, and his tongue slid between Jason's lips.

Jason no longer cared about Tech or losing his scholarship. His tongue tapped Kyle's in return and that was all that mattered.

Kyle took hold of Jason's hand, their fingers intertwining. And without a word, they climbed upstairs.

In Kyle's room the two boys stood beside the bed facing each other. Jason ran his tongue down Kyle's cheek and into the little hollows beneath his chin. Kyle moaned softly, his fingers digging into Jason's shoulders and up through his thick hair.

Jason tugged Kyle's shirt off, moving slowly at first. But as their kisses became more fervent, they were soon plucking eagerly to release each other's belts. An instant later Kyle's jeans dropped to the carpet, followed by Jason's.

rainbow high

Withdrawing his lips from Kyle's mouth, Jason gazed at their near-naked bodies, their desire evident beneath white undies. Quivering with excitement, his fingers slid beneath Kyle's elastic band, touching him. An instant later their briefs crowned the piles binding their ankles.

Stumbling sideways, they tumbled into bed, legs thrashing to kick off shoes.

While Jason's mouth devoured Kyle's chest and shoulders, wanting to taste every inch of him, Kyle gasped, "Wait," struggling to pry off Jason's sneakers.

He hurled the shoes to the floor as Jason yanked his jeans off. Free at last, they pressed close together, the contours of their naked bodies molding perfectly, smooth and hard.

Jason climbed on top of him, all his anguish about Tech and Kyle and his sucky life swelling inside him. And then they were heaving and moaning, as Jason clung to every part of Kyle, running his hands up to the curves of his shoulders, along his lean muscled upper arms, across his chest and down his back, wanting never to let go.

Kyle's hot breath whispered into his ear, "Let it out, boy."

Jason clutched him closer and harder, blood pounding in his ears, tighter and faster, until they were gasping and groaning, one followed by the other.

When it was over, they slipped beneath the sheets, their naked bodies sticky against each other. Jason pulled the sheet over their heads, wishing they could stay this way forever.

"I love you," Kyle said.

"Back at you," Jason whispered, as a quiet rivulet, first from one eye, then the other, trickled across his cheeks. He rubbed against the pillow, wiping his face. "I'm really sorry. About what I said earlier, outside. I can be a creep sometimes, I know."

"You're upset." Kyle kissed his cheek and brought his lips to Jason's, tasting of salt. "This whole thing really sucks."

Jason nodded. "What's going to happen to us?"

"We'll figure it out," Kyle said, his voice full of confidence. "My mom says if two people are meant for each other, they'll end up together eventually."

Jason felt his tears ebbing. "Can I come visit you at Princeton?"

"You'd better!" Kyle hugged him tighter and Jason squeezed him back.

They lay sniffling and wiping their noses, tears dripping down their cheeks, as they breathed in the warm air beneath the sheets, ran their fingers in gentle circles on each other's skin, and listened to the quiet hum of the aquarium.

"Hey," Kyle whispered, after some time. "My mom and dad will be home soon. You hungry?"

In the kitchen, they were devouring the final spoonfuls from an ice-cream tub when Kyle's parents came home—first his mom, then his dad.

Mrs. Meeks gazed at Jason head-on, with a curious look. Quickly he glanced away. Could she tell what Kyle and he had been up to? If she could, she didn't let on.

"Can you stay for dinner?" she asked.

Jason phoned his mom to let her know. But he didn't mention the scholarship—or rather, no scholarship—news.

During dinner, beneath the table, he rested his foot on Kyle's, while Mr. Meeks talked about the championship. After dessert, Jason didn't want to leave.

"Here, take my jacket," Kyle told him. "It's cold out."

"I'm not going to take your jacket."

"Don't worry. I've got another one." Kyle shoved the

rainbow high

jacket at him and said, "What are you smiling at?"

"You," Jason told him, pulling the jacket on. He'd miss Kyle fussing over him when he left for Princeton.

When Jason arrived home, his mom was sitting at the kitchen table, pasting news clippings about the championship into the scrapbook she kept of him.

Usually he would've kidded her, asking if she wanted his autograph. But tonight he kept silent and bit into a fingernail.

"Hi, hon." She glanced up cheerily. "Whose jacket is that?"

"Kyle's." He pulled a chair out and sat down across from her, leaving the jacket on. "I left mine at school."

His mom's eyebrows shot up like antennae. "How come?"

What was the best way to break the news to her?

"Um . . ." Picking up the glue stick, he turned it between his fingers. "Something happened and I left school without it."

Her scissors cut across the newspaper, her eyebrows still raised. "Are you going to tell me about it?"

Jason gritted his teeth. Was there a best way to say it? He put the glue stick down and cleared his throat. "Um, I got a letter from Tech. They . . . withdrew my scholarship."

The skin around his mom's eyes crinkled. She laid the scissors down and slumped back in her chair.

Jason looked down at the table and told her the rest. When he'd finished, he peered up at her.

She was gazing at him, tears quivering in her eyelids, her mouth clamped tight, clearly trying not to cry.

Jason shoved his hands into Kyle's jacket pockets, struggling to keep still.

His mom ran her fingertips along the edge of the scrapbook and began turning the pages—past certificates and news articles, postcards from basketball camp, and team photos. All the while she slowly shook her head from side to side.

"I know you're angry," he told her.

"I *am* angry . . ." Her voice trembled. "Because I want you to have the opportunities I didn't have. And not make the mistakes I made."

He knew she meant giving up college.

"I'll still go to college." He pulled his hands out from the jacket and reached across the table, touching her soft fingers. "It'll be okay. You'll see."

They talked about his possible alternatives and he promised he'd apologize to Coach for walking out on him.

She gazed at the jacket. "Kyle seems like a good friend."

"Yeah," Jason said, suddenly warm beneath the jacket. Was his mom finally coming to terms with his being gay?

She wiped her cheek and forced a weak smile. "I want you to be happy, Jason."

"I *am* happy."

Did he mean it? Being with Kyle had given him new hope.

They talked for a while and he told her what Ms. MacTraugh had said that time about being true to himself and honest with others. Later he kissed his mom good night and headed to his room.

On the bed lay his cat, curled into the nook between his pillow and the bedspread. Jason sat down to stroke it a moment.

Sometime after midnight he awoke to find himself stretched out on the bed, still dressed, and the light on. He considered that for an instant and turned the lamp off. Then he pulled Kyle's jacket more tightly around him and fell back to sleep.

jason   kyle

nelson

One evening that week, Nelson and his mom were watching TV together on the sofa, munching popcorn, when she asked, "Sweetie? Have you received any more information since your acceptance to Tech?"

Nelson nearly choked on a popcorn kernel. He had put off telling his mom he'd decided not to go to Tech, knowing she'd have a mental meltdown.

"Actually —" he grabbed hold of the armrest, bracing himself "—I decided not to go to Tech."

Out of the corner of his eye he watched Felicia begin quaking and shaking. Her face turned crimson. Her eyes bulged.

"When," she yelled, "did you decide that?"

"About a month ago. Didn't I tell you? I thought I—"

Before he could utter another word, she tore off on a rant. "If you think I'm going to pay for you to just lay around the house and sleep all day . . ." Blah, blah, blah. "You'd better get a job because you're going to have to pay rent . . ." Yadda, yadda, yadda.

Nelson kept waiting for her to pick up the phone and bring his dad into it. Yet she didn't. And for that, he was grateful.

After half a week of railing and raving, she began petering out, instead asking reasonable questions: "Why don't you want to go to college? Do you realize how necessary a university education is?"

"I know, Mom," he replied as he helped her carry the lawn furnishings out from the garage. "It's not like I'll never go to college. I just feel like I need a break, that's all."

"For how long?" His mom's tone was skeptical.

"I don't know." Nelson unfolded a chaise lounge. "A year maybe. A 'gap' year. Lots of people do it."

"Well, I won't have you just lazing around the house."

"I think you've made that clear, Mom."

By the end of the week the spring weather had turned warm enough for Nelson and his mom to wear shorts.

"Okay," she announced. "I'll agree to your so-called gap year on one condition. Before school ends—by graduation time—you have to come up with a plan. I don't care if it's a job, or volunteer work, or some sort of classes, but you have to do something productive, all right?"

"All right." Nelson nodded, wondering what the heck he would do.

"What do you think?" he asked Kyle as they walked home after school.

"Aren't you going to community college with Jeremy?" Kyle asked.

"Nah. That was before we broke up. What if—just my luck—

we ended up in class together? After everything we've gone through, it would feel too weird."

They walked quietly, kicking a rock down the sidewalk between them, while thoughts clunked around in Nelson's head.

"You know he was going to be my prom date. Now who am I going to take? I'll feel like a tag-along loser going by myself."

"Couldn't you still go with him as friends?" Kyle asked. "Didn't he say he wanted to be friends?"

Nelson lit up a cigarette. "Kyle, everyone says that when they break up. It's code for 'Later. Have a nice life.'"

Kyle's brow scrunched up. "But don't you want to be friends with him?"

Nelson took a deep drag from his cigarette and blew the stream of smoke out his nose. "Can we just drop it? This is really starting to get on my nerves. No, I don't want to be friends. And I'm not asking him to the prom."

When they got to Nelson's, Kyle worked on his calculus homework while Nelson peered in the mirror, spiking his hair with gel.

"Besides," Nelson said abruptly. "What if he says no? You may as well just put a knife through my heart right now."

Kyle turned the page of his math book. "And what if he says yes?"

Nelson glowered into the mirror at him. Sometimes he wanted to strangle Kyle.

Several days passed, and the GSA celebrated securing Mueller's approval for same-sex dates to the prom. Meanwhile Nelson kept turning over in his mind, should he call Jeremy?

One evening, after feeding and walking Atticus, smoking

three cigarettes, and surfing the web for an hour, Nelson finally summoned his nerve to pick up the phone and dial.

"Hello?" answered the friendly, familiar voice.

"Um, hi." Nelson paced the room with the phone to his ear. "It's me."

He waited. Would Jeremy recognize his voice?

"Nelson?" Jeremy said. "How's it going? I've been meaning to call you."

"Same here," Nelson said, as the tension left his shoulders.

They made small talk—awkwardly at first—about school, Kyle, Jason, Nelson's mom, Jeremy's friends.

Gradually Nelson calmed down enough to sit in his chair. But when it came time to say why he'd called, he stood up again. "Listen, did you mean it when you said you want to stay friends?"

"Yeah," Jeremy said, his voice genuine.

"Well, then, um . . ." Nelson began pacing again. "My prom's coming up? And, um, Kyle and Jason are going? And, um, I was wondering if you wanted to go with me—as friends? We could all hang out. I'll pay for your ticket, but you'd have to rent a tux."

Nelson waited, twisting his finger around his silver neck chain.

After what seemed like a million years, Jeremy said, "Well . . . I never went to my *own* prom. And my brother has a tux I can borrow. I'd like to see you and Kyle again—and meet Jason. Yeah, I would like to go."

"Awesome!" Nelson leaped up off the floor. He could hardly wait, though the prom was still several weeks away.

Immediately after hanging up, he called Kyle.

"Guess who's going to prom with me—as friends. You happy now?"

rainbow high

"Yeah," Kyle said. "Are *you*?"

"No. Now I have to decide what kind of tux to get. Okay. I guess I'm a little happy. Hey, thanks."

"For what?" Kyle asked.

"For making me call him."

When Nelson got off the phone, his thoughts returned to Jeremy. What would it feel like to see him again? Would he be able to accept being merely friends? Or would prom turn out a disaster?

chapter 23

jason nelson kyle

That week Kyle had his final swim meet of the season. In the weeks since the hotel room fiasco, things with the team had gotten loads better, thanks largely to a school meeting he and his dad had had with Coach Sweeney.

The three of them had sat across the desk in the pool office.

"Thank you for coming in this morning," Coach Sweeney said, shaking hands with his dad. "Kyle has always been a superb member of the Whitman team—both as an outstanding swimmer and helping with fund-raising projects. That's why I was very disappointed with his behavior during the trip."

"So was I." His dad followed her gaze across to Kyle. "But from what I understand this all began because of a note sent from a parent. Is that correct?"

"Not exactly," Coach Sweeney replied. "I believe it began because of Kyle's coming out."

Kyle sat up to protest but his dad spoke first.

"If he wants to come out, that's his right. Isn't it?" His dad's tone made it clear he expected agreement.

"Mr. Meeks . . ." Coach Sweeney drew an audible breath. "You have to understand that your son is not the only member of this team. Other parents hold different views."

"I appreciate that," his dad said firmly. "What I don't agree with is why my son should have to alter his showering simply because someone else feels uncomfortable with him."

Coach Sweeney massaged her knuckles. "What solution do you see, Mr. Meeks?"

"You're their coach. It's up to you to set the rules. But unless my son is doing something wrong, then maybe those boys and their parents are the ones who need to alter *their* behavior."

Kyle wanted to jump up and cheer as his dad pressed on.

"How has the basketball team handled their coming-out situation?"

"I don't know." Coach Sweeney squeezed her hands together nervously. "I haven't heard that it's been a problem."

"Then maybe—" Kyle's dad stood up "—you should ask their coach how he handled it. Anything else we need to discuss?"

Coach Sweeney shook her head.

Later that week, she called a meeting of the team. For an hour, they talked about name-calling and respecting others. Charlie Tuggs huffed, rolled his eyes, and glared at Kyle.

But for the remainder of the season, Kyle had showered together with the other guys, and Charlie left him alone.

One evening, when Kyle's dad was reading the paper, Kyle stepped up behind him and leaned over the chair, embracing him.

"What's up?" his dad said.

"Nothing." Kyle rested his chin on his dad's shoulder. It was the closest he'd felt to his dad in years.

Nevertheless, it was to his mom that Kyle turned when it came to asking for prom money.

One evening when she came to his room to say good night, he asked, "I was wondering if . . . Could you help me with money for a tux and stuff?"

She leaned against the doorway, smiling. "I think so." But then her brow rose, questioning. "Are you taking someone?"

"Yeah. Jason. Who else?"

"Oh." She nodded. "Okay."

Kyle hadn't *explicitly* asked Jason yet. He'd been waiting till the basketball season ended. But then he decided to wait till after the college decision fuss was resolved. And then he decided to wait till after the GSA secured approval for same-sex dates.

"When the heck are you going to ask him?" Nelson insisted as they waited for the metro one afternoon. "Fifteen minutes before the dance?"

"It's just . . ." Kyle peered down the track, searching for the train. "What if he doesn't feel ready to go to the prom with me?"

"Kyle! He kissed you in front of a whole stadium of people, didn't he? Of course he's going to go to the prom with you. You made me call Jeremy. Now you call Jason!"

"Okay. I will. Lay off."

But Nelson pulled out his cell phone and began dialing.

"Nelson, what are you doing?" Kyle reached to grab the phone but too late.

"Hi, Jason? This is Nelson. Yeah, wha's up? Hey, I'm with

rainbow high

Kyle. He wants to ask you something."

With a brazen smile, he extended the receiver to Kyle.

Even though Kyle wanted to kill Nelson, he took the phone. "Hi," he said tentatively.

"Wha's up?" Jason replied. "Nelson said you wanted to ask me something."

Nelson puckered his lips and made kissing sounds.

Kyle waved him away and spoke into the phone. "Yeah, um, you and I hadn't really talked about the prom yet? So, um, you want to go? . . ." He swallowed the knot in his throat and added, "with me?"

On the other end of the line he heard Jason chuckle softly. "I was going to ask you."

"Really?" Kyle asked.

Nelson stuck his forefinger down his throat as if to puke.

"Yeah," Jason said. "You want to go with me?"

"Yeah," Kyle said, uttering a sigh.

After they'd finished talking and Kyle flipped the receiver closed, Nelson exclaimed, "Thank God that's over with!"

Kyle lifted the phone as if to clobber him. But instead he wrapped his arm around Nelson's shoulder in a bear hug, just as the train arrived.

The following Saturday afternoon, Kyle and Jason rode their bikes to the mall to choose and reserve their tuxes.

At the formal wear shop, a perky silver-haired saleslady walked them around the cramped display floor, pointing out a variety of tuxedo styles: traditional, high fashion, and ultra formal.

When they reached the last mannequin, the lady clerk asked, "Do you boys know the color of your dates' evening gowns?"

Kyle and Jason stared at the clerk a moment, then at each

other. Jason turned again to the clerk and deposited his arm around Kyle. "*We're* our dates."

The clerk's brow furrowed a moment, then her eyes grew wide with comprehension as the blood drained from her face. "Oh." She cleared her throat.

With the warmth of Jason's arm resting on his shoulder, Kyle thought how much Jason had changed in the past few months—coming out to the world and coming to accept himself. It had been what Kyle wanted, but he'd never expected it to happen so fast.

While the saleslady nervously shuffled to the stockroom for tuxes, Kyle's mind drifted to his life's dream: to someday marry the guy he loved, have a house, raise kids.

The current moment seemed like one more step toward that dream.

If only the future weren't so uncertain. Where would Jason go to college? Would their relationship endure their time apart?

The saleslady returned and Jason pulled on the silky black tux jacket she handed him. In the three-way mirror his tall, handsome reflection extended time after time toward infinity. He turned to Kyle, his face glowing with promise.

And in spite of all the future's uncertainty, Kyle thought himself the luckiest boy on earth.

rainbow high

jason kyle

nelson

After having reserved their prom tuxes, Jason and Kyle hung out at the mall's food court, where over ice cream they joked and giggled about the saleslady in the formal wear shop.

As Jason bit into his cone, he spotted Coach Cameron with his wife and one of their daughters, talking and pointing in a store window while walking in Jason's direction.

Several weeks had passed since Jason apologized to Coach Cameron for losing his temper in his office.

"I'm really sorry for how I acted," Jason had uttered, head bowed. "I know you always did everything you could for me, Coach. That means more to me than you'll ever know."

He had glanced up to see Coach working a hand across his jaw, as if recovering from a blow. "Well, let that be the first and only time you go off like that."

That had been the last Coach spoke of it.

"Come on!" Jason now told Kyle. "Hey, Coach!"

Jason led Kyle across the mall and introduced him.

"Oh, yes," Coach said, shaking Kyle's hand. "I remember you from after the championship game."

The blood rushed into Jason's face as he recalled their postgame kiss. But even so, he felt glad to introduce Kyle to Coach—at least better than he'd felt introducing him to his dad.

"Thanks for talking to Coach Sweeney," Kyle said, recovering from his own blush.

"I hope it helped." Coach nodded and turned to Jason. "By the way, I want you to stop by my office Monday. I think I've found a college interested in talking with you."

"You serious?" Jason said, afraid to get his hopes up.

"It's still extremely preliminary," Coach warned. "But let's talk about it."

Jason's chest swelled with new optimism as he and Kyle biked home from the mall.

It had been hard for Jason to stay hopeful after losing his scholarship—especially when he heard Corey, Andre, and his other teammates talk about their plans for next year.

Dwayne served as a constant reminder of that loss, rousing Jason's nerves each time they passed in the hall at school.

"I heard about them pulling your scholarship," Dwayne commented one day, grinning ear to ear. "That's *so* too bad."

Jason wanted to pound him right then and there—may as well finish the "altercation" that had supposedly cost the scholarship.

But would that resolve anything? Wouldn't there always be a Dwayne, someone to goad him?

Summoning all his resolve, Jason brushed past him.

rainbow high

▼ ▼ ▼

With the end of basketball season Jason's schedule had finally eased up enough for him to attend GSA meetings. He carried his lunch tray to the counselors' conference room and recalled the first meeting, when a group of boys had harassed students going in. Now no one even seemed to notice.

This day the topic focused on ensuring same-sex couples had been able to get the "couple discount" on prom tickets. At the end of the meeting as students were leaving, Ms. MacTraugh told Jason, "I've missed seeing you. Why don't you stop by after school, so we can chat again?"

He agreed and after the last bell headed to her art classroom, where she was taking down paintings.

"Do you mind helping me?" She peered at him through her round wireframes. "It's time to start cleaning up for the end of the year."

He helped her pull down artwork and apologized for not having come to many GSA meetings. "I wanted to, but with practice and the team . . ." His voice trailed off.

"Coach told me what happened with your scholarship," Ms. MacTraugh said as she steadied a stepladder for Jason.

"Yeah." Jason handed her a painting. "I'm still a little bit bummed about it."

"I would think you'd be outraged." Her voice grew loud.

"Well, yeah," Jason muttered. "I was."

"And you're not anymore?" She adjusted her glasses.

"Maybe a little." He stepped off the ladder. "But what can I do about it? Coach already tried talking to the Tech coaches."

"That's enough for today." Ms. MacTraugh gazed at the half-bare walls. "I get too sad taking them all down at once. Have a seat." She pulled out a block of writing paper. "Why don't you write a letter to Tech and get it off your chest?"

That's a stupid idea, Jason thought. "It won't do any good."

But Ms. MacTraugh handed him a pen. "Come on." She patted him on the shoulder. "You don't want to carry this around the rest of your life. Write down everything you want to tell them. The important thing is to get it out."

Grudgingly Jason took the pen. While Ms. MacTraugh washed paintbrushes, he stared at the blank paper, with no idea where to start. Then a devilish thought crossed his mind. Hadn't Ms. MacTraugh said he could write anything he wanted?

Dear Tech a-holes,

You can keep your stupid scholarship . . .

Slowly, as the anger poured from his heart, down his arm, through his fingers, and into his pen, he wrote . . . and raged . . . and released . . .

By the time he finished, he'd filled up six pages. He looked at the clock. An hour had passed. He'd never written so much in one sitting. Like after a game, he felt exhausted. And he felt something else, though he couldn't quite put a name to it.

He glanced at Ms. MacTraugh, jotting at her desk, and recalled her statement to the GSA at the start of the semester: "Words have power."

Was this what she had meant?

It felt as though in writing these pages he'd reclaimed what Tech's retraction letter had taken from him: his power.

He'd known Tech might take his scholarship away. Coming out seemed like the hardest thing he'd ever had to do. But he'd done it. And no one could ever take *that* away from him.

Ms. MacTraugh looked up. "All done?"

He nodded. "What should I do with it?"

"Take a few days to think about it. You may want to send it.

rainbow high

Or you might want to hold on to it. You'll decide what's best."

He folded the letter into his breast pocket. "Thanks," he said, standing up.

"Thank *you*," she told him. "You've helped change the world, Jason."

Him? Change the world? Yeah, right. "I don't think so," he told her.

"You may not see it now." She smiled. "But some day you will."

Whatever, he thought. He did feel better, though. After saying good-bye, he headed home.

His mom was in the kitchen, sorting through mail. "Hi, honey. How was school?"

"Great!" He picked Rex up and started stroking him.

"What happened that's so great?" His mom gazed over her reading glasses at him.

Jason rubbed his fingers through the purring cat's fur. "I just feel great, that's all."

She gave him a curious look. "I spoke to the mailroom manager today."

Earlier she had mentioned to Jason that she'd try to get him a summer job at her company, so they could spend more time together.

"He said he wants you to come in for an interview, even though he already saw your interview on TV." She gave a nervous laugh. "I hope it works out."

He could tell she was trying to accept and understand him. "Me too," he said.

She smiled and returned to the pile of mail, holding out a hand-addressed envelope to him. "Here's one for you. It looks like more fan mail."

Jason waited till he got to his room to read it. Though he'd read some of the letters out loud to his mom, it seemed like they didn't hold the same meaning for her that they did for him.

He put his backpack down on his bed, pulled off his jacket, and gently tore open the hand-scrawled envelope.

Hi Jason,

It's taken me a long time to get the nerve to write. You see, when I heard you on TV, I knew . . . I also am gay. But I don't know how to handle it.

At my high school I'm the captain of the wrestling team. Every day I have to deal with homophobia. And yet in classes, sex hardly ever gets addressed, especially homosexuality, as if it doesn't exist.

Seeing you on TV inspired me a lot. I really want to come out to friends, but instead I find myself lying. I guess I'm afraid. What if they ditch me?

Maybe someday I'll feel brave enough to come out like you.

In the meantime, I just wanted to say thanks. It's nice to know I'm not alone.

Jason stared at the handwriting, wishing he could write back, but the envelope bore no return address. So instead, he simply held the letter for a minute and silently hoped the guy would be okay.

As he folded the sheet of paper up Jason thought about his own letter in his breast pocket. Yeah, it was true he had lost the scholarship he'd wanted so badly, but in the process he'd gained something far greater.

He had become a role model after all.

jason

kyle

nelson

One night at dinner Nelson laid his palms flat on the tabletop, preparing for his mom's guaranteed freak-out when he told her his prom plans. "Mom?" He tried to keep his voice steady. "I've asked Jeremy to go to the dance with me . . . as friends."

Her gaze moved across Nelson's face as if searching. At last she said, "That's fine."

Huh? Why wasn't she wigging out? Nelson chewed on his tofu, mulling over her response. Had she really decided to trust him? If they were going to have a show down, better to have it now than later.

"So . . . how do you know I'm not lying to you about just being friends?"

"Are you?" she said, calmly scooping more rice.

He pushed a piece of broccoli from one side of his plate to the other. "No."

"Nelson, I never said I didn't like Jeremy. I think he's a very nice boy. I just don't want you romantically involved with him."

Nelson poured soy sauce onto his plate, relieved to hear she still liked Jeremy.

"From the start he wanted me to mention the HIV to you. He felt bad I didn't."

"Well . . . I wish you had listened to him. How is his health?"

"Great, usually. Better than mine."

"I'm glad to hear that. Invite him over again sometime. I'd like to get to know him more. I think you can learn a lot from him—and become good friends."

Nelson poked at the food on his plate, still unsure. Could they be friends?

The week before the prom Nelson raced around in a whirlwind, hauling Kyle with him as he picked out a boutonniere for Jeremy, chose a predance restaurant, made dinner reservations, dyed his hair purple, and selected a tuxedo and accessories.

Saturday afternoon Nelson's mom dropped him off at Kyle's.

"I know this is a big night for you," she said, her eyes misting up with tears.

"Mom, why are you crying? It's just a dance. Chillax, *please*?"

Even though he'd stopped kissing her in ninth grade, he now leaned over and pecked her on the cheek. She wrapped her arms around him, nearly squeezing him to death. When she finally let go, he grabbed his prom duds and hurried up the sidewalk before she decided to throw herself at his feet or something.

"And don't wait up for me," he yelled, and waved good-bye.

In Kyle's bedroom the two boys cranked the stereo and began excitedly stripping and dressing. With each new garment Nelson strutted a make-believe fashion runway.

rainbow high

Although they were able to help each other with their cuff-links, when it came to the bow ties, they hit a snag. Kyle had a simple pre-tied one, but Nelson had the real thing. No matter how much they fumbled, neither he nor Kyle could tie it.

"Dad!" Kyle swung open the door. "We need your help!"

"Wow!" His mom whistled, leaning in the doorway. "You both look so dashing."

His dad clambered up the stairs. Facing Kyle's mirror, he circled his arms around Nelson, showing him how to tie the bow. It was a moment Nelson would've never imagined.

Mrs. Meeks took photos of Kyle and Nelson—some killer-serious poses and some goofy ones. Her car had been designated as the prom-mobile. After another mushy damp-eyed-mom good-bye scene, Nelson and Kyle hurried off to Jason's.

Melissa answered the Carrillos' door, gleefully jumping up and down.

While Jason and Kyle pinned each other's boutonnieres, Melissa giggled. "You look like you're getting married."

Nelson turned away, wanting to gag.

More photos flashed—of Kyle and Jason; Nelson with Kyle and Jason; Jason, his mom, his sister, and—at Melissa's insistence—the Siamese cat.

As the boys said bye, Jason hugged his mom, telling her something in Spanish, and she joined the weepy mother's league.

When the boys reached Jeremy's, Kyle and Jason waited in the car outside the apartment building while Nelson carried his little boutonniere box up the familiar stairway.

From inside Jeremy's apartment came the muffled chords of country music. Nelson's heart panged with reminiscence and filled him with doubt: Would he be able to get through this evening?

Straightening his tie, he rang the bell.

Jeremy's brother opened the door. "Hey, come on in." He shouted "Jeremy!" over his shoulder and went to sit in front of the TV.

The clack of Western boots came from around the bedroom corner as Jeremy hurried in, adjusting his cuffs and tux sleeves. "Hi."

"Hi," Nelson echoed, wondering if they were going to kiss or hug or at least shake hands. Unable to make the first move, he merely said, "You shaved your goatee off. Looks great."

"Thanks." Jeremy rubbed a hand across his chin. "You look great too. I like the hair. Cool tux."

They stared silently at each other like two penguins on ice.

"I, um . . ." Nelson held out the flower box.

"Let me get yours," Jeremy said, and retrieved it from the refrigerator.

As they moved close to pin each other's lapels, Jeremy's breath blew warm on Nelson's cheek, making Nelson ache to feel Jeremy's tender lips once more.

But Jeremy stepped back. "Ready to go?"

"No!" Nelson wanted to plead. But instead he mumbled a resigned "Okay."

Outside he introduced Jeremy to Jason and they climbed in back of the car. Although they sat side by side, merely inches apart, to Nelson it seemed like a million miles.

For dinner Kyle and Nelson had selected a swank seafood-and-steak place traditional with prommies. Jeremy sat diagonally from Nelson. Each time their knees bumped accidentally, Nelson nearly jolted off his chair.

He tried ordering a cocktail to soothe his nerves, but the waitress carded him, so he had to endure his confusion sober,

rainbow high

barely able to look at—much less speak—to Jeremy. Nelson didn't want to be mean and ignore him, but this whole situation was just too freakin' awkward.

Maybe things would get better once they got to the prom. They couldn't get much worse.

In the hotel lobby the sound of Madonna blared from the ballroom. A cloud of perfume and cologne wafted over Nelson as he led the way through the prom crowd.

On the dance floor, schoolmates bounced like mad as the twinkling reflection from the mirror ball sparkled across tuxes and gowns. Cliques circled the edges, chattering and checking out one another's outfits.

"There's Debra!" Jason shouted.

Nelson turned to see her squeezing through the crush in a smoldering ivory strapless, pulling Lance behind her. Cindy and Corey followed.

Debra embraced Jason, kissing his cheek, and said something in his ear. In turn, Jason gently squeezed her hand.

Nelson watched, marveling. How had Jason and Debra managed to stay friends after breaking up?

"So are you guys really going to dance with each other?" Cindy asked the boys, direct as ever.

"Absolutely!" Nelson yelled, hoping the music and dancing could snap him out of his Jeremy weirdness.

"Why is it," Cindy remarked, "two girls can dance together and no one says anything? But if two guys do it, everyone goes crazy!"

"'Cause two girls are hot!" Corey beamed.

"Oh, we gotta dance to this!" Nelson shouted to the group as the song changed. He jostled toward the mirror ball, Jeremy and the group trailing after him.

To Nelson's immense satisfaction, as the boys began dancing

together people gaped and pointed. Ever since freshman year Nelson had imagined this moment.

A couple of swaggering guys from the football team, straining in their tuxes, puffed their chests out and raised their fists in threatening gestures. One of them yelled something, but the music was too loud to hear it.

Jason and Corey turned toward the guys, as if ready to take them on, but just then Mueller showed up, scowling daggers, and the football boys backed down.

"You did it!" Cindy said, high-fiving Nelson.

For the next dozen songs Nelson jumped and bounced to the music, trying to shake off all his mixed-up impulses toward Jeremy. But he could barely look at him in the eye. Anyone watching would hardly have known they were dancing together.

Then the fast set of songs ended and a slow series started. Cindy leaned into Corey. Ditto Lance and Debra. Then Kyle took hold of Jason's hand and Jason hesitated but then put his arm around Kyle.

Jeremy and Nelson were the only couple left standing apart on the dance floor.

"Want to dance?" Jeremy extended his hand.

Nelson glanced at the other couples holding one another close. That had been Nelson's dream too—prom with someone he loved, not with an ex from a breakup.

"No, thanks," he said.

Jeremy's hand fell to his side. He gazed at Nelson, downcast. "I'm going to the lobby for a bit."

Nelson stayed behind, too confused to stop him, feeling like total Loserville.

"Why are you standing here by yourself?"

Nelson whirled around to see Kyle's face set in a sharp frown.

rainbow high

Jason stood next to him. "Did you two fight?"

"I never should've done this," Nelson grumbled. "I should just go home." He started to leave but Kyle grabbed his shoulder.

"Nelson! We've been talking about this night for four years!"

Nelson wavered. He turned to Jason. "Tell me something. Isn't it hard for you and Debra to still be friends?"

Jason gave him a puzzled look. "Sometimes." He gazed at Debra and Lance slow dancing. "But I wouldn't want to stop being friends with her." He cracked a smile. "Not that she'd let me, even if I did." He glanced toward the lobby door. "Don't you care about him—Jeremy, I mean?"

"Yeah," Nelson said.

"Then get over yourself," Jason ordered, reaching over to adjust Nelson's collar.

"You'll never have this night again," Kyle murmured, and following Jason's lead, he brushed off Nelson's jacket.

"But you don't understand!" Nelson protested.

Ignoring his complaint, Kyle and Jason gently pushed him toward the door.

In the middle of the lobby filled with groups of jabbering prommies, Jeremy sat alone on a flat bench. His eyes gazed down at his hand. Between his thumb and forefinger, he held the boutonniere Nelson had given him.

Oh crap, Nelson thought, suffusing with guilt. As he walked over, Jeremy glanced up.

"Can I ask you something?" He gazed at Nelson dead-on. "Why did you invite me tonight? All evening you've ignored me. If you did this to get back at me, mission accomplished."

"Get back at you?" The accusation rang in Nelson's ears. "For what?"

"For breaking up. For things not working out. You tell me why."

Doubts surged in Nelson's mind. Was Jeremy right? Was he trying to get back at him?

"No! It's not that. It's just . . ." Nelson struggled with words.

Jeremy waited, twirling the flower between his fingers.

"This is hard for me . . . I still care about you."

"You've got a weird way of showing it." Jeremy tossed the boutonniere on the bench. "This is hard for me too, you know? If you want me to leave, just say so."

Was that what Nelson wanted? If not, then why had he been such a jerk with Jeremy tonight? He tugged on an earring and tried to clear his thoughts.

"I'm sorry." Nelson gazed down at the flower cast aside. "Please don't leave."

Sheepishly he sat on the edge of the bench beside Jeremy, closer than they'd been all evening. "I don't know why I'm acting so weird. I guess I . . ." He gulped a deep breath, swallowing the lump in his throat. "I guess I don't know if I can be friends with someone I fell in love with."

It was the first time—excepting Kyle—that Nelson had ever uttered to a boy that he loved him. Only in Nelson's topsy-turdy universe would it happen to be a boy he'd already broken up with.

Nelson leaned back on the bench, hating his sucky life and forgetting the bench had no backrest. Bam! He promptly fell off. Just like that.

Not again. He covered his face, feeling totally stupid. Who else but Nelson could admit his love one instant and crash onto his butt the next? He rolled over on the carpet, wishing he could disappear.

"You okay?" Jeremy's voice sounded beside him.

"Just perfecting my technique," Nelson muttered. He peered between his fingers.

Jeremy knelt next to him, restraining a smile. He extended a hand and pulled Nelson upright. "Dude, look. I'd really like to be friends with you. But it can only work if you want it to."

Nelson gazed into those puppy brown eyes. *Could* he be just friends? Well, if Jason could do so with Debra, why couldn't he with Jeremy?

He picked up the flower lying on the bench and took a deep smell, strengthening his resolve. "I *do* want to be friends," he told Jeremy, and pinned the boutonniere back into his lapel.

A moment later he was two-stepping with his ex past a tide of couples on the dance floor—not exactly the prom fantasy he'd dreamt of all those years but . . .

It was real.

The remainder of the evening he and Jeremy talked and joked, almost like old times, and they danced like crazy.

At one in the morning the DJ cranked up the music. Recognizing the starting chords immediately, Nelson leaped with a whoop, thrusting his arms high into the air. Trumpets blared. Drums banged. And gesturing initials, Nelson led the Walt Whitman High School senior class in a full-fledged rendition of "YMCA."

After a final slow, mushy song, Mr. Mueller chased everyone out of the ballroom. Cindy wrapped her arms around Nelson and insisted the boys come up to the hotel room she and Corey and Debra and Lance had rented.

During the next several hours the eight of them devoured twelve bags of chips, cookies, and pretzels; drank fifteen soft drinks and half a fifth of cheap vodka; told crude jokes; played music so loud that the management called them to turn it down; giggled and shrieked through three rounds of Secrets and Lies; rearranged the room furniture; trampolined between the double beds to *MTV After Hours* and got called by the manager again.

In between all that, Nelson tried on Debra's evening gown while Debra put on his tux; Cindy convinced Corey to let her paint his toenails; Jason taught everyone the words to "La Cucaracha" in Spanish; Kyle confessed to having ridden his bike past Jason's house, hoping to catch a glimpse of him, a million times during freshman year; Jeremy led everyone in a cha-cha line dance to Cher's "Do You Believe in Life After Love?"; and Lance got sick, after which he crashed dead asleep.

Shortly before dawn the boys finally left for Jeremy's, where Kyle and Jason said good-bye to him in the car and waited while Nelson walked Jeremy to the front door.

"Well . . ." Nelson glanced down at the sidewalk. "Sorry I acted like such a megaturd tonight."

Jeremy smiled. "We got through it."

"Yeah," Nelson agreed.

They stared at each other for a long, unforgettable moment. Then Jeremy opened his arms and Nelson flew into them, clutching him in a fierce embrace.

When they finally let go, Jeremy said, "Hey, my gang's been asking about you. Come to coffee with us sometime."

"Okay!" Nelson nodded eagerly. He watched Jeremy go inside. Then he skipped back to the car.

In the front seat, Jason and Kyle sat wrapped around each other, tongues to tonsils. *Quelle surprise.*

Leaning onto the back fender, Nelson lit up a cigarette, watching the sky turn aquamarine as birds began chirping.

He drew in a deep drag of smoke, proud of how he'd gotten through the night, and thought about all he'd come through this past year: the unexpected incursion of Jason into his friendship with Kyle; the HIV scare; his disappointment that college with Kyle wasn't going to happen; and now, his acceptance that there would be no big R with Jeremy.

Yet in spite of it all, in a weird way he felt stronger—as if he could handle anything the future might bring. And for that, maybe it had all been worth it.

"You coming?" Jason called, leaning out the window.

Nelson flicked his cigarette away. "Can I sit up front with you guys?"

Jason moved over, letting Nelson squeeze in.

Kyle started the engine and asked, "What's the big smile for?"

"Nothing." Nelson shrugged, watching the first golden rays of sun splash onto the road ahead. Then he added, "And everything."

for more information about . . .

organizing a peer group

GLSEN (Gay, Lesbian and Straight Education Network)
121 West 27th Street, Suite 804
New York, NY 10001-6207
Phone: (212) 727-0135
Fax: (212) 727-0245
www.glsen.org (Please visit this Web site to find the chapter in your region.)

The Gay, Lesbian and Straight Education Network strives to ensure that each member of every school community is valued and respected regardless of sexual orientation or gender identity/expression. GLSEN believes that such an atmosphere engenders a positive sense of self, which is the basis of educational achievement and personal growth. Since homophobia and heterosexism undermine a healthy school climate, we work to educate teachers, students, and the public at large about the damaging effects these forces have on youth and adults alike. GLSEN recognizes that forces such as racism and sexism have similarly adverse impacts on communities, and we support schools in seeking to redress all such inequities. GLSEN seeks to develop school climates where difference is valued for the positive contribution it makes in creating a more vibrant and diverse community. We welcome as members any and all individuals, regardless of sexual orientation, gender identity/expression, or occupation, who are committed to seeing this philosophy realized in K-12 schools.

GLSEN combats the harassment and discrimination leveled against students and school personnel. GLSEN creates learning environments that affirm the inherent dignity of all students, and, in so doing, teaches them to respect and accept all of their classmates—regardless of sexual orientation and gender identity/expression. GLSEN believes that the key to ending anti-gay prejudice and hate-motivated violence is education. And it's for this reason that GLSEN brings together students, educators, families, and other community members—of any sexual orientation or gender identity/expression—to reform America's educational system.

GLSEN's student organizing project provides support and resources to youth in even the most isolated of places, supporting students as they form and lead gay-straight alliances—helping them to change their own school environments from the inside out. A Gay-Straight Alliance (GSA) is a school-based, student-led, noncurricular club organized to end anti-gay bias and homophobia in schools and create positive change by making schools welcoming, supportive, and safe places for all students, regardless of sexual orientation or gender identity. GSAs help eliminate anti-gay bias, discrimination, harassment, and violence by educating school communities about homophobia and the lives of youth, and supporting lesbian, gay, bisexual, and transgender (LGBT) students and their heterosexual allies.

issues with parents

PFLAG: Parents, Families and Friends of Lesbians and Gays
1726 M. Street, NW, Suite 400
Washington, DC 20036
Phone: (202) 467-8180
Fax: (202) 467-8194
www.pflag.org (Please visit this Web site to find the chapter in your region.)

Parents, Families and Friends of Lesbians and Gays promotes the health and well-being of gay, lesbian, bisexual, and transgendered persons and their families and friends through support, to cope with an adverse society; education, to enlighten an ill-informed public; and advocacy, to end discrimination and to secure equal civil rights. Parents, Families and Friends of Lesbians and Gays provides opportunity for dialogue about sexual orientation and gender identity, and acts to create a society that is healthy and respectful of human diversity. PFLAG is a national nonprofit organization with a membership of over 80,000 households and more than 440 affiliates worldwide. This vast grassroots network is developed, resourced, and serviced by the PFLAG national office, located in Washington, D.C., the national Board of Directors, and the Regional Directors' Council. The parents, families, and friends of lesbian, gay, bisexual, and transgendered persons celebrate diversity and envision a society that embraces everyone, including those of diverse sexual orientations and gender identities. Only with respect, dignity, and equality for all will we reach our full potential as human beings, individually and collectively. PFLAG welcomes the participation and support of all who share in, and hope to realize, this vision.

violence and hate crimes against gays and lesbians

The New York City Gay & Lesbian Anti-Violence Project and the
National Coalition of Anti-Violence Projects
240 West 35th Street, Suite 200
New York, NY 10001
Phone: (212) 714-1184
Fax: (212) 714-2627
Bilingual hotline based in the New York area: (212) 714-1141
www.avp.org (Please visit this Web site to find a branch and phone
contact for your region.)

The New York City Gay & Lesbian Anti-Violence Project (AVP) is the
nation's largest crime-victim service agency for the lesbian, gay, transgender, bisexual, and HIV-affected communities. For twenty years,
AVP has provided counseling and advocacy for thousands of victims of
bias-motivated violence, domestic violence, sexual assault, HIV-
related violence, and police misconduct. AVP educates the public
about violence against or within our communities and works to
reform public policies impacting all lesbian, gay, transgender, bisexual, and HIV-affected people. The NCAVP is the nationwide network
of anti-violence projects of which the New York's AVP is a part.

human rights campaign

919 18th Street, NW, Suite 800
Washington, D.C. 20006
Phone: (202) 628-4160
Fax: (202) 347-5323
www.hrc.org

As America's largest gay and lesbian organization, the Human Rights Campaign provides a national voice on gay and lesbian issues. The Human Rights Campaign effectively lobbies Congress, mobilizes grassroots action in diverse communities, invests strategically to elect a fair-minded Congress, and increases public understanding through innovative education and communication strategies.

HRC is a bipartisan organization that works to advance equality based on sexual orientation and gender expression and identity, to ensure that gay, lesbian, bisexual, and transgender Americans can be open, honest, and safe at home, at work, and in the community.

HIV (human immunodeficiency virus) and AIDS (acquired immune deficiency syndrome)

Centers for Disease Control
National AIDS Hotline: 1-800-342-2437
www.cdc.gov/hiv/hivinfo/nah.htm

The Centers for Disease Control and Prevention (CDC) is recognized as the lead federal agency for protecting the health and safety of people at home and abroad, providing credible information to enhance health decisions, and promoting health through strong partnerships. CDC serves as the national focus for developing and applying disease prevention and control, environmental health, and health promotion and education activities designed to improve the health of the people of the United States.

Behavioral science has shown that a balance of prevention messages is important for young people. Total abstinence from sexual activity is the only sure way to prevent sexual transmission of HIV infection. Despite all efforts, some young people may still engage in sexual intercourse that puts them at risk for HIV and other STDs. For these individuals, the correct and consistent use of latex condoms has been shown to be highly effective in preventing the transmission of HIV and other STDs. Data clearly show that many young people are sexually active and that they are placing themselves and their partners at risk for infection with HIV and other STDs. These young people must be provided with the skills and support they need to protect themselves.

teen sexuality

Advocates for Youth
1025 Vermont Avenue, NW, Suite 200
Washington, DC 20005
Phone: (202) 347-5700
Fax: (202) 347-2263
www.advocatesforyouth.org

There is much to do to improve adolescent reproductive and sexual health in the United States and in the developing world. Recent declines in teenage pregnancy and childbearing are threatened by growing political battles over adolescent sexuality. Societal confusion over sex and a growing adult cynicism about youth culture further fuel the debate. To date, conservative forces have successfully censored sexuality education in over one-third of American schools, confidential access to contraception is under attack in the United States and routinely withheld from adolescents in the developing world, and adolescent access to abortion is almost a thing of the past. Concurrently, poverty, homophobia, and racism continue to confound the battle against HIV, leaving gay, lesbian, bisexual, and transgender (GLBT) youth, youth of color, and young people in the developing world particularly vulnerable to infection.

Advocates envisions a time when there is societal consensus that sexuality is a normal, positive, and healthy aspect of being human, of being a teen, of being alive. Advocates for Youth believes that a shift in the cultural environment in which adolescents live—from one that distrusts young people and their sexuality to one that embraces youth as partners and recognizes adolescent sexual development as normal and healthy—will yield significant public health outcomes for youth in the United States and in the developing world. To ultimately have the largest impact on improving adolescent sexual health, Advocates believes its role is to boldly advocate for changes in the environment that will improve the delivery of adolescent sexual health information and services.

gay and lesbian teen suicides

The Trevor Helpline: 1-800-850-8078 and 1-866-488-7386
www.thetrevorproject.org

The Trevor Helpline is a national 24-hour toll-free suicide prevention hotline aimed at gay or questioning youth. The Trevor Helpline
is geared toward helping those in crisis, or anyone wanting information on how to help someone in crisis. All calls are handled by
trained counselors and are free and confidential.

The Trevor Helpline was established by the Trevor Project in
August 1998 to coincide with the HBO airing of *Trevor*, hosted by
Ellen DeGeneres. *Trevor* is the award-winning short film about a
thirteen-year-old boy named Trevor who, when rejected by friends
and peers as he begins to come to terms with his sexuality, makes an
unsuccessful attempt at suicide.

When *Trevor* was scheduled to air on HBO, the film's creators
began to realize that some of the program's teen viewers might be
facing the same kind of crisis as Trevor, and they began to search for
a support line to help them. When they discovered that no national
twenty-four-hour toll-free suicide hotline existed that was geared
toward gay youth, they decided to establish one and began the search
for funding.

gay and lesbian teen services on the internet

Youth Guardian Services, Inc.
101 E. State Street
Ithaca, NY 14850
Phone: 1-877-270-5152
Fax: (703) 783-0525
www.youth-guard.org

Youth Guardian Services is a youth-run, nonprofit organization that provides support services on the Internet to gay, lesbian, bisexual, transgendered, questioning, and straight supportive youth. At this time the organization operates solely on private donations from individuals.

The YOUTH e-mail lists are a group of three e-mail mailing lists separated by age groups (13-17, 17-21, 21-25). The goal of these lists is to provide gay, lesbian, bisexual, transgendered, and questioning youth an open forum to communicate with other youth. The content ranges from support topics in times of crisis to "chit-chat" and small talk. Each list is operated by a volunteer staff made up of members who are in the same age group as the list subscribers.

The newest addition to the YOUTH Lists is the STR8 List for straight and questioning youth aged twenty-five or younger who have friends or family members who are gay, lesbian, bisexual, transgendered, or questioning. The list provides a safe space and supportive environment to talk with other straight youth in similar situations about the unique issues facing straight youth who have friends or family members who are gay, lesbian, bisexual, transgendered, or questioning.